TETHERED TO SHAME

The Search for Grace

Judy Hudson

Cover design by Angela Matlashevsky

Author photo by Cassandra Hampton

Tethered to Shame: *The Search for Grace*

Copyright ©2018 by Judy Hudson

ISBN-9781731532954

Independently published

10 9 8 7 6 5 4 3

Books by the author

Tethered to Shadows: *The Healing Journey of Six*

Tethered to Shame: *The Search for Grace*

Untethered Heart: *Redeemed by Love*

Acknowledgements

Thank you to the many people who provided feedback after reading the first book in the *Tethered series*. Hearing how some part of it *touched your hearts* has encouraged me more than you will ever know.

For this second book in the series, many thanks go to Chris Hollaway and Colleen Skaggs for critiquing every chapter along the way and keeping me on track.

To Susan Keltner, my friend and colleague—your review of the manuscript from the perspective of psychology, recovery, and how we humans behave, was invaluable.

Michelle Meeker—thank you again for attention to nuances and plausibility.

Kenneth E. Rodgers – your discernment amazes me. Thank you for your critique and suggestions to make the characters and story stronger.

And to my family who has supported my writing, encouraged me without fail, and given excellent feedback, I am forever grateful.

Prologue

Rachel untied the GOR-TEX® jacket from around her waist and slipped her arms through the sleeves, shrugging it over her head and day pack. The temperature had dropped at least five degrees in the last half hour, chilling her damp shoulders.

Herbert Glacier loomed ahead, proudly displaying the streams of silt and rock it had carved out along its ancient journey. Boulders spread out across its front like a giant river bed.

Rachel was again struck by the intensity of the turquoise blue showing through the great fissures. Being this close to such an enormous frozen river made her feel insignificant — as if her short life was no more than a fleck of granite.

Dan Jordan stepped closer, putting his long arm around her shoulder, and squeezed her to him affectionately. They stood quietly a few moments before Dan spoke. "Pretty impressive up close, isn't it?"

Rachel nodded, taking a ragged breath before she whispered, "It's like, if we can be still enough, we'll be able to see it move — pick up a boulder and nudge it toward the center. Maybe even hear it groan as the ice shifts and moves along the path."

They watched as two bald eagles circled high above the forest that had followed the glacier's retreat of the last few centuries. The clear blue sky stretched out overhead.

"Thank you, G-Dan. I'm so glad you made this hike with me. It means a lot."

"I wouldn't have missed it for the world, sweetheart. But it's a good thing you got me working out these last six months. It would have been a long trek with that extra ten pounds."

Rachel leaned into him and chuckled, "Just wait — next year I'll get you on the ski slopes!"

Dan shrugged off his backpack and motioned to some

waist-high boulders nearby. "How about some lunch while we contemplate the route these rocks have traveled."

"Sounds good."

Rachel shed her jacket and day pack, retrieving two bottles of water. Digging in a side pocket, she produced two cloth napkins and two protein bars, offering one of each to her grandfather. As she leaned over to take a sandwich from him, she laughed, "My mother would never have allowed a lunch to leave her kitchen without proper linens! And here I am of legal age...she's twenty-five hundred miles away...and I'm still packing proper linens in the wilds of Alaska! Am I hopeless or what?"

Dan laughed at Rachel's pantomime of her mother's persnickety nature. "I guess we're all creatures of habit to some extent. I'll try not to get it dirty."

The easy banter and obvious affection between the two belied the freshness of their relationship. It had been less than a year since their genetic connection was discovered. What a shock to them both! Dan had given up on the idea of ever having a grandchild, and Rachel had never known a grandfather. Then Rachel moved to Alaska and their relationship was discovered—Rachel was the child Dan's daughter had given up for adoption while away at graduate school.

Since the discovery, Rachel and Dan took to each other like kindred souls, trying to make up for the lost twenty years. Their affection filled some empty spots in each other. They found reasons to simply hang out, watch a movie, or work out together at the gym. And Rachel was learning to get her hands dirty as she watched Dan putter in his makeshift work shop.

Their dialogue was relaxed as they soaked up the afternoon sun, taking a break from the first half of this nine mile trail. "I can't believe you never hiked before I came into your life, G-Dan. It's such a necessity for me...like, I *have* to climb the mountains. Explore all the trails. It's like breathing to me."

Dan shifted his position, re-crossing his long legs before he spoke. "There's so much I missed out on. Maybe it would have been different..." His head shook imperceptibly as he let his words drift off.

After a moment of quiet contemplation, Rachel attempted to lighten the sense of loss. "Maybe I wouldn't have learned to love hiking, G-Dan. Maybe I would have been a stinky little fisher girl, hanging on your hip pocket, refusing to venture very far from the boat."

He gave a half smile, winking at Rachel. "Maybe."

"Are you ever going to forgive her, G-Dan? I mean…I didn't even want to meet her at first, so I figure I had good reason to drag my feet, but you…she's your daughter. I thought you two used to be tight."

Dan sucked at the side of his mouth, seemingly distracted by something lodged between his teeth. His Adam's apple pistoned a few times before he spoke. "Some day, I guess. It just seems that everything for the last twenty-one years has been a lie. That's a hard one for me to reckon."

"Was my grandmother like her, G-Dan?"

As soon as the words were out of her mouth, Rachel knew it was a mistake to bring up the topic of Dan's lost wife. Although he tried to hide his emotions, she could see his forehead flush and his jaws clench. "I'm sorry…I shouldn't have asked."

He looked sideways at her. "Naw, you got a right to know. You carry her blood."

Returning his gaze to the glacier, his voice was hoarse. "Yes, Dana is a lot like her mother. And I guess you remind me a lot of her too. Pretty. Tall. Beautiful skin. Full of life. Soft." Dan's voice had trailed off to a whisper. He stared ahead as his granddaughter waited.

Rachel could sense the terrible sadness in him, and wished again she had kept her curiosity in check. She adored this man, and had recognized early on that the topic of his wife was off-limits.

After several moments, Dan scanned the glacier before him, as if taking it in one last time. "I suppose we ought to head back down the trail, don't you think? It'll be a few hours to your rig."

"Yes, let's. This has been a fabulous trail, G-Dan. And I'm glad I got to see it with you."

The two quickly packed up the remnants of lunch, strapped on their packs, and settled into a quiet steady gait with Rachel in the lead. After thirty minutes, the open area gave way to denser vegetation. Dan started singing a ditty at the top of his lungs,

"A frog went a courtin' and he did ride, uh huh, uh huh…"

Rachel guffawed, turning to applaud his humor. "Is there some self description there, G-Dan?"

They both laughed and bantered as they continued down the trail. Dan jogged to catch up closer to Rachel, "Hey, missy, let's stick a little closer together. And make lots of noise. There's plenty bear in the area, and we don't want to surprise them. In fact, I'd be happier if you'd let me take the lead."

Rachel swept out her arm, motioning for Dan to pass her. As her eyes followed her hand to the curve in the trail ahead, two playful bear cubs tumbled onto the path. They weren't much bigger than Labrador pups. After regaining their footing, they turned in unison to stare at Rachel several yards distance.

Rachel's instant delight at seeing these precious cubs in the wild turned quickly to fear. She heard rustling in the bushes just outside her line of sight, and knew they were in trouble — the cubs were ahead; their mother was to her left and behind. She stood immobilized as her mind raced through options. *If she moved to reach for her pepper spray, would the movement invite an attack? What was G-Dan doing behind her? Should she run? Play dead?*

Rachel turned slowly as the bear sow roared, lifting up on hind legs, not thirty feet to Rachel's left. Her splayed claws looked longer than Rachel's own fingers. Strings of saliva flung from the sow's ferocious mouth as she again roared her outrage at their intrusion.

Time slowed to a crawl. Rachel mentally took measure of how much taller the upright sow was compared to her, and at the same time, thought it ironic that she could think of such a detail in the midst of imminent danger. The bear's thick black coat rippled as she tossed her head. *How did the experts say to handle situations like this? Wave your arms and back away slowly, yelling at the same time?* Somehow that didn't seem to fit now…she was too close.

She could sense G-Dan's presence, but couldn't see him. A choking sound escaped from her throat as the sow roared again and dropped to all fours.

Chapter One

THE MATANUSKA FERRY BLASTED its fog horn announcing arrival at Auke Bay. Clusters of people had gathered at the ferry terminal to welcome the four hundred or so passengers this late summer evening as the sun held steady over Lynn Canal.

Dana's face reflected the same anticipation as many of the people waiting on the landing, necks stretched up toward the boat deck, eyes searching the faces of the people looking back. She scanned the crowds hoping to spot her dad. His height of nearly six feet and self-assured bearing made him easy to pick out in a crowd, but tonight he was missing from the throng.

"He must have gone down to the car deck already." The disappointment in her voice was apparent.

Hub gave her shoulder a reassuring shrug. "He'll be here soon enough. We'll catch him after he drives up from the hold."

Dana scrunched her hands and shoulders like a little girl trying to contain herself. Her dreams were finally coming true — her dad was moving back to Juneau. She could look after him now; spend more time as a family. And even more, he would be the glue to bond the tentative relationship with her adult daughter.

She had given Rachel up at birth, and for the last twenty years, had longed to meet her again. That meeting had finally happened, but instead of the joyful mother-daughter reunion she had hoped for, Rachel was reticent with Dana. Thankfully, she had quickly fallen in love with Dana's dad and had established herself as the cherished grandchild Dan thought he would never have. Now, it was time to build on that foundation.

Hub and Dana studied the people who walked up the ramp following the luggage cart. Hikers, tourists, locals and people from the villages. Young and old; tired and energetic. She and Hub waved or spoke to many who looked familiar. Dana

1

thought, *what a beautiful sampling of Alaskans and visitors.*

The foot traffic thinned out, followed by the parade of cars, delivery vans and motor homes. Finally, Dan's green Dodge pickup appeared, pulling his fishing boat. He nodded to Dana, and pointed to the parking area ahead.

They caught up with him just past the staging area. Dana reached through the open window to hug her father. "Welcome home, Dad. I'm so glad you're finally here."

Dan patted her arm, then reached through the window opening to shake hands with Hub. "Thank you. You didn't need to meet me here at the dock. Were you afraid I couldn't remember how to find your place?"

"I just couldn't wait the extra five minutes, Dad! I wanted to see for myself that you were coming off that ferry with your pickup and your belongings. You've actually moved home!"

"Well, I'm here lock-stock-and barrel. And I'm looking forward to that nightcap you promised me."

The interchange quickly wrapped up so the three could shuttle a few miles further out the road to Dana and Hub's.

Home was a modest log house on the shores of the vast Lynn Canal, a ninety-mile fjord that separated Juneau and a string of discontinuous communities from open waters of the Pacific Ocean. A wide, covered deck offered full view of the ever-changing scenery before them. Tree covered islands dotted the miles of water that hosted hump back whales and orcas, salmon, seals, and occasionally sea lions; ferries, ships, and smaller vessels for fishing or sight-seeing.

It was a well lived-in home. Rustic. Simple. Functional. Hub's shop invited opportunities to get grease under the nails rebuilding a small motor, or to relax while tying flies for stream fishing. Inside, the kitchen opened to the living room, dominated by huge windows overlooking Lynn Canal.

Lionel, the fat cat that claimed ownership of the back of the couch, gave the briefest glance at the people who intruded on his domain.

Hub, Dana and Dan settled on the deck while the midnight sun denied the late hour. Dana served drinks and a bowl of almonds.

"Dad, you look a little tired. Are you feeling alright?"

"I'm fine, Dana. I'll probably sleep well, though. It took a lot more than I thought to wrap up a decade of living in Haines. Didn't know if it would all fit in that mini-container. My neighbor was glad to take the crab pots, and that helped. I'll never go back to that commercial size."

Dana could see the tiredness around Dan's eyes, but there was something else. His normally robust conversation was subdued. He avoided eye contact with her. She checked her excitement about the housing options she'd found for him, and stifled her questions about connecting with Rachel.

"Well, your room is ready anytime you're ready to crash, Dad. Don't let us keep you up. We'll get to talk more over breakfast."

Left alone, Dana and Hub nestled into the porch glider, quietly watching the sun dip into the watery horizon. Hub was the first to break the silence, approaching the unspoken concern they shared. "He's probably just tired, Dana. This is a big change for him. He's used to his own routine. Friends. Independence. We need to not crowd him."

It was a few minutes before Dana responded. "I know. There's something else, though, Hub. He's never been so…so aloof with me. Never. I feel like I'm being punished."

They watched as a bald eagle lifted from the huge Sitka spruce next to the house, settling in its flight plan to the small Gull Island a short distance from shore.

"He said he understood, Hub, but I don't think he does. It's hard for him to talk about things of the heart, and I don't think he knows how hard it was for me to keep Rachel's existence a secret all those years. How it impacted me."

"Give it time, Dana. It's not every day you welcome a twenty-year old baby girl into your world. And now his move on top of that…it's got to be hard — even for a tough old bird like him.

"Let's get some sleep and start fresh in the morning."

The smell of bacon permeated the house when Dana woke up. Savoring the sound of her husband and father talking in the kitchen, she lingered under the light quilt. Although she couldn't make out their words, she sensed the camaraderie between the two men. Dan had been a father figure to Hub since high school, and she counted their triad as a blessing. Now it would be a foursome.

Dana slipped on last night's clothes, gathered her long hair up in a band, and walked bare footed to the kitchen.

"There you are. I wondered if you were going to show yourself this morning!" Hub squeezed her with one arm, while reaching for her favorite mug.

Dan gave the briefest nod before returning his attention out the window. He was fully dressed, his shirt ironed and tucked into blue jeans that appeared fairly new. Dana could smell his familiar aftershave.

She reached over to where he sat, hugging his head to her shoulder. "Morning, Dad. Are you ready for the day?"

His response to her affection was a brief hug and reach for his coffee.

Breakfast was cordial, but lacked intimacy. Dana's nervous banter seemed loud compared to the men's voices. She reached over to the sideboard for a folder and placed it on the table.

"Dad, I've got a list of all the vacancies in the valley and Lemon Creek here. The ones in yellow are out here. The pinks are in Lemon Creek. And the checks are the ones that are for sale. We can go look at them after breakfast if you want—I took the day off."

Dan shifted in his chair before he spoke. "I appreciate your doing this, Dana, but I think I've already got a place settled. Rachel called the other night about a vacancy in her apartment complex. They've got a storage shed for some of my stuff, and I can rent a storage unit for the rest. So I think I'm going to go with that."

Dana sat back in her chair, her expressive face bracing her disappointment. She attempted to mask her feelings with her words. "Oh. Okay. I didn't know."

She returned the folder to the sideboard, and folded her hands on the table. "So…is there anything we can help you with?"

"Well, I 'spect I could use some help unloading when that container gets here. I'm sure there will be other stuff—I'll let you know." Dan briefly touched Dana's hands, showing the slightest amount of reassurance.

"Well, maybe you and Rachel could come for dinner after you get settled in, if you decide this is the place for you. I'll fix up some halibut and sourdough rolls."

"Maybe. I'll check with Rachel. I'm not sure if she's working tonight, but she said she'd meet me at the complex and show me around. I'll let you know. But don't count on us — it'll be a busy day."

Dana was devastated. No invitation to join him. No involvement in the plans that were obviously being made behind her back the last few days. No consideration for the time she took off work. No opportunity to be with her daughter.

After Dan left, Dana retreated to the deck, arms crossed, tears slipping down her cheeks. *Is this the way it's going to be, Lord? Now that I've found my daughter, I don't get to love her, and I lose my father in the process?*

Hub stepped out to the deck and kissed the top of her head. "Give it time, honey. I'll see you about noon if you're here."

Dana sat staring across the water for several minutes after Hub left for the shop, allowing her thoughts to bounce around all corners of her mind. She felt so grateful that her father and Rachel had already established a close bond. Surely that bond would eventually reach out to encompass her. Hopefully, it would develop into love — love from Rachel, that is. Dana already loved her beyond reason. *She's my child.*

There had only been the briefest moment to hold her before Dana released her daughter to be raised by strangers. She agreed to a closed adoption thinking it would be best for her child. That decision haunted her for the next twenty years as she questioned her motives, doubted her decision, and longed to know how it turned out for her daughter.

When Rachel moved to Alaska just after Christmas, she met Hub on the airplane returning from Seattle. Over the months, they developed an easy friendship, fostered by interaction at the local coffee shop where Rachel found a job. Dana initially avoided contact with Rachel because of a conflict of interest — her adoptive mother was Dana's client.

But in the last few months, it became evident that Rachel was the daughter she had relinquished at birth. What a mixed blessing! Her daughter was finally found — a delightful, competent, beautiful young woman. However, she had no interest in locating her birth mother. For reasons unknown to Dana, Rachel resented her.

Initially, Dana thought it could be enough — just knowing

Rachel through Hub and her father; knowing that she turned out okay; that she had a normal upbringing. But as the weeks dragged on with no contact, Dana longed for more. *I'm in the middle! For goodness sakes, I deserve some spill over.* It rankled her that her father hadn't been more inclusive of her. *He could have at least told me about the apartment! He knows how I long to be part of her life.*

Dana stood up abruptly and stomped into the house. She threw some bottled water and snacks into the cooler, as well as a package of herring. She quickly gathered her socks, sunglasses, cell phone and jacket. Punching in Hub's number on her cell phone, she tripped down the steps to the beach behind their home where her skiff was secured to a buoy just off shore.

She tried to normalize her voice. "Honey, I'm going to go out on the water for awhile. No use sitting around here feeling sorry for myself. I think it'll do me some good."

"Okay. Do you want company?"

"Umm…not really. Unless you have a burning desire to go with me."

Hub's response was measured. "Not really. I'm backed up here. Where are you planning to go?"

"North of Shelter Island. The water is beautiful. Hopefully I'll see some critters."

"Okay. Keep me posted."

In short order, Dana had pulled the skiff in close, loaded it with a fish cooler, fishing pole and tackle box. Planing across the water, she knew exactly where she wanted to be.

It took almost thirty minutes to get there, but she was not disappointed. It looked like there were six Dall porpoises, and they were making a b-line for her skiff. They swam close together, their sleek black and white bodies surfacing in unison. It reminded Dana of a synchronized flying performance at an air show.

The porpoises disappeared momentarily, but Dana held a steady speed, certain they would join her. Sure enough, she was rewarded when two porpoises surfaced in front of her boat, crossing within inches of the bow with split-second accuracy. The first two were followed immediately by another pair, and another. She counted five rapid loops in succession, before a brief intermission, then two appeared on her starboard side.

They disappeared together in the depths of the canal, but not before one turned on its side and flipped water at her as if to say goodbye.

The encounter with these beautiful creatures left Dana breathless. Unconsciously, she reduced her speed as she considered the intimacy of the moment. There were no other boats within a half-mile—it was just her and the porpoises on this glistening expanse of blue water. She had again witnessed God's playful and exquisite choreography.

As she adjusted her direction to head for North Pass, Dana noticed how serene she felt. This morning's tension was so unimportant. Things would work out. She knew who was in control, and *He had plans for her good*.

Chapter Two

DANA STOOD IN FRONT of her office assessing its appeal from the viewpoint of a new client. The square house with a simple peaked roof was one of three on this block built closely together in the early 1900s. The two front windows looking out at Gastineau Channel reminded her of sleepy eyes shadowed by burgundy awnings. The simple concrete steps leading to the front door had moss in the cracks, typical of older structures in Juneau.

Some weeds had found footing between her office and the bookstore uphill. She made a mental note to tend to them during her first break.

After making some phone calls, Dana welcomed a new client, Ruth Gunderson. She looked about forty, solidly built, about five foot-ten. Her chestnut hair, pulled back over her ears in an attractive bun at the base of her neck, brought out the speckled colors in her matching sweater and slacks.

Standing up to shake hands with Dana, she said, "Thank you for seeing me. You have a nice office here, even though the parking is not ideal. I guess that isn't too important when you don't host a lot of people at one time, though."

Dana tilted her head, "Did you have trouble finding a place to park?"

"Uh, no…I parked out front. I'm just aware of things like that—I cater events, so I'm always aware of parking capacity, especially in downtown Juneau."

"Oh, okay. Well, I'll give you a few minutes to complete the paper work, then we can meet in my office. There's bottled water in the little frig, and hot water for drinks on the counter there if you'd like. I'll be back in a few minutes."

When Ruth joined Dana, she sat stiffly in the wingback chair. She seemed to scrutinize Dana while Dana recited insurance and administrative essentials, as well as the privacy act exclusions.

"And what about you, Dana, do you have accountability to a broader authority—someone who oversees your work?"

Ruth's commanding voice gave Dana pause, and she momentarily felt like a child in trouble. Recovering quickly, she responded, "That's a good question, Ruth, I've never been asked that before. You must do your homework well."

At Ruth's matter-of-fact nod, Dana continued. "Not accountability *per se*, but I do meet the requirements of the state's licensing board for continued education. I would report any misconduct allegations to that board, although I have never had any. Um, more directly, I meet regularly with a group of my peers, which is of enormous value. We not only help each other with therapeutic modalities, situations that get murky, and share ideas to help clients' progress, but we watch each other for signs of burnout. We're all about being ethical, skilled practioners...and supportive of each other."

"I'm glad to know that. Well, where do we start?"

With open hands gesturing toward Ruth, Dana nodded, "Tell me about yourself and why you're here."

Pointing to the paper work she had just completed, Ruth said, "I guess you can see I'm forty-three. My family and I have been here fifteen years—my husband works at the airport. He services aircraft, which is what he did in the Navy. We have three daughters, two are on their own.

"I cater weddings and events mainly...that's my work anyway. My church is very important to me...we do meals at the Glory Hole one day a week and on Thanksgiving. And I help out where I can—since I have flexibility, I can step in when families are going through troubled times. Do you have a family, Dana?"

"Um, yes, I'm married, and we dote on the four-legged critters that claim pre-eminence."

"No children?" Again, Ruth's clipped words seemed judgmental.

Shaking her head, Dana responded, "I...ah...didn't get to raise any children..." She watched Ruth a moment to see if that was sufficient information for her. When she appeared satisfied, she asked gently, "And what brings you here, Ruth?"

Ruth's imposing demeanor changed as her eyes seemed to search her thoughts. "Well, I don't know if you can help me with this since you haven't raised children of your own. My youngest daughter is seventeen, and she's being defiant."

"What do you mean by defiant?"

Grasping one knee with clasped hands, Ruth's eyes studied the air to the side of Dana's face, then released her knee. She folded and unfolded her hands a moment before looking directly at Dana again. "She's a good girl—no drugs or drinking. Smoking. I'm sure she's not sexually active. She's a good girl. Gets good grades. We have doted on her, of course. She's the youngest, and we're able to do that now. We've planned for her college after graduation—she's a senior at JD High. She always wanted to be a pediatrician. But...she is getting more and more stubborn, defying me.

"She used to be so helpful in my catering business—she was my right-hand." Ruth's face softened as she interrupted herself to brag, "She's so efficient, and has good social skills. My clientele always comment on how responsible she is for her age."

With that aside, Ruth continued her crisp narrative. "She's a Christian, and has always been active in our church, but lately, she gives me grief about everything—help with catering, even though I pay her. And I have to argue to get her to church. She talks back to me...she's disrespectful. Lately, she quit coming to the dinner table when we eat—we always have meals as a family. And now she tells me she's going to take a year off before she starts college—go live with her oldest sister in Portland. And that is not an option, Dana. Mary, my eldest, is not a good influence on Angie. She would not encourage Angie's professional goals, or being involved in church. Mary lives life...according to Mary. She works at a bar. I don't even know what all she does, but she's not living up to her capabilities. Or how she was raised!"

Ruth's breathing was shallow, her hands clasped. "We don't talk often...she doesn't want me in her business. And I'm afraid if Angie goes to live with her, she'll throw her future away."

Dana breathed deeply, silently willing Ruth to follow suit to relieve some tension, as she waited for her finish. When Ruth sat back in the chair and looked directly at her, Dana assumed she was handing the baton off to her. "I can understand what a big worry that is, Ruth. It sounds like she's got great potential and opportunity, but she might...side-track. How does she get along with other family members? And school leaders?"

"Good. Her teachers love her. She has friends. Her father doesn't say much about the change — he expects me to confront the issues, so he's the good guy, and they're close. I'm more the disciplinarian."

"So...the different roles that you and your husband take...is that no longer working for you? Do you need to redefine how you parent together?"

"You know, Dana, for not having children, you're asking some very pointed questions. They're...thought-provoking."

Dana chuckled, but waited for Ruth to go on.

"It works for us. Les is just...he's not firm. It's not in him. He'll step in when I ask him to, but...generally he makes it worse, so...so that's why I'm here!" Ruth's tone was cordial, but her frustration was apparent.

"Ruth, I can understand how worried you are about Angie's choices and future. And even though I've not raised a daughter, I'm pretty good at asking questions that hopefully will help you discover what's best for you and your family. So, if you're comfortable with me, we can do some individual work over the next few weeks."

At Ruth's definite nod, Dana approached another option. "I'd like you to consider something else. I'm starting a therapy group next month for adult women. It's a confidential setting, and you're not likely to know any of the other women at first, but I believe groups are a really good way to learn about ourselves and how we interact with others. I suspect you might learn some things that will help with your daughters.

"It's a closed group that will last until spring. That means the same five or six women will be together for the duration. So, it's a small, safe setting where we can examine things of the heart — our identities and ways of thinking; our histories and what interferes with healthy relationships.

"You don't have to make a decision now, but it's something to think about."

Ruth shrugged. "That might be worth looking at. I'll see how it fits in with my catering business

After the session ended, Dana sat back in her chair to consider Ruth's situation, personality, and demeanor. *Hmm. At one time, I would have envied Ruth's predicament because it meant I got to be a mom. And now my own daughter is back in my life — with barriers. Who knows how we'll learn from each other…if I can keep her from bulldozing me. I don't want to fight for leadership if she joins the group.*

Chapter Three

DANA LAUGHED AS HER colleague, Phyllis Barton, finished her story about being propositioned during the whole flight back from Seattle.

"I mean…this little pipsqueak would not take a hint! I thought, are you blind? Can you not see that I make two of you? We are not *even* a potential match!

"He kept saying, *just go to dinner with me. I can show you a good time. Show me your Juneau.* Pfft. I thought—good time baloney—I would spend the whole time trying to keep from patting him on the head." Phyllis' rosy cheeks were moist from the humor leaking from her eyes.

"How did you finally get rid of him?" interjected Lisen.

Phyllis's silent laughter shook her generous mid-section a full minute before she could catch her breath. Finally her words burst through her attempted restraint, "Like any teenage girl would…I hid in the bathroom for forty-five minutes!"

When the shared laughter died down, Amy Smith added, "Oh Phyllis, you are so funny. And so beautiful. He saw that— he just wasn't the right *knight-in-shining-armor* for you. When the right one comes along, you won't feel the need to hide in the bathroom!"

Phyllis wiped the tears from her face and finally settled back in her chair. "Oh my dear friends…you are so gracious. Thank you. I just don't want to go through that again. Actually, I've gotten quite settled as a solo person, and it's okay. I miss my husband, of course, but I really don't think I will marry again. And certainly not to a guy half my size with twice the ego!"

The affection these women shared for each other was obvious. They were all mental health professionals who met monthly to lend support—professionally and personally. They processed difficult cases, shared treatment modalities, and gauged the burn-out potential in each other.

Lisen, the moderator for the month, finally asked for check-ins to get the group back on track. "Dana, what's happening with you? How's it going with that daughter of yours?"

"Oh, Lisen, you zeroed right in on the hot spot." Dana's demeanor tumbled from the lightness of laughter to the heaviness of her heart. "My daughter. My beautiful daughter is still very gun-shy. She avoids me. I even called her adoptive mother to see what might be the obstacles, but so far, I'm at a loss."

Marla interjected, "The mother was your client at one time, wasn't she?"

"Yes. Once she got used to the idea that I am not only her former therapist, but that we share a daughter, she acted like it was a bonus. She said Rachel has *some issues* and thinks I can help." Dana rolled her eyes, knowing her colleagues understood the dilemma that dual relationships create. "Yeah. I assured her I cannot, and will not be a therapist to Rachel, or even to her any more. She seems to think things will work out. Actually, that's quite a change from who she was as a client. Then, she was very anxious...and controlling about how things would roll out in her daughter's life. But, here we are."

Dana stalled before continuing. "I...what is unsettling now is more about my dad. He and Rachel are becoming really close. He actually moved to Juneau. After all the years I asked him to, he finally does, but it's really for Rachel, not me."

Her arms crossed as she grappled with how she felt. Her voice faltered, "It's like he's excluding me...he doesn't invite me to join their budding relationship. The two of them arranged for him to move into the same apartment complex, and didn't even tell me about it beforehand. I took the day off and planned to help him look for a place, but she had already taken care of it.

"I don't know. It's not a big thing. I can see how he might have forgotten to tell me, or include me. I just...I just want to build a relationship with Rachel now that I've found her, and he isn't helping. I can't believe he's not helping to make that happen."

The room was silent for a moment. "Ouch," was all that Phyllis offered.

"Anyway, that's what's happening personally. And I'm hopeful it will all work out. I'm praying for patience — right now!

"Professionally, about the only thing on my radar screen is a new therapy group. I'll be starting a women's group in August if you have any clients you want to send my way for group work."

Marla Anderson spoke up. "I might have a referral. In fact, I'm certain of it. I've got a gal who needs group work desperately. She'll be court-ordered. She's tough on the outside, history with lots of drugs, but clean now for six months. She's developed some good skills with that...but she's so damaged. Inside that tough exterior, she's very vulnerable.

"She'll be a challenge, Dana, but I really hope you can take her. You're the only *game in town* when it comes to psychotherapy groups."

"Do you think she can handle group dynamics when addictions aren't the core issue?

"I don't know. But I do know she needs to integrate...step out of that *bad-girl* mentality. Desperately."

Dana was hesitant. "Have her call me. I'll see what we can work out."

Chapter Four

HUB AND DANA LINGERED over coffee Friday morning. He was dressed in Levis and a work shirt, ready to go to his boat repair shop. Dana was barefooted and in pajama shorts, her toes reaching under the table to rub his calf. "Now don't do that! I'll never get to work."

Dana giggled, glad for the time to flirt with her husband. "You know...you could take the day off and we could play."

Hub stood up as he chuckled, leaning over to kiss her forehead, "Don't tempt me! I, madam, do not have the luxury of a four-day work week...unlike present company."

His mental shift was apparent as he nodded toward the rocky shore behind their house. "I got the materials in to replace that mooring buoy—new buoy, pennant and chain. I'd like to get that done tomorrow afternoon if the water is decent. The forecast is good. It's the lowest tide we'll get for awhile. Your dad said he could help, but we could use you if you're free. I need you to hold the boat steady while he hands down the chain."

"Of course. Are you going to suit up?"

"Yeah. I'll need to dig out my dry suit in order to connect the chain."

"I wonder if Rachel might want to be a part of that operation. Didn't you say once that she scuba dived?"

"Mmm...yeah. I don't plan on using the tanks, though. With low tide, I think I can hold my breath long enough to hook the chain to the anchor. Now that I think about it, it would be too many people to work around, so we'd better not invite her this time."

"How about we invite her to fish the derby? We could spend some time with her that way. Maybe she wouldn't feel too uncomfortable around me, ya think?"

"Yeah, maybe. I could do that." Hub's attention had already shifted to the work ahead of him.

Dana's hopes soared, her mind making plans as soon as Hub left for work. Even if they could fish only one of the three days, it would give her the opportunity to interact with Rachel. To get to know her...show her how much she cared.

Later in the day, Dana reached Rachel's voicemail. Trying to control the excitement in her voice, she invited Rachel to go on the boat with her and Hub, and probably her dad, to fish the derby. It promised to be great fun, and maybe someone on the boat would win the $10,000 prize for the biggest salmon.

Dana called to invite her father also, but only reached his voicemail. Checking her disappointment, she got dressed to walk the dogs.

By noon Saturday, Dana's spirits tanked. She hadn't heard back from Rachel or Dan, and began to imagine the two of them conspiring against her. Maybe they were searching for excuses to avoid her. By the time Dan arrived to help maintain the mooring buoy, she was in a foul mood.

Dan and Hub quickly settled in to the task before them, discussing how to get the job done most effectively. They were both skilled mariners, like-minded in how to use the weight of the chain to take Hub down to the anchor.

"Are you sure you can still hold your breath that long, son? Even at low tide, you're working at ten feet below."

Hub's nod was short of reckless. "Yeah, I think I've still got it. I can always surface and try it again. Might need something to warm me up when we're done, but I think I can get it."

"Well, don't take any risks, son...promise me that."

"I won't."

Dana's apprehension about doing maintenance on the buoy moor overrode her angst about not hearing back from Rachel. She trusted that Hub and her dad knew what they were doing, but there were always risks in working under water. She double checked the skiff's equipment, assuring the presence of sufficient floatation devices should they get into trouble. The small outboard motor was available should they get separated during the buoy change. The little anchor was onboard, as well as oars and the safety kit.

She watched as Hub positioned the anchor shackles on the end of the chain in such a manner that he could quickly open the steel connector below and attach it to the concrete anchor. He glanced at her with his boyish grin, saying so much without words — *don't worry; trust me; I can do this.* Still, Dana was glad her dad was there in case anything went wrong.

Hub stepped overboard holding a length of chain to help him descend. The water splashed up, drenching Dan's shoulder as he managed the bulk of the chain. He concentrated on the murky water where Hub disappeared, although visibility was limited to just a few feet. Dana easily held the skiff steady over the anchor with just the oars. This close to low tide, the wave action was minimal.

Seconds passed. Dana found herself not breathing, willing Hub to surface. She looked for signs of worry in her father, but he seemed calm. Another fifteen seconds passed. She thought of the possibilities — getting wrapped around the chain and not able to pull himself back up, blacking out...maybe a mammoth halibut! Finally, she couldn't stand it anymore. "Shouldn't he have surfaced by now?"

"He's okay. I think I can feel him on the other end of chain. Just hold us steady like you're doin.'"

Dana's eye tooth worried her lower lip, her scrunched eyebrows showing her uneasiness. She wished she would have set her phone to time Hub's submersion. *He should be surfacing. He's not twenty-five anymore.* She slipped out of her boots, preparing to dive in.

Suddenly, Hub broke through the surface of the water, his head thrown back gasping for air. Before his lungs were fully recharged, he spewed, "I got it! I got it!"

Dan beamed at his son-in-law. "Good job! I knew if anyone could do it, it would be you."

Relieved, Dana held back to balance the boat as she watched her father give her husband a hand up. She threw a towel his way, then watched as he shed his dry suit. The men turned to the last task of securing the new blue-striped buoy to the pennant, then to the line that stretched to the beach.

"Thanks, Dad. You were a great help. It was just the right length of chain to work with."

"Glad to help, son. You were down there a long time. I got to wonderin' if I'd have to get a shark hook to pull you back up."

Dana watched as the men bantered, grateful for their close relationship, but a little jealous of not being part of it.

"Dana, can you pull us in on the line? Let's try it out."

She stuffed the hurt feelings while she went about storing the oars and pulling the skiff by the line attached to the shore, reaching arm-over-arm.

The men collected their tools and continued to talk about mooring options as they walked up the beach ahead of Dana. She nurtured the feeling of being excluded. Unappreciated.

When there was a break in the conversation, Dana asked Dan if he wanted to stay for supper.

"I think not, Dana. Thanks, but I'd better get back."

"Well, did you get my message about the derby?" Her irritation was thinly disguised.

"Yeah, I got it. I think I'll pass, though, unless you need a deck hand. You know I don't like to fish around idiots, and there's always a fair share in the derby."

"But what if Rachel wants to come…?"

"You can handle it."

Dana grumbled, "Thanks for letting me know," before turning on her heal and stomping up the beach, leaving the two men behind.

Chapter Five

THE ANNUAL GOLDEN NORTH Salmon Derby was scheduled to start in three days. For local fishermen, it was the Super Bowl event of the year. Cash prizes were given for the biggest salmon turned in—$10,000 for first place, plus goods and services donated by local businesses. Proceeds from the derby went to a scholarship fund for local students.

Dana had missed only one derby since she moved to Juneau as a teenager. Even though her life had been about commercial fishing, the derby was special. The camaraderie among fishermen as the boats came to the weigh stations seemed like a family reunion to her. A great deal of banter and bragging floated among the boats as they compared catches and stories. It was the competition that charged her adrenaline, though—Dana liked to win!

Her emotions undulated from irritation that Rachel hadn't at least called to acknowledge her invitation, to grief over being so unimportant in Rachel's life. It was fear, really. *What if she never wants to be part of my life?*

Returning home from work, Dana threw her tote in the corner, and quickly changed into comfortable clothes to take the dogs for a walk. Mica and Nikki would help her run off some negative self-talk and the unsettled feeling in her gut.

When they returned, Hub was just pulling into the drive with a big smile on his face. "Rachel said she'd like to go with us on Saturday—she's got one day off during the derby."

Dana was so glad, she pushed the last of her pity party to the back of her mind.

"Oh that's great. Just the three of us—we'll have such a great time."

"Well, she asked if it would be okay to bring a friend. I said *sure.* It'll be more fun for her to have someone her own age." Hub jostled Dana's shoulders affectionately.

Dana's face showed her disappointment at having to share Rachel, but she responded, "Of course. She's young...and still nervous about me, I'm sure. Did you see her at the coffee shop?"

Hub nodded, but continued to study Dana's face, holding eye contact.

Finally, she sighed, "It's just so hard to be patient. Thank you, Hub, for keeping me reigned in. I'm glad she trusts you — my dad sure isn't helping!"

***

Dana was up at four-thirty Saturday to get things ready to load onto the boat. Hub had brought it around to the mooring buoy out back, and was readying the skiff to transport them and supplies to the bigger boat.

Her ear was attuned to the arrival of Rachel's Jeep. The last time Rachel had come to their house — the only time — it was for a planned fishing trip with Hub, Dan, and one of Hub's mechanics. *I wonder if that's who she asked to come along this time.*

The memory of her last visit still made Dana wince. Rachel had showed up early, joining Dana on the deck where she was working on the house. At that time, Dana had a suspicion Rachel might be the daughter she had given up at birth, but had no proof. As their conversation led to birthdays, Dana knew — this was her daughter.

When she told Rachel what she suspected, Rachel reacted with anger, accusing Dana of deceiving her; condemning her for giving her away to strangers. Rachel had no interest in finding her birth mother, and the revelation had been overwhelming.

Later they met once to confirm their biological relationship, but Rachel had avoided being alone with Dana since. *Dear Lord, please make this the day we can start building bridges. Perhaps today is a big step for Rachel. Give me patience.*

Dana checked the cooler again to make sure there was sufficient food and drinks for four. At the last minute, she added a forth package of frozen herring for bait.

Jackets and totes were stacked on the cargo lift ready to send to the beach below. She tried to think what she might be missing, but her thoughts were scattered as she listened for Rachel's Jeep.

Finally, she heard the crunch of tires out front. Her stomach did flip-flops. *Calm down, Dana. It'll be all right.* She forced a confident smile as she stepped out the door to welcome her daughter and a tall young man with a patchy beard, intense aqua blue eyes, and a huge goofy smile.

"Good morning! You're just in time...I can hear the salmon splashing out on the water—calling to us."

Rachel's tentative smile was interrupted as she looked up at the young man. "I'd like you to meet my friend, Eric Mortenson. Eric, this is Dana."

After shaking hands and offering more welcomes, Dana motioned to the cargo lift at the edge of the deck. "Put your gear on the lift, if you want, and we'll load up in a few minutes. You can use the facilities...refill your cups if you'd like."

Dana knew she was talking fast and tried to slow down.

When he spoke, Eric's voice sounded like a drawl in comparison to hers. "Thanks for letting me go fishing with you, ma'am. This is totally cool. And your place is rad. You've got a front row seat for storms, I bet."

As small talk continued, Dana watched Rachel glance around the interior of her home. She realized this was the first time she had actually been inside. A large framed photograph on the wall had captured her attention.

"That's the *Adelaide*," Dana offered tentatively, "the boat we fished on when I was growing up. I was about twelve when that was taken."

Rachel acknowledged Dana's description without comment, stepping away from the pictures. "Can we help with anything?"

"No, I think we're all set. If you two are ready to go, we can join Hub below and get loaded."

The three made quick work of hauling gear to the skiff, meeting up with Hub, and transferring to the larger boat. Once on their way, Eric was talkative, engaging Dana and Hub in conversations about fishing techniques and their past success in the derbies. Rachel appeared to divide her attention between their dialogue and the water stretching out before them. Her face was unreadable.

There was more boat traffic than usual since it was the derby, but once they got north of Shelter Island, it thinned out. Hub cut the engine. "Let's see what kind of luck we have trolling for awhile. We can anchor up if you kids don't catch the winning salmon pretty quick. Eric, do you want to keep us pointed toward that little island north of us while I lower the trolling motor?"

Dana had put one package of herring in the bait bucket, lifted down two fishing poles, and proceeded to thread the double hooks through the herring. She was aware of Rachel's scrutiny.

"You want to have just a slight curve in the herring so it'll *swim* better. Would you like to try it?"

Rachel hesitated. "I think I'll watch you a few more times first. Is that okay?"

"Certainly. Or I'll bait your hooks all day if you'd prefer— I'm glad to do it."

"Umm…that's okay. I'll try it a little later."

Rachel let out her line counting the number of pulls, keeping the movement steady to keep the flasher from tangling. She obviously had done this before. Dana gave a few suggestions to Eric as he got his line in the water.

Within twenty minutes, Eric's line dipped, suggesting a bite. Dana coached him on how to set the hook and loosen the tension on his reel to allow the salmon to run without breaking the line. The others reeled in their lines and watched expectantly as Eric played his catch. It took a good ten minutes before it tired out.

Dana netted the salmon and dropped it in the fish hold for everyone to inspect. Eric and Rachel almost danced with excitement.

"It's a nice one, Eric. Good job. You handled him like you knew what you were doing." Hub chucked Eric's shoulder.

"Thanks. That's a big fish! I've fished a lot, but mostly in the streams. For trout—about one-tenth that size. He sure put up a nice fight."

Dana hooked the fish scale onto an eye screw protruding from the cabin overhang for just that purpose. "It's a nice coho. Let's see how much he weighs."

Hub lifted it onto the hook, reading the scale. "Seventeen pounds! Nice. Let's keep it on ice – it'll be a good one to turn in, but probably won't be the winner. If we get one in the twenty-five pound range, we'll pull up and run it to a weigh station before it can lose any weight."

Rachel's camera was busy catching shots of Eric and his fish. She handed it to Dana, "Would you take a picture of us...with the salmon between us?"

Dana obliged, grateful that Rachel had initiated the slightest communication with her.

She watched throughout the morning as Rachel interacted comfortably with Hub and Eric. She wasn't rude to Dana, but definitely aloof.

Hits were sporadic – just enough to maintain everyone's excitement. During interludes, Eric shared that he was from Nevada, but had to return to the University of Arizona in a few weeks. He was spending the summer in Southeast Alaska, hiking all the trails he could.

He grinned at Rachel, "I planned to make it to Skagway, but I met a fellow hiker who makes a mean latte, so I'll have to catch Haines and Skagway on another trip."

Eric's easy manner endeared him to Dana. He was intrigued by her work as a counselor, and they fell into a comfortable dialogue, to which Rachel listened.

"Are you an Alaska Native, Dana?"

Dana leaned back against the cabin wall, her long legs stretched out before her, crossed at the ankles. "Well, I'm a native Alaskan, but not a part of the Alaskan Native culture. I was born in Ketchikan, and grew up in Southeast Alaska. My dad raised me – largely out on these waters. I didn't have my own room until I was in middle school. Or a television or bicycle or a dog. We just fished when we could, and I stayed with family friends during the school year when Dad found work during the off-season. Some years we lived on the boat year-round.

"It was solitary in a lot of ways, but I wouldn't trade it for the world."

"What happened to your mom?"

There was the slightest catch in Dana's voice, "She left when I was very young. I don't really remember her."

"Bummer. How 'bout you, Hub...and how did you get the name Hub? Is that short for Hubert?"

Hub chuckled, scanning the water for boats ahead. "No, not Hubert. It's Robert if I have to get particular about it. *Hub* is a nickname that stuck when I was just a little guy interested in anything on wheels. It started as Hubcap, and was shortened to Hub somewhere along the way. Never got away from it, I guess."

Just then Rachel's line started peeling off her reel—that familiar sound that assured a good sized fish was on the hook. As Rachel lifted her pole from the holder, the other three quickly reeled in their lines.

"Oh, you got a nice one there, Rachel. Keep your tip up. Give him some line. A little less tension." Hub stood next to Rachel as he coached her. "That's it."

Rachel's smile was radiant. Dana noticed how strong she was—her arms bearing the weight of the salmon's fight; her legs holding her steady on the deck. Her focus never left the water, watching as her salmon jumped and dove until it was worn out and she could easily reel it in.

As Dana netted the coho, Rachel's sparkly eyes were directed at Hub. "Wow! That was a ride! Thanks for helping me.

"It's huge, isn't it? Sorry, Eric, but it's bigger than yours. Is it a male or female? It's beautiful, isn't it?"

All four admired Rachel's catch while her torso shimmied with excitement. She asked Dana to take pictures of her and her salmon, and also with Eric. Dana's heart beat a little faster.

The four debated whether to pull anchor and run the catch in to be weighed by derby officials or wait awhile to see if they caught more. Rachel ultimately decided she wanted to keep it on ice and continue fishing.

The excitement tapered and the four fishermen settled back into their respective spots on the boat over sandwiches and chips. Eric picked up the conversation again, showing great interest in Hub and Dana's history. "So how did you meet and how long have you been together?"

Hub grinned at Dana, signaling for her to respond. "Well, we were high school sweethearts. I had just moved up from Ketchikan...feeling pretty desolate and alone...and Hub rescued me." When she looked back at Hub, the slightest blush colored Dana's cheeks. "He asked me to join him for lunch, and the rest is history. We've been married seventeen years."

"Do you have any kids?"

Dana couldn't breathe. Her eyes darted to Rachel for clues on how to answer, but Rachel looked away, showing no emotion. *Obviously, she didn't tell her friend how we are connected. Now what?*

Without making eye contact with Eric, Dana stammered , "Uh, well...no, Hub and I haven't had children. We...we...it just didn't happen."

She stood up abruptly, offering to get refills and more chips from the galley. Hub turned the conversation to Eric's career plans.

After a few moments, Rachel stepped down to the galley. Standing across from Dana, she avoided eye contact. "I...I'm sorry. I didn't see that coming. I didn't say anything to Eric because...I just didn't."

Dana nodded, but continued to stand there, holding her breath. The two women studied each other, started to speak at the same time, then again waited for the other to speak. Finally, Dana asked, "How...what ..."

She took a deep breath and splayed out her hands as if starting fresh. "That's okay, Rachel. I know it's awkward for you, and I will do whatever makes you comfortable. I...just hope we can...spend some time figuring out what our relationship can be."

"You're doing that." Rachel pointed to her own face and mimicked Dana's nervous habit of pulling her lower lip under her canine tooth. "That's what I do. Hard to believe something like that is genetic. But we have the same teeth, don't we?"

Dana nodded slowly, tears forming in her eyes.

Rachel looked away, her voice hesitant. "My mom says that now she knows you're my biological...mother, she can see all kinds of similarities between us."

She swung away from Dana, "I don't see it, but that...that lip thing...struck me." She paused with one foot on the step, not looking back. "I'm curious some...but I'm not ready, Dana. I don't know why, but I just can't go there yet."

After Rachel joined the men on deck, Dana spoke softly into the silence. "That's okay, my darling girl. I'll wait until you're ready."

Chapter Six

DANA WAITED FOR THE school bus ahead to load the last of the grade-schoolers. She wondered if Rachel had ever ridden a school bus. Had she been driven to school or walked? Had she gone to private schools? *I know she was a good student to have graduated early, and she's so bright. Articulate. Beautiful. There's so much I long to know about her.*

As the stop sign closed against the side of the bus and traffic began to move again, Dana turned her thoughts to the therapy group starting today. She mentally checked through the list of six women who would begin their nine-month journey together. As far as she knew, none of them knew each other. In fact, they were quite different in their histories and needs.

Brandi, a young working mom who hasn't found her identity and voice. *She could have been a model with her beauty and bearing.*

Sheryl, a red-headed high school teacher whose nervous laughter might become annoying. *She seems too scatter-brained to be a teacher. It'll be interesting to see how she establishes herself with the other women.*

Ruth, a devoted mom facing the empty nest soon. *Hmm. Good heart, but almost…an overpowering presence.*

Susan, a single woman who's nearly reclusive. *She's so withdrawn…from any social connection. I hope she'll come out of her shell.*

Kimberly, somewhat of a party gal who struggles with depression. *Hopefully she's committed enough to be consistent.*

And Beth, who goes by Genie. Dana's brow furrowed, her mouth scrunching. *Lord, I don't know if she's a good fit for this group. I'll need your wisdom every step of the way.*

Dana recalled the intake appointment with Genie, a referral from her colleague who was the addictions counselor. Beth showed a very tough persona—distrusting of everything. She dressed like an insolent teenager, yet her face revealed the harshness of life on the streets. She claimed she wants to work with this group—needed to—yet there was a guardedness about her that worried Dana.

She sighed heavily and spoke out loud, "Well, we shall see."

***

At five-thirty, Dana peeked through her office window at the group room. Five of the women had arrived: three were seated; one was on her cell phone by the front door; one was fixing a beverage from the hostess bar.

Dana slipped her shoes back on, took a deep breath, and opened the door. All eyes turned to her except Brandi, who motioned she was wrapping up her phone call.

"Welcome, ladies! We have one more person yet to arrive. Grab a beverage, if you'd like—there's tea, water and hot chocolate."

"No coffee?"

"There isn't tonight, Genie, but if you're a coffee drinker, I'll have it ready in the future."

Her voice sounded to Dana like a grunt. "I am."

The women quickly settled into the circle of chairs. There was little interaction among them, which was typical of a gathering of strangers who were probably nervous about the unknown course set before them.

"Great. Let's get started. We're still missing one person. If she arrives yet this evening, or by next session, we'll have a group of six, otherwise, it will be just the five of you."

Dana looked around the circle, briefly holding eye-contact with each person, one at a time. To her, it was a silent connection—a physical reassurance of each person's importance. She felt herself settle, knowing she was good at doing group therapy. She would set the stage, and attend to the process, trusting that as empowered women, they would stretch and grow at their own pace and in their own way.

"I'm so glad you are here—each of you. It's probably scary on some level to commit to a nine-month group with people yet unknown to you, with the expectation that you will share personal aspects of your lives and goals, and allow yourself to be vulnerable in some ways. It's a very courageous first step, and I applaud each of you for taking it."

The women were attentive as Dana spoke, continually moving her eyes to maintain contact with everyone. She crossed her legs and scooted to one side of her chair, although her hands continued to emphasize her words.

"I've been leading groups for almost eleven years now, and each group is unique—just as we human beings are. But the constant in each group is this: It's a microcosm of community where we come together as strangers with a common purpose. We get to know each other, and over time, learn to trust each other...at least within this context.

"We will establish boundaries to provide emotional safety for ourselves and each other so that we can be free to *be* who we are. We can examine our hurts and hang-ups, and how we interact in a communal way that validates our thinking. We can even experiment with who we want to become.

"We can examine our histories, or make conscious choices about behaviors and reactions, and discard habits that are no longer working for us."

Dana's arms stretched out as if to encircle all that had been said. "The beauty of group interaction is that you learn to set boundaries and be in relationships that are affirming. And you take what you learn here to your world outside of this group. Does that make sense?"

The women nodded in response to Dana's question. She launched into the required information about confidentiality and the exceptions in case of certain disclosures or potential harm to self or others. "And part of the safety of this group is each of *you* maintaining its confidentiality. Certainly you can discuss what you're getting from the group with your loved ones, but be careful to protect the identity of each other outside the group setting.

"We'll take a break for two weeks at Christmas and perhaps other times if the group decides, but my hope is you'll each be here every week, unless it's unavoidable. It's like we're traveling in a raft together...paddling, and if one is absent, the group is less powerful and it's harder to stay on course."

Ruth interjected. "That's a relief. I have a lot of catering events over the holidays, so I won't have to miss any meetings."

Dana continued with the topic of personal boundaries, which created discussion among the women. "Boundaries create the safe place, so you can be *real*. That includes predictable start and stop times, speaking for yourself only, taking turns speaking and listening...and underlying it all is respect. Even though we are all very different, and have come to this point in our lives travelling dissimilar roads, we are each unique and precious. So...by honoring ourselves and our internal wisdom, we can honor the individual journeys, perspectives and solutions of others. Does that make sense?"

"No cross talk! It's as simple as that." The volume of Genie's voice seemed incongruent with her small stature, accentuated by ripped jeans that was a popular style with teenagers. "At NA we don't allow that either."

The vigilance in the room ratcheted up a notch with Genie's pronouncement. "Thank you, Genie. Yes, it's similar. And that brings up another characteristic of this group that's different from the twelve-step groups, which by the way, I support wholeheartedly. Whereas the twelve-step groups are open to changing attendance each week, this group is what we call a closed group. We begin and end with the same individuals. You five, plus the missing person if she gets here by the next session, will make up the group for nine months. What happens then, is you come to know and understand each other on a deeper level."

Dana received nods from Sheryl, Brandi and Ruth, and a glance from Susan. Genie didn't acknowledge her. "Okay, any questions? Or something I've not covered that would make you feel more comfortable in group?"

Ruth spoke right up again. "What are the rules about bad language? I really don't appreciate it."

Genie scowled at Ruth, but Dana spoke up before she could match words with her disapproving look. "That's a good point, Ruth. We all have different comfort levels with swearing, and probably speak differently in different settings. I generally don't say *damn* when I am in church, but it seems to fly out of my mouth fairly easily at times. So let's talk about what our behavior—and tolerance needs to be in this setting, this group...to make it safe for everyone."

Sheryl's laughter announced her intent to respond and continued as her words bubbled out in its midst. "*Oy vey.* As a teacher, I've had to get used to a lot of freakin' language." Her gangly body shook as she laughed even more. "Those high-schoolers can embarrass a drill sergeant, I tell ya. But I don't want to hear it in my classroom either, so the kids curb it. Either that or I threaten to start a rumor that we're BFFs."

After another wave of laughter ebbed, Sheryl added. "I'm sure we can do some curbing and some tolerating here since we're likely to become BFFs."

"What's BFF?" Susan asked quietly.

Sheryl's laughter salted her response, "I'm sorry...you can tell I spend *waaay* too much time with teenagers. Best Friends Forever—even though in the teenagers' world, that might mean two days!"

Dana interjected, "I like how you married up *curbing* and *tolerating*, Sheryl. That strikes a nice balance, doesn't it? We can curb our language that might be offensive to others, and we can tolerate some slippage and differences. How does that sound— each of you?"

Ruth sat back in her chair, "I guess that sounds fair enough."

Susan shrugged and nodded, her eyes appearing large behind her glasses.

Brandi said it was fine.

"It's just like a classroom to me," offered Sheryl.

All eyes turned to Genie, who responded condescendingly. "I can't say I won't offend someone, but I'll try to have my Sunday manners on."

Dana decided to go with that concession, even though there was *attitude* behind Genie's words. "Okay, any other boundaries or guidelines we need to make this a safe place for everyone?"

Hearing no other comments, Dana launched into the next topic with some playfulness in her voice. "Okay. I'd like us to introduce ourselves to each other in sort of a fun way. On the counter over there is card stock and a variety of craft supplies for you to use. I'd like you to make a name card with just your first name, and decorate it in a way that says something about you."

She noticed that Susan looked anxious. "Now this isn't an art class, and I'm no teacher, so don't worry about it being artistic. It's just a backdrop to help us talk about ourselves a little bit. Who we are—not deep dark secrets, but what we do; what we like; how we recreate…that sort of thing. Oh…and what you hope to gain from this group over the next nine months."

After several minutes, everyone had crafted a name card and returned to their chairs. "Great. It looks like everyone's ready. I'll start us off and give you a moment to collect your thoughts.

"I'm Dana, and even though I won't normally share my personal life in group—this is your time, not mine—I will tell you that I am married to my high school sweetheart. Our kids are four-legged creatures—Mica and Nikki, the dogs, and Lionel, the fat cat who owns us.

"I like to fish just about as much as I like to sleep," she held up her name card shaped like a fish, "so I watch the tides and get out when I can. And I hike and pick blueberries; go to the high school plays when they're offered. And sometimes I sit and knit—it's relaxing to me.

"And…what I'd like to get from this group: My desire is to help each of you meet your personal goals; to gain insight about those things that hold you back from living your life freely—untethered. I want to help each of you discover your personal strengths and the qualities that make *you* uniquely *you*.

"There's scripture that says, *I praise you for I am fearfully and wonderfully made. Wonderful are your works.* That's you. You were each awesomely and wonderfully created, and my desire is that you come to know that, if you don't already.

"So, enough about me. Who would like to go next?"

Ruth sat up straighter. "I will. And that scripture is from Psalms 139.

"I'm Ruth. I've been married for twenty-five years come November. Les, my husband, and I have three daughters. The youngest is seventeen." She looked over at Sheryl, "She might even be one of your students, hopefully not one of those who uses foul language.

"I've always loved to cook, so I developed a catering business—weddings and events. Plus I cook at the Glory Hole every week—it's my church's mission. And I take meals to people who are sick or grieving, and try to help in other ways. And that's about it."

"It sounds like you're a busy gal, Ruth. What would you like to get from this group?"

Ruth surged on. "My youngest daughter is being very obstinate, and I don't seem to be able to reach her. It's a critical time for her—her senior year and going off to college. I've got to make her understand the impact of her choices..." Her confident demeanor faltered as she continued, "It seems I say the wrong thing, and I'm afraid...Dana has helped me these last few weeks to understand that I can only change me. So that's what I hope for...to learn more about communicating with my family."

"Thank you, Ruth. Your daughters are lucky to have your determination to find solutions."

Scanning the other group members, Dana asked, "Who would like to go next?"

Sheryl flashed her name card, rocking her head back and forth causing her red curls to bounce. "I'll jump in. I can't swim, but I'll go down tryin.'"

She pointed to her name card in the shape of an apple. "I'm Sheryl—Mrs. T. to my students. I've been a teacher almost twenty years. I teach trigonometry, so my students are typically more serious about learning, which helps. Some of my colleagues have it a lot worse, but I like my kids.

"I'm married to an old curmudgeon. He's kind of a homebody, so I go about my business without him. He's into fishing too, Dana, so you've probably seen him out there on the bread line. But I like to go to movies and concerts; book readings at the library and such. I tell ya, there's a lot to do in Juneau for next to nothing.

"We've got a son in the Coast Guard." Freeing her lip from the braces on her teeth, she continued, "I guess I want to do life a little differently. I'm pretty stressed out. I have to take a pill to get to sleep and another to calm me down." At that, Sheryl sat back and laughed so hard tears, came to her eyes.

"Ay-ay-ay. I guess I'm hopeless." Taking a deep breath, she became more sober. "Dana tells me that stress may be causing some of my problems, so that's why I'm here. Sometimes I think I'm getting Alzheimer's—I forget things that are important, and can't remember if I'm coming or going. And I'm on edge."

She looked around before continuing quietly. "The final straw was...I lost my temper at a student who was just being a teenager. That's not like me, and I feel horrible about it. So...I've gotta get on top of it...or cut my throat." Her chuckle signaled that was enough of her serious side!

"Well, I applaud you, Sheryl. Working with teenagers all day would tax just about anyone, I think. You're doing important work.

"Who would like to go next?"

"I'll go next." Brandi's striking dark blue eyes revealed no emotion, although she held eye-contact with the others. She spoke properly, holding her body erect as if addressing a Toastmasters' gathering.

Holding up her name card with four stick figures, she recited, "I'm Brandi. I am married and have two children— Miranda is six and Robbie is four. I work part time at the hospital. In the billing office.

"My husband works for the government and can set his own schedule, so he keeps the children while I work early mornings. I'm up when the east coast is buzzing, but home by seven-thirty. That way we don't have to leave the children with strangers. I don't have much time to recreate with two children, but I do like to work out—I guess that's my recreation."

She took a deep breath, less certain of her words. "I'm here...because... My husband and I have been fighting a lot but I don't want to go to couples counseling. I think I need to figure some things out first." She pushed her lush blond hair back from her face, flipping the long waves over her shoulder. "I guess that's what I want to take from the group—understanding of...myself, and...what's what."

Dana's nod seemed to punctuate Brandi's last statement. "Okay! I hope we can help you with that.

"Beth or Susan...which of you would like to go next?"

The response was swift and loud. "It's Genie! G-e-n-i-e, as in Aladdin and the magic lamp." Beth's forceful clarification of her nickname startled Dana.

"My apologies, Genie. I knew you preferred your nickname and I messed up. Please forgive me. Would you like to go next?"

Genie's arms were crossed, her elbows extending beyond the sides of her slim body. Her skinny jeans accentuated her thin legs crossed at the knees, with one lace-up boot wrapped back around the other. She let her arms fall back on the chair arms. "Well, I'm a drug addict. I've been clean and sober for one hundred eighty-three days."

Ruth interjected, "Good for you."

Genie flashed a sideways glance at Ruth, her furrowed brows scrunched even more, before she continued. "I have a sponsor, and that's what I do—twelve step meetings. Except when I work. I deliver auto parts around the valley. And I'm here because I have to be."

Dana cocked her head at Genie with a questioning look.

"Well, I guess I don't *have* to be. I could just die." She looked back at Dana demurely before she continued. "My drug counselor wants me here. She thinks some of your manners might wear off on me."

Dana raised her eyebrows, gently asking, "And what do *you* want to gain from this group, Genie?"

It was a moment before she responded, her voice giving the slightest hint of vulnerability. "I want to get better. I don't ever want to go back to where I was."

"Thank you, Genie. I'm really glad you're here.

"Susan...we come to you. Will you share with us?"

Susan's straight brown hair created a perfectly straight line above her eyebrows and just below her ears. She pushed her heavy-framed black glasses up on her nose before she started, her voice timorous. "I work for the school system as a reading specialist. I'm single."

She shrugged her shoulder, dipping her head as if apologizing. "I like to read...science fiction mostly. And ancient history."

She continued in monotone. "I'm here because I have some anxiety....and OCD. It keeps me from flying. I need to go to San Francisco for a summer semester for some advanced education. So, I want to get over my anxiety. That's all."

"Okay. Thank you, Susan. You're very courageous to be here…in this uncertain setting, in spite of your anxiety. I'm proud of you."

Dana took some time to look around the group, contemplating all that had been said thus far. She sat back in her chair, comfortably crossing her arms. "Wow. We've covered a lot of territory tonight, haven't we? What a gathering of interesting, courageous, accomplished women you are. I'm honored to be working with you.

"Before we end the session tonight, I'd like to hear from each of you—how are you feeling right now? What are your thoughts about the first group session—are you committed to being here next week? Notice what your body is telling you—where are you holding any tension? Then give us your thoughts."

Sheryl was the first to speak, her laughter reduced to a chuckle. "I'm glad I'm here. I don't know how you all can help me with my stress, but I'm actually more relaxed now than when we started. I'll be here next week."

"I will be too." Brandi seemed to study her hands as she rubbed one with the other, posture still erect. "I'm…I'm good."

Dana noticed that Brandi's eye-contact seemed warmer to the other women. "Ruth?"

"I'm still a little nervous, but less so than when we started. I think it'll be all right. I plan to be here next week."

Susan's facial expression didn't change, but she nodded firmly and said she would be back. All eyes shifted toward Genie.

Her posture was more relaxed with both boots on the floor. She lifted her chin as she spoke, her brows still furrowed. "I'm game. It's different than I expected, but it'll probably be okay. I'll be here next week."

Dana sat in the circle of chairs after her clients left, still contemplating the dynamics of the group. She thought, for the initial start up, it went fairly well. Each person showed at least a slight improvement in comfort level. Each was fairly direct with her issues and goals, without too much disclosure. *That Sheryl will be a good buffer between Genie and Ruth. I can't let her become the referee and lose track of her own healing though. Those two will be my biggest challenge.*

Chapter Seven

"DAD, I'D LIKE TO SEE your new place. When are you going to have us over?" Dana had swallowed her pride and reached out to her father again. He hadn't called even to hear the details of the derby. Although their fish hadn't been in the top weights, Rachel had won a barbeque grill donated by the local hardware store.

Dana knew he had stopped by for coffee with Hub a few times, but he had avoided her.

"You can come any time, Dana. Check it out. I'm not up to fixing a meal, though. I've been pretty busy."

"What's going on?"

"I've just got things going on, Dana." The irritation in his voice came through loud and clear. "Putting the place together. Getting settled."

There was a heavy silence on the line before Dana broke it with a serious tone. "Dad, we've got to talk. This isn't like us to be so distant. We're family."

Dan's response was biting, "Families don't betray each other then spend twenty years lying about it, Dana."

She yelled back, "I didn't betray you, Dad! I tried to protect you! I *lived* the loss of my daughter alone! Can't you understand what that was like for me?" Dana couldn't catch a breath to release the deep sobs held in her heart.

Her dad's silence was finally broken with his quiet words. "I'm sorry you chose to do it your way, Dana. There's nothing I can do about that."

After a brief silence, Dan added, "I have nothing more to say. I'll talk to you later."

Dana sat for a long while, holding her cell phone after her father hung up. Her grief turned to anger as she thought about her father's inability to discuss hurtful things—things of the heart. As she reflected on the events over her lifetime, she could see where he deftly side-stepped conversations that came too close to his heart. He was okay with all the celebratory times, funny times, superficial discussions, but not things of personal importance. *Was it always like this? Have I just not seen it before? Or was it convenient...easier for me to not see it?*

She thought about the greatest pain of her young years— growing up without a mother. *But we almost never talked about it.* It was only when Dan was still drinking that he even mentioned her name. *And that wasn't to comfort me...it was his own sorrow spilling out.*

Or guilt.

"Well Father, I learned well from you, didn't I?"

Dana dropped her phone on the counter and began to pace around the kitchen island. *He's like some of my clients, afraid to confront emotional pain – but he's not doing anything about it!*

Dana dropped down on the couch, folding her legs beneath her. Absently stroking Lionel, she studied the overcast day out her window. The silver blue water was calm. A few fishing boats trolled just beyond the nearest islands.

She spoke out loud to the cat, "Well, I guess that's the way it's going to be." Dana could feel the wall begin to form around her heart. Invisible. Strong. Necessary to keep her from falling apart.

***

The women arrived for the second group session appearing less circumspect than the previous week. Brandi, Sheryl and Ruth were having a dialogue about the school sports programs, while Genie and Susan listened.

As Dana joined them, they each gravitated to the seat they had chosen the week before, and looked expectantly at her. "Good evening! It's so good to see each of you again.

"Before we get started, I wanted to let you know the other gal who was going to join us said she couldn't make it after all, so it will be just the five of you for the duration. And that's probably just as well since we got a good start last week in getting to know each other.

"So...what I'd like to do for starters is to do a check-in. Share what you'd like about how your week went, what thoughts or questions came up for you since last week, or anything that might be troubling you."

Looking around the circle, she connected visually with each person. "Who'd like to start?"

Dana had learned to out-wait the silence. It was often hard to be the first to speak, especially in the early stages of group development.

Sheryl slapped her knee, chortling as she spoke. "Well, I'll jump in. I'm never one to think first. My week has been great...if you like hanging from a fast moving train! I'm trying to learn the peculiarities of one hundred hormonal teenagers, and at the same time, remind them how to at least spell trigonometry. Maybe even recall what they've forgotten over the summer so we can move on to new material. *Oy vey*. I don't know why I didn't become a truck driver."

After a laughing spell and wiping the tears from her eyes, Sheryl added, "But it's great. Really. I love those kids...most of them."

"You must have the gift for it, Sheryl. You obviously love what you do. What helps you get through the rough spots?"

Sheryl's response bubbled with her laughter. "I've not taken up whisky yet, but I might need to some day." Seeming to notice that the others weren't laughing with her, Sheryl became more serious. "Oh, I don't know. That's what I'm here for, I guess. It used to be enough to laugh it off, but... It helps when I can get out and walk...talk things through with another teacher. But I'm so busy, that's impossible."

Dana summarized Sheryl's point, nodding. "Sounds like walking and talking are pretty important."

She let that settle before asking, "Who's next?"

"I'll follow." Susan pushed her glasses up on her nose. "I don't have nearly as many students, but it is busy setting up reading plans for each person. It takes extra hours."

"And how are you doing with it all, Susan? Is it stressful?"

"Not too bad. I'm doing okay."

Dana decided that was all she could pull from Susan today, so looked around the circle to see who might volunteer to go next.

Genie finally spoke up. "Everything's just peachy. Good job. Nice digs. A little honey on the side. Lots of twelve-step meetings."

"Have you got a good sponsor, Genie?" After seeing her nod, Dana asked, "Are you working with her regularly? Working the steps?"

Genie affirmed with a nod, but offered nothing further.

"Okay, Brandi, how about you?"

"I'm doing fine. Adjusting to the kids being in school. Having to line them out before I go to bed and help with their homework when they get home from school. We're getting into a routine, though." Her forged smile signaled the end of her statement.

"Okay. Ruth?"

Ruth took a deep breath, then spoke matter-of-factly. "I'm okay. It hasn't been the best of weeks. My teenager has her own car now, and prefers to study at her girlfriend's, so it makes it easy for her to avoid me. I'm pretty irritated, but trying to leave her alone."

"What are you doing to cope, Ruth?"

"Staying busy. Picking blueberries." She pointed over to the counter. "I brought some blueberry tarts for everyone tonight."

"Nice. Thank you.

"Okay. I'd like us to talk about boundaries tonight. Limits. They're all around us—stop signs; fences; rules. We see clearly where the property lines are, which delineates what is ours; what is not. Where our rights and responsibilities begin and end. But in our personal lives, it's often hard to figure out:

"Can I loan my partner's pickup to the neighbor without checking with him first?

"Do friends need to call before they stop by?

"Is it okay for someone else to get into my purse?"

Dana's eyes walked around the circle as she offered more examples.

"If my family member needs money, and I just got paid, am I obligated to loan them money?

"If he wants sex and I don't, what's okay?

"If I don't have plans, am I obligated to work an extra shift when asked?

"I see some nods and smirks, so I'm sure you've each got opinions on the topic, or some challenges. So...let's explore...what are boundaries? When is it hard to set a boundary...a limit...to say *no* when you determine you want to? And to say *yes* when you decide to."

"I say *no* whenever I want to. No guy's gonna dictate my wants—for sex or anything else. I'm in control, thank you." Genie's pronouncement and raised chin left no room for debate.

"Okay. So you're very clear about the power of your *no*. Other thoughts?"

"I think it's different when you're married. You've got to *give and take*." Brandi's voice was not condemning, but certain. "I mean, with children, I'd never be in the mood for sex, but that wouldn't be fair to him. He has needs. So...sometimes it's okay to say *no*, but sometimes you just need to...think of him."

Sheryl's chuckle proclaimed her turn. "I just wish the old curmudgeon and I would have some arguments about sex, but that's not the issue for me. *No* is not a word that rolls off my tongue easily. I've got more magazine subscriptions than Safeway. Every time a kid does a marathon of some sort, they know I'm an easy mark. Or if the principal needs an extra chaperone, he knows he can count on Mrs. T. Sometimes it gets to be too much!"

Ruth shifted in her chair. "I think we're called to serve God through helping others...to give. We're supposed to serve...use our blessings. So I avoid *no* whenever I can."

Genie glowered at her, but remained silent.

Dana acknowledged Ruth's opinion with a nod and turned to Susan. "Susan, do you have some thoughts about boundaries?"

"Not really. I just do what I can and decline when I don't feel I can."

"All right. So it sounds like there's a balance, isn't there? Sometimes we need to say *yes* even when we might not feel up to it, and sometimes we need to say *no* even when it's hard. What makes it hard to say *no*?"

Sheryl and Brandi spoke of the difficulty of disappointing others, the fear of being rejected, or judged, and how difficult it is to hold ground with a persistent or demanding person. Genie flippantly inserted, "Just tell them all to go to hell." Susan observed the discussion without comment.

Ruth watched the others but didn't speak up.

Finally, Brandi turned to Dana and asked, "How do you know where to *draw the line*? When is it okay to say *enough already*?"

Dana chuckled at her perplexed expression. "I don't know. I think we each have to decide for ourselves. But in deciding, don't we need to consider our own needs as well as those we care about?

"How often do you make decisions based on your personal energy, priorities, goals, preferences, and internal value system rather than someone else's expectations? Or fear of someone's disapproval or judgment?"

Even though Genie was quiet, Dana could tell she was thoughtful about what had been said. "Okay. Before we end for the day, I want to give you an assignment: Pay attention to your thought process when you make choices this week. In fact, write down at least three choices you make, and what were the factors you considered in making that choice. They don't have to be major decisions, perhaps what program you watch on television; what time you go to bed — that sort of thing. Then next session, let's see what we've learned."

Dana noticed the increased interaction among three of the women as they left her office. Genie and Susan remained separate and left quietly.

Chapter Eight

DANA STOOD IN LINE at the grocery store watching the little boy in a football uniform. He was covered with mud—a testimony to the amount of rain that had soaked the ball field. He seemed oblivious to his condition as he concentrated on the ice cream sandwich taken from the package in his mother's grocery cart.

She wished she could capture the image that said so much about the stamina of a rough-and-tumble boy in an environment where rain dominated. Only the hardy ones thrived in southeast Alaska—magnificence wrapped in dreary weather and darkness at times. Depression and addictions were common here, one of the highest rates in the nation.

I wonder why it's such an issue with some, yet people like this little guy thrive in spite of the mud.

I hope Rachel is a thriver.

Dana had finally had a telephone conversation with Rachel that was almost normal, *whatever that is.* Dana asked about Rachel's classes and how she was getting settled in school. Resisting the temptation to pursue a face-to-face visit, Dana acknowledged that, for now, impersonal communication might be all that Rachel could handle. *If that's all you can give right now, my darling, I will be content with that...and pack my schedule to over-flowing to keep myself from obsessing about you.*

The next day rained off and on—light but steady. Dana stepped out of her office before the group arrived, drinking in the fresh air. The low-lying clouds blocked the view of Mount Juneau looming above the city, and the vast waters to the south. Dana brought her focus to the immediate surroundings. The block seemed bleak and tired. Lonely. Dana tried to shrug off the dreary feel of it.

After everyone was seated, Dana asked, "So, let's do check-ins…how are you doing? How's your week been? And, what did you notice about the choices you made this week?"

Brandi responded without hesitation. "I'm sort of angry. I don't know that there's anything in particular, but I have been more aware of my decision-making process. And what I see, I don't like."

Her blonde hair tied up in a messy bun bounced as she spoke her indignation. "I decided to keep track of my choices about household chores. It's one of the major arguments with my husband, so I thought I'd do some research, sort of. Well, I ended up doing over half his responsibilities just to avoid an argument. And now I'm pis…mad. I don't know if that was your intention with this assignment, Dana, but it has sure stirred me up."

Dana gulped aloud for effect. "Well…I guess if that's what it takes to gain insight, that's what it takes! So…from a boundary-setting concept, what does it tell you?"

"That my husband isn't doing his part, which I have known all along. I'm just madder now."

"Okay, but what does it say about you? About the choices you make?"

"That I do his responsibilities to keep the peace." Brandi slumped back in the chair. "I know…I do it to myself. But if I don't do it, it'll just pile up, or won't get done. I can't stand the mess — that's even worse than the arguments."

"It's a common problem in relationships, and I don't pretend to have the answers, but I think awareness is the first step to finding solutions. Awareness of your feelings, and how you react. So…how do you typically react when you have arguments about it?"

Brandi's voice sounded less irritated as she examined her routine. "We yell at each other; he accuses me of everything I've ever done wrong; or he promises to be better. But it never lasts. It's just the same thing all over again, and I resent him."

"Aha. Resentment. A very telling emotion, isn't it? Usually, when I feel resentment, it's because *I* have failed to set a boundary, even though the resentment is directed toward him. Is any of that true for you?"

Brandi huffed as she looked directly at Dana, her voice in contrast with her tough expression. "Yes, but I don't know what to do differently."

"I understand.

"Maybe some ideas will come to you as we go around. Who would like to check in next?

Sheryl rolled her eyes in reaction to what Brandi had just said. "You'd flip out if you had to live with me and my mess! But my husband and I don't argue about that. Stuff just stacks up until one of us is forced to take out the trash. Sorry, but we're pretty close to slobs, I guess."

She chuckled before continuing. "One of the other teachers asked me for the umpteenth time to give her a ride home after school. It's not that big of a deal, but it takes an extra hour by the time I wait for her to get her stuff, then veer off to her neck of the woods, and hang around to chitchat about the world's problems. I don't mind once in awhile, but last year it got to be a fairly regular thing.

"I'm ready to go home! I'm tired and cranky, and it does add to my stress level...but I can't seem to say *no*. I don't want to hurt her feelings."

Dana probed. "Because if you hurt her feelings...then what?"

Sheryl stammered, her eyes moving in a circle as if chasing the answer. "I...well, I wouldn't want to hurt anyone's feelings."

Dana took a deep breath before she responded. "It seems like there's a balance somewhere between being overly generous and being protective of your personal time and energy."

Sheryl's head shook side-to-side as she looked skyward before she nodded. "I know. I'm a wimp."

Genie leaned to one side of her chair stretching out her legs; her hands clasped. "I don't have a problem saying *no*. If it doesn't fit with my priorities, I don't do it. Simple as that."

Dana hesitated before asking, "So, you don't have trouble setting boundaries with anyone? Friends, bosses, salesmen, family?"

Genie shook her head firmly with each category, her lips pursed for emphasis.

Gently, Dana asked, "How about with yourself, Genie? Do you ever have trouble setting boundaries with yourself?"

Genie's furrowed brows suggested a challenge to what Dana had just said, but when she finally spoke, her voice was tentative. "I don't know what you mean."

"Well, in a way, we set boundaries with ourselves too, don't we? We choose how to behave in public. We set limits on our actions, time, activities. Maybe I'd prefer to read all night, but choose to turn the light out because I need to get up early. That sort of thing."

Genie shrugged one shoulder. "Anybody has trouble saying *no* in that case. That's self-discipline. I don't...I have trouble like anybody else. If you mean my drug stuff, I'm good now. I've been clean two hundred and four days."

"I didn't mean to insinuate drug use particularly. I was thinking that...sometimes it's easy to set limits with other people, yet difficult to set limits for ourselves. Or vice versa. Maybe it's a dichotomy...if we're good at one, the other is difficult?"

She stared at Dana a moment before responding. "Maybe. I'll think about it."

"And how are you otherwise? How'd your week go?"

"All right. No biggies."

"Okay.

"Ruth, how's it going with you?"

Ruth looked perturbed. "Not so good. I forgot all about the assignment, frankly. It's been...difficult this week.

"My seventeen-year-old left the house. Packed up her clothes and is staying with her girlfriend, which we don't really approve of. We had a family function at the church, and she refused to go. I insisted, and she left. She hasn't returned any of my phone calls, and that was last Wednesday."

"That's gotta hurt. How have you been coping with it, Ruth?"

She shrugged. "I keep busy. Pray. Eat chocolate."

"Are you and your husband discussing it at all?"

"Yeah. He's at a loss for what to do, but he goes off to work and doesn't think about it. I'm so..." Her eyes closed briefly, her jaws tightened. "I'm so afraid she'll throw everything away. Like my oldest daughter. She did the same thing."

"Ruth, if you could rewind last Wednesday, what would you do differently?"

She shook her head slowly, her lips pursed. "I don't know. I can't have her flaunting our family values and structure. She can't just do her own thing and simply ignore what we believe. She's got to give some."

Genie's disgust exploded. "She's seventeen! I was on my own...making my own way when I was fourteen! You act like she's a baby! No wonder she can't stand to be in your house!"

Ruth's eyes sparked, then narrowed, boring into Genie as she snarled, "That is exactly why I try to set rules for her—I don't want her to be like...like so many young people today, to go down that road. I don't want her to end up pregnant or with some abusive man, or...worse!"

Dana held her hands up, fingers splayed. "Hold on now. We're talking about two different people and completely different circumstances. Let's not cross-talk." She shifted her body directly in line with Ruth to discourage further comment from Genie, but not before she saw Genie toss her head and sit back in her chair like a pouting child. "It's got to be tough for a mother to watch a near-adult child make choices that are not what you want. What is the emotion that goes with that, Ruth? What are you feeling right now when you think about her?"

Ruth's eyes searched the space in front of her, her voice unsteady. "I'm angry. And afraid. I'm...just scared of what might happen to her."

"And where do you carry that fear in your body, Ruth?"

"My chest." Ruth put her hand on her breast.

"Okay, take some deep breaths." Dana exaggerated her breathing to encourage Ruth to deepen hers. "You might tap your feet back and forth—it helps to calm us. Sort of like the comfort of an old rocking chair."

After several deep breaths, Ruth's face began to relax and the crunch of her shoulders released.

"Ruth, setting aside the fear you have for your daughter, what is the fear you have for yourself?"

Her head pulled back as if rejecting the idea outright, then her words stepped out hesitantly. I...don't...think I'm afraid for myself. Maybe that I won't be in her life? Maybe that I won't know my grandchildren, if she or Mary ever have children."

Dana continued to exaggerate her deep breathing, watching Ruth as she followed suit. "What control do you have over those things, Ruth—not having her in your life as an adult, and not knowing your grandchildren?"

Ruth's shoulders slumped, but she still sat straight in her chair. "None really. Once Angie's eighteen and out of my house, I have no control over her."

"I wonder how much control you truly have even now, Ruth—influence, yes—you're her mother, but control? Isn't she the one who decided to leave? I'm certain she loves you even if it doesn't feel like it right now, but isn't she making the choices, even though she's not yet eighteen?"

Ruth stared at Dana. "We're still responsible for her. If she does something stupid, we're the ones who have to clean up the mess. But, no, we can't force her to live with us." Her lower jaw shifted as if chewing on that thought. "What would you do, Dana? She's still a minor. How do I *influence* rather than *control* when she is not willing to meet me half way?"

Dana's voice was as steady as her penetrating look. "I don't have those answers, Ruth, but I am absolutely certain you will find them. You've taken a very courageous step in that direction this evening by admitting your sense of helplessness. We can't change what we don't acknowledge. Can you tolerate that uncertainty for a bit while you explore the question of *control* versus *influence*?"

Ruth nodded even though doubt showed on her face.

Dana made a mental check of the time left in the session and decided to not address Genie's cross-talk or revelation about being on her own at age fourteen. She prompted Susan with a questioning look. "And how are you doing, Susan?"

"I'm okay. Just more anxious this week. I've got a lot of new students." She picked at her cuticles as she looked directly as Dana.

"And how does anxiety manifest itself, Susan…what are your symptoms?"

Susan's answers were clipped, direct. "I stay in my room more. Reading. Sometimes I'm late for work, even when I'm up early. I have to do stuff…check the tire pressure in my car, the lights, fluid levels. I do equations in my head. It's tiring."

"I'm sure that's exhausting, Susan. And does your vehicle need attention when you do this checking?"

"Sometimes. The tire's mainly. I know it's not...urgent, but I can't leave without checking."

"Are there times when you can tell yourself to ignore the compulsion to check things?"

Susan nodded. "When I'm less anxious. I take medication, but sometimes it isn't enough."

"And what helps in those times? Have you noticed anything that makes a difference?"

"My sleep. Eating right. If I eat too many sweets, it seems worse."

"And you see your medical practitioner regularly, don't you, Susan...for the medication part?"

Susan nodded.

"You seem to have a good awareness of the changes in your body, and what some of the triggers are. That's good."

Dana had already shifted to a pattern of deeper, slower breathing as she spoke. "Okay, let's all do some belly-breathing as we wind down this evening. It's such a powerful way to remind our bodies to return to neutral...not racing our engines when there isn't the need for racing." She made eye contact with each woman as she exaggerated her breathing and stretched out her arms, using her hands to show the release of tension with each out-breath. She observed as each person ratcheted her stress level down a notch. All but Genie closed their eyes.

"Keep breathing as I say a few things.

"I think we made good strides tonight. Each of you has been very courageous to open yourselves up to this group."

Her breath as well as her words came slower. "To admit vulnerability in some aspect of your lives—it's uncomfortable. We often spend so much time hiding our problems from others that we bury them from our own awareness. That is until the stress level gets so high that we explode.

"I'd like you to each do a check-in with yourself...notice your body; where are you tense or relaxed; warm or cool; soft or firm?" Dana's voice and steady deep breaths were calming. "Do you notice any change? Note what's running around in your mind; and then share what you're feeling right now."

Dana watched as each person's eyes shifted focus from internal to the space immediately in front of her. After a moment, she asked, "Genie, how are you feeling right now?"

Genie looked startled at being called upon. She grumbled, "I'm fine. It's nothing I'm not used to."

Dana didn't respond right away, letting Genie's comment hang in the silence. She nodded, deciding that was probably the extent of how much attention Genie could tolerate right now. She looked questioningly at Susan, going around the circle in the opposite direction of how they had shared.

"I'm a little more relaxed. That breathing helps."

"Ruth?"

Ruth hesitated then seemed resolved to plunge in. "I'm...perplexed. Angry. There's a lot of arguments going around in my head, and I don't know where to light. I bared my soul and that's not something I do. But I'm not sorry. I'm counting on everybody to respect the rules we spoke about and to not gossip about me." She glanced at Genie before directing her words at Dana again. "You said we can't change what we don't acknowledge. I think that's probably true, so I'm going to pray about that a bit. But I'm fine."

When Dana's eyes settled on her, Sheryl flashed a fleeting smile, her red hair dancing as her head darted about. "I'm good. This has been thought-provoking. I've got a lot to think about. I am calmer though." Her chuckles spurted out as she motioned for Brandi to take it from there.

Brandi looked thoughtful, a dimple showing above her right eyebrow. "Well...I'm not as angry, but I still don't know what I should do. I know my problem is different than any of you, and I need to decide my own approach. I'm just not sure what that looks like. But that's why we're here, right? To figure it out?"

Dana nodded and assured Brandi and the other members of the group that answers will surface. She said she was confident that each person would find her own unique insight and plan of action, but inside, she couldn't wait for the women to leave her office. It felt like this session had bombed and she was anxious to have it end. *What if the hostility between Ruth and Genie can't be bridged? I could lose one or both of them — it could mean success or failure of the whole group.*

Chapter Nine

IT WAS DANA'S MONTH to facilitate the group of her peers. They had just finished updates on their personal lives and had discussed a suicidal patient of Lisen Velvick's, the Psychiatric Nurse Practitioner.

Lisen concluded, "Thanks, guys. It really helps to hear your ideas about treating him. Hopefully the meds will keep him stable 'til you can help him with better coping skills."

Dana looked around the room for signals that anyone else had anything to say before she spoke. "I guess I'd like to talk about my new group, if we've got time yet."

She combed her fingers through her dark wavy hair before settling in a posture with her hands on her head. Her voice was rhythmic. "I think I just lived through the worst group session I have ever experienced." She threw her hands up, shaking her head with chagrin before she slumped in her chair.

"Oh I hope I didn't lose anyone.

"The group is still in the formative stage—not yet trusting each other. Some vulnerabilities were exposed the last few sessions. Two gals especially seem to rub each other the wrong way—a domineering mom whose daughter is rebelling. Then there's a street-smart gal, who's had it pretty tough." Dana flashed a knowing glance at Marla Anderson who had referred Genie to Dana's group.

"*Street Smart* hasn't revealed much yet. Projects a tough exterior—she's almost arrogant about it—and caustic toward the mom. Well, the mom shared her fear about being rejected by her seventeen-year old daughter—she already has an estranged older daughter. Anyway, *Street Smart* insinuated that *Mom* was treating her like a baby since she herself was on her own at fourteen."

Raised eyebrows and knowing looks were shared among the therapists. A fourteen-year-old on her own usually meant neglect, abuse and trauma.

"Yeah. So, the comment, and attitude behind it, created more strain between the two gals. We were in the last minutes of the session, though, so I couldn't open another can of worms.

"We muddled through it, but...I guess I'm afraid of what that might mean. *Street Smart* isn't open to individual sessions — she says she's on overload with her NA program, this group, and work."

Dana paused to organize her thoughts, looking down at her now folded hands. "The other women would probably be sensitive if *Street Smart* does have a blow out — even the mom, but I don't know if she could handle much empathy at this point. I think she's afraid to allow a crack in that huge wall she's got wrapped around herself — afraid she'll crash.

"I know I need to address it in group...right away. But I don't want to run either of them off. Any ideas?"

Her peers looked thoughtful for a moment before Marla spoke up. "I assume *Street Smart* is the client I referred to you, which is irrelevant, I guess, but do you think the other group members will truly be empathetic...even if she reveals something shocking to their experience? Like prostitution or whatever she might be hiding? I don't know that prostitution is part of her history, but with a kid on her own at fourteen and a history of drug addiction, it wouldn't be surprising."

"Good point." Dana grimaced as her mind clicked through each group member's personality. "It might be a stretch at this point for the mom. I think they can get there — it could be healing for them both to work through their judgment of each other, but it might be too early in the group process for that level of acceptance."

Phyllis' hands went to her heart, her face exuding empathy. "That poor kid. I realize the drug treatment program is demanding, but is there truly no room for some individual sessions? Does she have an individual therapist even?"

Marla responded, "No...she's just got aftercare sessions with me, twelve-step meetings, probation requirements, and then Dana's group. It is a lot, but I couldn't tell you if there's more room for some one-on-one. She also has a good job."

Amy Smith offered tentatively. "I don't know how you would get to this in a group, but if there's a way to help *Street Smart* contain the trauma—somehow, without going into it—acknowledge that you've touched on a nerve, but it's premature to bring it to the group.

"On second thought …that might raise the level of curiosity in the others and make her reinforce the walls. I don't know how you do it, Dana."

"No…no…this is good stuff. Really. The use of a container to hold the toxin until there's greater trust in the group is a good idea. I've used that in individual work."

Marla's body language signaled that she was wrestling with an idea. "Dana, what if…what if the mom, or the other women aren't as gracious as you hope? What if they come across as condemning? It could set her back a long way. My recovery people are used to the twelve step traditions read at the beginning of every meeting, so they're reminded about personal recovery being linked to group unity. I don't know what framework you might have set up, but maybe you can borrow from the twelve step traditions."

"We do set boundaries at the beginning of group, but I wish I had emphasized them more since. Yeah, I'll need to do that now. Hopefully without *Street Smart* or the mom feeling picked on.

"Thank you for all your help. You gals are marvelous…reminding me once again why I need and love you!"

Chapter Ten

THE TIDE WAS HIGH as Hub and Dana walked along the beach with Nikki and Mica running ahead. Sounds were amplified by the fog — gulls and ravens declaring their presence; the crunch of rocks beneath hiking boots. The soft blanket of clouds seemed to embrace the earth ever so softly, hiding the vast waters that lapped within meters of the couple's trek and the mountains that dominated opposite the water.

Hub had been quiet for most of the walk from their house. He reached for Dana's hand. "You know...there are only a few more days to fish this year. I'd like to get a day or two on the water with you, my love."

Dana drew closer, putting her arm around his waist. "Sounds interesting."

"And while we're talking about it, I think we should plan a get-away." Dana stiffened beneath Hub's arm, but he continued. "We've not had a warm vacation for a few years — what do you think about Hawaii? Or American Samoa?"

"Could we wait until things are better with Rachel? And my dad? I want to go...I just feel so unsettled right now."

She stopped and turned to face her husband. "Hub, I don't want to miss an opportunity to...to have time with Rachel. Her birthday is coming up. Thanksgiving. Christmas. There might be an opportunity for family connections. I don't know, but I'm hopeful. I don't want to miss the chance. Is that all right?"

Hub's pursed lips suggested his irritation. "I guess."

They walked another few minutes before he continued. "I need some time with my wife, however. I understand how...uncertain this all is to you, Dana, but I don't want to get lost in the shuffle. We can't put our lives on hold until our girl figures out how lucky she is to have two moms. And your dad will come around. He's solid."

"I don't know, Hub. He has never—in my whole life-- treated me like this. Never. I've always felt so confident of his love, but right now it feels very conditional. Like I'm no longer important since he has a granddaughter to dote on. He has purposely excluded me from their activities. Did you know he joined the fitness club with her? *He* never told me that...I heard it from my hairdresser! My dad in a fitness club!" Dana's exasperation resounded through the fog.

"I'm glad for him—it's got to help his heart condition, but why not say something? I don't know...it's just that it's so different, and yet he's...he's not including me in any of his life changes."

A raven cawed from a tree top somewhere above them in the fog.

"Give it time, Dana. You're still his little girl. He'll figure it out."

***

Rachel's phone beeped over to voicemail. *Rachel. I'm out. Leave it!*

Dana was startled at the abruptness of her message. "Umm...hi, Rachel. This is Dana. I know you're probably busy with school. I just wanted to say *hi*. If you get a chance, give me a call...if you would."

Dana checked her disappointment, and turned her attention to the day unfolding. This was her late day since her group ran until seven.

Even though she had rehearsed her opening several times, she was nervous about tonight's group. It could get out of control so easily. Genie's contentious manner was a characteristic that often intimidated Dana, yet she knew that beneath that tough exterior was a hurting child. *Lord, please enable me to help her. Give me your wisdom.*

As the women assembled, they seemed subdued to Dana. *Am I imagining that? Is something else going on, or was last week even worse than I thought?*

It threatened Dana's self confidence, and she again questioned if she could address the conflict without creating more alienation among group members.

After they had each settled in their usual seats, Dana began tentatively. "I'm glad to see each of you here." As she looked around the circle at each person, Genie was the only one who refused to make eye contact.

"Before we start check-ins, I'd like to say a few things. We are settling in to four weeks now…getting to know each other better. Sharing more openly than in the beginning. Dealing with even more personal aspects of our lives.

"That's the beauty of women coming together in a supportive, safe setting—we get to understand ourselves better, perhaps look at ourselves through a different lens as we are more candid with each.

"With that openness comes risk as well. We spoke in the beginning about boundaries to create a safe environment. Because any time we allow ourselves to be vulnerable, we are taking a risk. We risk being hurt, rejected, misunderstood. That's the difficulty and the beauty of any close relationship, I believe. When I open myself up and am understood and accepted, I am affirmed as an individual. I'm stronger for it.

"At the same time, I am more open to being judged. Rejected.

"So when others see my idiosyncrasies…and flaws, if they will be patient and compassionate with me rather than judge me, I am free to examine myself. I don't have to defend myself. I can be open to different thinking because I know I am accepted—imperfect as I am."

Dana's expressive hands emphasized the points as she named them. "It's a predictable stage that every intimate relationship must go through to build trust. Families, friends, co-workers, and certainly couples must work through those differences—showing respect for each other in spite of disagreement—in order to have true intimacy. Closeness."

Although Genie continued to avoid eye-contact, Dana could see that she, as well as the other women, was listening.

"And in most groups, there will be personality conflicts. I suspect we saw some of that last week between you, Genie…and you, Ruth. And tensions are okay. It's the nature of human beings. While it challenges us, it also gives us opportunities to stretch and grow; to learn new ways of relating."

Dana put her chin on her hand, leaning toward Genie. "I may be reading this wrong, and please forgive me if that's the case, but I had a sense, Genie, that Ruth's worry about her daughter touched a raw nerve with you. Perhaps that's a topic you're not ready to share in group yet. And that's okay."

Sitting back in her chair, Dana spread her hands, gesturing to include the entire group. "Part of setting boundaries is to decide how much to share...and with whom. Trust is built when I have the right to be me, with my own opinions, flaws, dreams, values, priorities and choices. And it's safe for me to share them without being judged."

Dana's gut churned as she turned the floor over to the group. "I've said more than I like to...but does any of this strike a chord?"

The women quietly fidgeted. Then Genie looked directly at Dana, scowling. "You're wrong about the raw places, Dana. I know the church lady has her own worries — I get that. And I'm sorry if I offended anyone by mentioning life in the real world." She nodded once toward Ruth. "That's the way I see it. That's the way I lived it. But I'll keep my thoughts to myself from now on."

Dana's heart sank. This is exactly the response she feared. She opened her mouth to speak, but was interrupted by Brandi.

"I, for one, hope you won't keep things to yourself, Genie." She looked back to Dana, "I hear what you're saying, Dana...about being different, and that we go through levels of trust — I understand that well from my marriage." Turning back to Genie, she continued, "but we can't clam up when it gets uncomfortable. That's what my husband does, and we don't get anything solved!"

Brandi's thick eyelashes flashed as she cocked her head, compelling Genie to make eye contact. "I mean...we're all so different. It can't be sweet all the time, but that's why we're here. I admire your toughness, Genie, and I think I can learn from you — don't withhold from us!"

Genie crossed her arms, her thin legs entwined from knee to ankle. The edge to her words were softened by the raising of her right eyebrow. "You might not like to hear about my world, princess. I doubt you have ever touched the street side of life."

They held eye-contact a moment before Brandi responded, her husky voice steady. "Maybe." She lifted her chin. "But I think I can handle it. And maybe I'll learn something that will help me."

Dana stammered, "Uh...okay. Thank you. Um...other thoughts?"

Susan's eyebrows bounced above the top of her glasses, her face placid, yet her words were clear. "I think it's good to be reminded of the boundaries, and that it's natural to go through stages. My students have to get used to me sometimes before they buckle down to business. I'm persistent about them making progress, and they settle in after a few weeks and start learning. It's uncomfortable at first...to keep them on task."

Sheryl's laughter was softer than normal. "*Oy vey*, can I relate to that. I have to act like the tsar at the beginning of the school year so those teenagers don't roll over me, but once we get used to each other, I can slack off and enjoy them."

Her red hair shook as laughter percolated before it erupted, "I didn't mean to insinuate you're a tsar, Dana. Really, you're not. It just struck me funny. Genie, I bet you have a name for each one of us!"

At the arch in Genie's right eyebrow, Sheryl teased, "You do, don't you! What's my nickname?"

Genie pursed her lips, but she couldn't hide the humor as just her eyes moved sideways. "Maybe not everyone, but Grumpy fits you to a tee."

The sudden laughter from Sheryl and Brandi, as well as Dana's chuckle took moments to settle, eliciting a half smile from Genie. Ruth's and Susan's faces were neutral.

"Laughter is good. But I don't think I'm ready to hear your nickname for me yet, Genie." Dana's quick reading of the somewhat more relaxed mood encouraged her, but Ruth was still unreadable. "Ruth, what are your thoughts? This doesn't seem funny to you."

She shrugged her shoulder before she looked directly at Dana. "I don't know what to say. You all seem to think it's funny, but I wouldn't call someone a name with caustic intent. It feels disrespectful to me."

There was a long pause before Dana spoke quietly. "Thank you for your candor, Ruth. You're right—a nickname can be fun, or it can be hurtful. And you were hurt by the one Genie gave you last week, is that right?"

She nodded.

Dana's mouth moved slightly as her eyetooth worried the inside of her lower lip. She looked toward Genie, hoping for some level of accord. "What are your thoughts, Genie? You've got a sharp sense of humor...very funny. And yet it can have barbs too, can't it?"

Genie uncrossed her legs and grabbed the arms of the chair, her face set, her eyes tracking her thoughts. Her chin jutted out. "Yes."

The stillness in the room was interrupted only by the gentle pulsing of Genie's knee.

Dana asked quietly, "Would you like to expand on that a little bit, Genie?"

She seemed to think about that a moment before replying, "No."

Dana's thoughts swirled, her stomach in knots. She desperately wanted both women to continue in the group, but this felt like a pivotal moment. She feared she would lose one if it appeared she sided with the other.

"I have to admit...I'm not sure where to go with this. You are both so important to this group, yet for whatever reason, there's a tension between you. It might have nothing to do with each other in reality, but it's being triggered here. I wonder if this is an opportunity to...respectfully confront the tension...in a way that can be healing." Dana leaned into the group, her arms crossed on her knees. Only her fingers tapping against her elbow betrayed her nervousness.

"Can we explore it further? Ruth, you've said how you felt...it feels hurtful. Genie, what do you make of that?"

Only Genie's eyes moved under her furrowed brow — from Dana to Ruth. Her expression didn't change. Her voice was flat; her words measured. "I didn't mean it to be funny. Or hurtful. It's just something I do. I attach names to people and things based on the way I see it. I'm sorry if I offended anyone. I'll try to refrain in the future."

Dana thought about what a concession that might have been for Genie, and prayed it was enough. She turned toward

Ruth, trying to read her expression. She asked softly, "Ruth, how does that settle with you?"

She took a deep breath before nodding. "It'll have to do." But Ruth's jutting jaw and narrowed eyes said more than her words.

Searching for a clue as to how to proceed, Dana finally asked, "Ruth, you don't look like *it'll do*. Is there something else?"

Ruth's face flushed as she sought to maintain control of her emotions. She licked her lips before speaking. "It's...it's probably me. I get accused a lot of having no sense of humor. Maybe that's true. Sometimes I don't know how to...how to tell *funny* from...*sarcasm*. It all seems to be a putdown to me."

Her voice was almost a whisper as she added, "Maybe that's...part of the problem with my girls."

The empathy from the other women was palpable, but no one spoke. When Genie finally broke the silence, her voice was firm, yet not biting. "It was sarcasm. You weren't misreading it.

"And I apologize. I was out of line."

Ruth raised her head slowly, looking at Genie as if studying a specimen. Although her face remained unreadable, her eyes revealed deliberation. "Thank you, Genie. I accept your apology. I think that's the first time someone has...validated my feelings. As hard as that is to accept, under the circumstances."

Dana sat for a moment, savoring the gratefulness she felt for the tentative concession the two women had given each other. She was afraid to speak, fearing she would break the spell. Finally, she said quietly, "Wow. Thank you both for your grace. And the way you reached out to each other. That...that's great."

It was nearing the end of the session, so Dana asked the group to participate in a   deep breathing exercise before wrapping up, leaving all the tensions of the day at their feet. In-between breaths, she narrated, "Notice where the tension is in your body, and on the out-breath, let it drain right out your toes." In just a few short minutes, she could see the change in each woman as their breathing became slower and deeper, their shoulders relaxing.

At the end of the exercise, she sat back in her chair, making eye-contact with each person, a gentle smile on her face. "I wonder...could we go around the room and each share what you're feeling right now, this moment?" Her eyes looked around for who might start.

Brandi sat up straighter, appearing contemplative. "I feel really good. I wish...I wish I could have that kind of honesty with my husband. That kind of confrontation. Resolution, really. Not defensiveness. It was difficult for both of you ladies, I would think, but you...you were both very honest. I admire that."

Dana's eyes focused on Susan sitting next to Brandi, her eyebrows raised in question.

"I'm relieved. It was kind of uncomfortable, but it's okay now."

Next to Susan, was Ruth. She sighed deeply before she responded, "Tired. I don't know why, but I'm very tired."

Uncharacteristically, Sheryl didn't laugh or even show the braces on her teeth. "Good. I'm good. Good job, ladies."

Genie took a moment before responding quietly. "Fine. I'm fine."

Without further commentary, Dana closed out the session and locked up the office, feeling relieved and hopeful herself.

Chapter Eleven

"YOUR DAD SAID HE would help me get firewood Saturday. Are you interested in joining us?" Hub and Dana sat at the counter with their morning coffee, both dogs watching intently from their bailiwick in front of the wood stove.

Dana stood up, emptying her glass of water in the sink before she responded. "I think not, Hub. I'd probably throw a block of wood at him. You go and have some guy time. Maybe some of your common sense will wear off on him."

The disappointment was obvious in Dana's demeanor as she looked distractedly out the window.

Saturday morning brought clear skies and crisp clean air that compelled Dana to fill her lungs and treasure the moment. Standing on the deck in her robe and lambskin slippers, she watched as Hub backed up to the wood trailer, positioning the receiver ball directly under the trailer hitch.

How many times had she watched in amazement as he expertly backed his pickup to a trailer, gauging the distance as if he could see the two objects draw close enough to fit perfectly together. It was so like him—the vehicle almost an extension of his movements—measured, precise. It's one of the things Dana admired about him, even as a teenager. His pace was steady. Deliberate. Whether it was in conversation or repairing a motor, he was intentional. If he built or repaired it, you could count on it being quality. If he said it, you could trust it was exactly what he meant.

Dana returned to the kitchen for the thermos of coffee and hardy lunch she had packed for her husband and father. Hub met her on the deck, accepting her gift and setting it aside. He took her cup of tea, set it aside, then wrapped her in his arms.

They stood entwined for a few moments, rocking gently. Finally, he whispered, "Are you sure you don't want to go with us this morning?"

Without releasing him, she nodded. "I'm sure. You two have fun. If I can get some prep work for my class done, I might curl up with a good book this afternoon. I'll help you unload the trailer when you get back."

He kissed her temple, and playfully declared, "Okay, my love, I shall return...with wood to warm your hearth!

Dana smiled as she watched Hub check the trailer and cargo straps on his chainsaw and equipment once again, the eager dogs dancing in the pickup bed. She waved as he climbed into the pickup and pulled out.

They were such a perfect match. His deliberateness reined in her glibness. Her spontaneity challenged his reticence. They worked well together. Dana thought of their symmetry when they split and stacked firewood. He would load the rounds onto the platform of the wood splitter while she operated the controls pushing the plunger to split each round. Anticipating his movements, she would push the plunger at the perfect time to minimize his effort. Their rhythm was efficient; intimate.

It was a comfortable role for Dana. She enjoyed working with him in this way, each movement complementing his. She knew it was a skill that not everyone had — being an effective helper around equipment. She was attuned to the sounds and nuances of the motor and gears. She grew up with it — functioning as first mate to her father on the fishing boat. Helping him with whatever needed to be done.

I learned it well. Being the helper...the mate. Anticipating his needs. Dana had walked to the back deck and was leaning on the railing, but the magnificence was lost to her this morning as she considered the building blocks of relationship with her father.

Is that all I was to him? The convenience of a helper? As long as I did what he wanted me to do, or I adapted to his world, his objectives, I had value? Her face clouded at the possibility her dad was that self-serving, even with his only child.

She had always believed she was the center of his world — most important in his life. Yet as her thoughts skimmed over the years, she could not think of a time when she defied him. Not directly. She complied with his will. He seemed supportive of her...attentive to her needs, but was he really? *Did I just not assert myself? Did I never give him the opportunity to show his true colors?*

Dana sat back in the deck chair to contemplate her growing up years. Her chin trembled as she thought about her mother, and the unanswered questions about what happened to her. It had been such a taboo subject, Dana had stuffed the longing to know more about her mother somewhere deep in her heart. *But I'm a part of her too – I deserve to know more. It isn't right he keeps it a secret, no matter how it distresses him. She was my mother!*

The more Dana considered her past – the accommodating girl child raised in a man's world – the angrier she got. *How dare he refuse to honor my need to know my own history, and then chastise me for keeping my secret from him! Of all the self-serving, self-centered, narcissistic, bull-headed...damn him!*

Dana could no longer sit still, her anger and grief propelling her to stomp around on the deck. "No wonder my mother left him!"

Her spoken words stopped her in her tracks. She had never allowed that thought to fully form in her mind. Her mother had disappeared and destroyed their lives. Her father had been devastated for years, thrown into depression and several years wasted in the bottle. She had been left to grow up without knowing a mother's comfort. The blame had always belonged to her mother. Even though Dan never spoke about it, it was understood that it was her mother's fault they were left adrift.

But now Dana looked at it objectively – through the lens she encouraged her clients to look through. What might the other possibilities be? Dana paced from one end of the deck to the other, looking at the bald eagle in the spruce tree above the beach, yet not seeing it.

Marriages seldom fail without culpability on both parts. *Why would my mother leave...disappear without explanation? Leave her child behind?*

Dana gave way to her anguish, shouting, "She left me with him. How could she do that?" She directed blame back to her mother, but gave vent to the pain and frustration that had been bottled up inside. Her thoughts hurled about, contending with her memories of growing up in her beloved southeast Alaska verses the foreign state of Montana, the last known trace of her mother. The idyllic view of her relationship with her father was clouded by the realization that maybe it was an illusion. *Maybe it was perfect only as long as I was passive. I had no dreams of my own. I married the guy any father would love. Pursued an education and respectable profession. Returned to Juneau. He's the one that moved away!*

But once his little girl makes a decision he disapproves of, I'm...he..."

Dana's ranting was spent. She collapsed on the chair, her head in her hands, and cried out her frustration. She was angry at herself for being forty-two without confronting it before. She was angry at her father for not understanding how painful it was to have a child alone, with no support, and to make the disastrous decision to give her up. How could he not understand why she kept the secret from him? And now that it was known, he was undermining her relationship with Rachel. How could she have idolized him her whole life when he was so undeserving?

The heat from the sun was now uncomfortable. Dana's robe and lined slippers were smothering. Forced to attend to her physical needs, she walked in the cool house, kicked off her slippers and rinsed her cup. Looking out the kitchen window, she resolved to find some answers.

* * *

Dana was surprised to hear the crunch of gravel, not realizing she had been on the internet for two hours. She had found her mother's name associated with a Cecil Thompson in Havre, Montana. The age fit—sixty-three. But there was no other information.

She slipped on her boots and grabbed her gloves, intending to help Hub and Dan unload the wood. As she stepped out the door, she noticed another vehicle parking at the end of the drive while Hub backed into the yard. Rachel's Jeep!

Dana was stunned. She stood at the door trying to make sense of the scene before her. Had Rachel just happened to drive up at the same time the guys came home? Had they called her? What was their intention? And why was she left out of the equation all together?

She steeled herself, putting on a smile and determination to be friendly to her father.

Rachel spotted her and waved. As they walked toward each other, Dana noticed how cute her daughter looked in local attire—blue jeans tucked into her red rubber boots, a sage green chamois shirt exposing a cream colored tee, and a camo baseball cap.

When they got within hearing distance, Rachel exclaimed, "Oh, Dana, it was a beautiful day. You should have joined us!"

Dana tried to control her voice, fearing she would come across peevish. "Darn, Rachel, I didn't know you were coming. I certainly would have joined the party if I'd known you were part of it."

"Oh. Well, I hadn't planned on it, but G-Dan promised a day in the woods if I'd at least pretend to help, so it was an easy choice to put the books aside. We saw two black bears. Hub said it was a sow and yearling. It was so cool!"

Rachel's enthusiasm was so genuine Dana couldn't help but be happy for her adventure. She was just irritated that she missed another chance to spend time with her.

"How are you doing with school, Rachel, are you settling in okay?"

"Yeah. I have more fun at the coffee shop, but I'm trying to be mature about it." She spit the word *mature* out like it was distasteful. "It's a lot of chemistry and math, so I have to focus, but I'll get to take ecology and some more interesting classes next semester."

"Are you making friends?"

"Oh...some. Some I know from the coffee shop. We're so busy on campus, I don't socialize much."

The men had removed the tie downs and begun to unload the wood. Rachel and Dana fell into step with them, lifting the round cuts off the trailer and tossing them in a pile to dry. The banter was relaxed, including Dana in the venture as if she had been a part of it all along. The movement felt good to Dana, releasing some of the aggravation she held toward her dad, although she avoided getting near him.

When the wood was off-loaded, and the men were putting the chainsaws away, Dana decided to approach Rachel. "I know you've got a birthday coming up, Rachel. If you're okay with it, Hub and I would like to take you to lunch, or have you over for a meal…if you're comfortable with that. I…don't want to crowd you."

When she didn't answer right away, Dana realized that in spite of the camaraderie they had just experienced, she was probably moving too fast. "I'm sorry, Rachel…I didn't mean to put you on the spot. It's okay to take a rain check."

"No…no, you didn't …" Rachel avoided Dana's gaze for a moment. She blew out her breath, her cheeks bulging as she did so. "I guess I could meet you at a restaurant. Sunday after my birthday?"

Dana tried to contain her excitement. "Fabulous. Do you like fish? How about the Twisted Fish…two o'clock?"

Little more was said after the date was set as Hub thanked Dan and goodbyes were exchanged. The two Jordans were able to part without their tension spilling onto Hub and Rachel.

Dana shared the news with Hub as they walked to the house arm-in-arm. She was so grateful to have a date set… one step forward with Rachel. Underlying the gratefulness was just a little spite that her dad would not be included.

Chapter Twelve

DANA'S PEER GROUP WAS meeting this week at the addictions center where Marla worked. They toured the offices and were introduced to some of the other therapists and staff before settling into one of the small group rooms. Marla was obviously proud of their new center, describing the different out-patient groups for teenagers and adults, as well as family support classes.

"The twelve-steppers are starting to use the building a lot for their meetings. There's an AA or NA group scheduled almost every day of the week. Then there's an Al-Anon group for people who are affected by a loved-one's addiction. Oh, and an ACOA group just started up—Adult Children of Alcoholics and other dysfunctions. I hope it'll take off because there are so many—addicts and others—who perpetuate the addiction dynamics generationally. Especially the control issues. Good grief, you wouldn't believe the dynamics surrounding that issue. Sometimes I think if they don't get out of my office, I'll start drinking again myself!"

Marla's hands made an imaginary circle and shook as if she were strangling someone. "I 'bout lost it with one of my dads this week. He could be the cover boy for GI Joe, and he's not even in the military! He's got the sweetest son anyone could ever want, but the two of them are at war. Dyl claims control by acting out, and Dad tries to fix him by adding more restrictions. The kid has no cell phone or electronics of any kind, no wheels, no time with friends, no sports. He doesn't even have a door on his bedroom! That's the latest *restriction*." Marla made air quotes with her fingers and pronounced the last word with disgust.

"The thing is, this kid is not aggressive or violent. I think he's just reactive to his father's suffocating controls. I try to remember Dad is probably scared, or just doesn't know any better, but I'm afraid his kid is going to take something that'll blow up his heart one of these days. In the meantime, I try to facilitate some understanding between them, but it's not going well. Dad is so stoved up, he's unaware of his own feelings and motivation, yet he can't tolerate Dyl having an independent idea."

Shaking her head as her frustration wound down, Marla concluded, "I don't know what I'm gonna do with that guy."

The other therapists were thoughtful as they waited for Marla to signal if she was seeking advice or just venting. When she didn't continue, Phyllis interjected, "Well, bless you for doing what you do, Marla. Those teens — and their families — are hurting. You must have the patience of Job.

"Do you do much with the Boundaries Circle concept? I use that diagram at least once a day, I swear." She looked around at the others questioningly, using her hands to demonstrate circles ratcheting out from small to large. "You know, the one that shows *You* in the center, then intimate relationships in the next circle, then guarded relationships, then superficial ones?"

With the nods from a few of the women, and blank looks from two, Phyllis offered, "I'll bring a copy next meeting and go over it if you want."

Marla verbalized the nods from the others, "That would be great. I've seen that, but a refresher would be good. I use a simple emotion model, especially for the teens...and adults like this dad! It's a more basic model."

Dana's furrowed brow suggested she was still examining a thought, but it took her a moment to speak. "You know...when you describe that dad, I see myself in that image. Not the autocratic parent, but the frustration of wanting something so bad, yet being helpless to...I started to say *obtain* it, but it really is to *control* it.

"It's not my daughter--I have a glimmer of hope there — but it's my dad. I am so angry at him, I want to wring his neck! And talk about being *stoved up*, he...he's *Mr. Friendly and Social* to everyone he meets, yet I'm beginning to realize how superficial he is.

"I've always thought we were close, but this...conflict, this unforgiveness, if you will, is making me see things differently. I don't know that I ever gave him cause to show his true colors with me. I guess I was more compliant than I realized. But now...his reaction to the secret about Rachel is to reject me. He simply will not discuss it.

"I called him and said we need to talk. Do you know how he responded? He said, *I'm sorry you made the choice you did*...to give Rachel up. He has no idea of what it was like for me as a young woman trying to please him...protect him...and make the hardest decision of my life alone. I didn't want to disappoint him, but I was pretty traumatized by the rape."

With the quiet support of her colleagues, Dana continued. "The more I look at him objectively, I realize it's always been about him: Being attuned to *his* moods, doing the right thing according to *his* perspective. And most of all, not talking about my mom.

"A lot has been surfacing for me during these last months. I can understand that he was hurt—his wife disappeared. I understand it's hard for him to talk about it, but damnit, she was my mother! I deserve to hear some answers, uncomfortable for him or not.

"I've always thought there was something fundamentally wrong with her—how else could she abandon us—never look back? But I'm wondering—did he treat her like he's treating me now? Was she emotionally starved? Was she isolated and just fell into a depression that overwhelmed her? Did he drive her away...tell her to leave?"

Dana looked up at the other women. "You'd think I would have dealt with this a long time ago, but here I am in my forties—clueless about my heritage. And I want to punish my dad—do something to get him to fess up. And since he won't, I distract myself with my work...all the while, my gut churns."

After a few moments, Phyllis' gentle reassurance broke the silence. "You know, Dana, being in your forties does not guarantee perfect insight. It's not at all unusual to reach this stage of life before looking at your life from a different perspective. Start with being kinder to yourself. You're looking at your history through new lenses, and that can be pretty daunting."

Phyllis' beautiful face took on an impish grin. She looked sideways at Dana, her long eyelashes flashing a wink, "It's possible this will be a life-changing time for your father too. Even though he's way past his forties, his persistent daughter just might cause some of his barriers to break down."

Marla's scrunched face showed her hesitancy to speak. "Dana, have you ever thought about doing the twelve steps yourself? I mean, almost everybody can benefit by reflecting on their lives from the perspective of what control we truly have over our lives. Some of the things you've said about you and your dad make me wonder if you got caught up in some ACOA dynamics...you know, *learning to step around the elephant in the living room,* but never talk about it? I'm not saying your dad is an alcoholic, but you can learn a lot by considering the way an addiction, or dysfunctional behavior, controls the family system...and creates cognitive distortions. I've got several books on the dynamics of adult children if you're interested—in fact, I've got one in mind especially that might be a good match."

Dana took a deep breath before answering. "You may be right, Marla. My dad did drink heavily for a few years after my mom disappeared—there, I said it again! *Disappeared*—like she was beamed up to Starship Enterprise. But the hole in my life, the huge void in our family, was not supposed to be there, so we ignored it."

She rolled her big brown eyes before concluding. "Yes, Marla, I think I will borrow your reference. Thank you. Even though he didn't drink for all that many years, we still walk around the *elephant in the living room.* Maybe it's time we stomp on a toe."

* * *

Over the next several days, the borrowed book stayed on the coffee table as Dana focused on Rachel's birthday. Her desire to provide just the right birthday present became all-consuming. Should she approach it as if it was her daughter's first birthday and give her something memorable that a one-year-old would receive belatedly—a treasured book? Should she start a tradition of numbered gifts that represent the beginning of their relationship...perhaps C. Alan Johnson figurines, beginning with the youngest child, and in future years, give progressively aging children? *It's her twenty-first…what would represent coming of age?*

Dana spent hours perusing the gift shops, and thinking about different options. Hub indulged her frenetic exploration, offering little comment on fleeting solutions. Finally, Dana brought home a silver bracelet crafted by a Tlingit artist with the orca design.

"I think you've got a winner there, Dana. It looks like something Rachel would wear."

"I hope so. I want to give her something personal and Alaskan. Unique. But her mother owns that gift shop downtown, *Arts and Treasures*. And they seem to have money. It might not mean anything to her, but it is beautiful, isn't it?"

Hub nodded like an indulgent husband trying to give the right amount of support that would allow for a possible change in direction. Dana's expression suggested there was something else. Her eyetooth nagged her lower lip, her crossed legs pulsed as she tapped her foot.

"What if…do you think it would be too much…is it too early to give Rachel a picture of me and my parents?" Dana reached beside her and brought out a three inch square faded photograph of Dan and the woman Hub had never met holding Dana as an infant.

They studied it together. Although Hub had seen it before, Dana seldom brought it out. "You look quite a bit like her. I can see Rachel's cheek bones and mouth in her. All three of you have the same nose."

Dana took the photo back, studying it as she centered over her tucked legs. "There's a guy in town that restores photos. He said he could take out the crease and fine-tune it a little. Enlarge it. Enhance the color. Frame it for me."

She sat back with the resolve of a decision made. "I'm gonna do it. Two of 'em. One for her and one for me." Having that settled, Dana kissed Hub's cheek and jumped off the couch like a teenager on a mission.

* * *

Sunday finally came. Dana had refrained from texting Rachel a reminder about their luncheon date to celebrate her birthday. She talked fast as Hub drove, asking when she should give

Rachel her gifts — before or after their meal, and in what order. "What if she forgot? Oh, Hub, I hope she doesn't forget. Or change her mind. This really is a big step for her, isn't it?"

Hub simply grinned and put his big hand over hers without comment.

The Sunday crowd had diminished by the time Rachel joined Dana and Hub in a corner table of the restaurant. As Rachel walked toward them, Dana thought what a classic beauty she was in every way — her stature and carriage; her subtle yet perfect makeup that highlighted incredible hazel green eyes. The casual clothes she wore were understated, but Dana knew they were way above her budget. She could feel the pride swell in her core as she considered that she had given birth to this magnificent beauty.

Rachel smiled at the birthday greetings and sat down opposite Hub. She scooted the chair to center across from him and Dana, and placed her chin in her hands. "Thank you. This is very sweet of you to...I haven't had a...a family birthday celebration since I was seventeen. Not that my mother didn't try...it just...didn't work out."

Dana was stunned. The thought of her daughter missing any birthday without great celebration was unthinkable, especially when she had brooded over each and every one missed, longing to know where Rachel was and what was happening in her life. She wanted to empathize with her now, but not implicate any lack on her adopted mother's part. Dana quivered inside — *she said* family. *She intimated that we're family!*

While Dana searched for a neutral starting place, Hub jumped right in, "Well, this is a special celebration then — besides it being your twenty-first! We are glad to be part of this one, and hope we won't miss another!"

Rachel's response to Hub was affectionate — a sweet smile that deepened her dimple, her eyes saying *thank you*. Dana was grateful for their bond and hoped it would soon expand to include her.

The server, a young man about Rachel's age, brought menus and recited the specials of the day. He was overtly attentive to Rachel, but she seemed oblivious to his attempts at flirtation.

With drinks served and an appetizer on its way, the table conversation slipped into safe topics — the outcome of the fishing derby, school, the Seahawks unimpressive performance. Dana found herself very comfortable with the pace, letting Hub lead the conversation while she tried not to be obvious about studying Rachel's every movement and expression. Rachel's glances at Dana suggested she knew she was under scrutiny, but her grin gave her approval.

After the main course, the three sipped hot drinks. Rachel held her latte with both hands, her eyes seeming to study the contents during a lull in the conversation. She glanced at Dana. "My mom said to tell you *hi*. I told her you were taking me out for lunch. She's glad we're getting to know each other a little bit. I still can't believe she actually went to a therapist…and it turned out to be my…you."

Rachel shook her head as if trying to clear it. "That one still blows me away. But I guess it's a good thing — we've found some common ground, and have gotten closer as a result.

"Mom and I are exact opposites, so sometimes we don't get each other. But we did commit to spending Christmas together this year…either she'll fly here or I'll fly to Minneapolis. Probably I'll do the flying since she's such a wuss…and I mean that in a fun way. My dad and I always teased her about being scared to do the things we liked to do, but…" Rachel shrugged her shoulders. "I guess that's just who she is."

Dana's eyes were misty as she interjected, "I'm forever grateful to her for raising you — protecting you." Her voice cracked, "for doing what I wish I could have."

Rachel smiled in acknowledgement, but glanced away to signal a change of topics.

Reaching into her bag, Dana retrieved a small box, wrapped elegantly with silver ribbon on azure paper. With a lighter voice, she offered it to Rachel. "Well. Hub and I want to give you something to celebrate your birthday…and your Alaskan connection. We hope you'll like it."

Rachel expressed her excitement about the wrapping and the idea of a present. She was child-like in anticipating what it might be, and then showed delight once she saw the piece of jewelry.

She slipped it on her left wrist and studied it carefully, while thanking Hub and Dana. "It's beautiful. I've never seen anything like it. It's an orca, isn't it? I love it! Thank you."

After several more comments, Dana brought out the framed five by five photograph of her and her parents. She was hesitant as she handed it to Rachel. "This isn't a birthday present *per se*...but I thought you might like to have it. It's the only picture I have of the three of us, and well, you might...see some of yourself there."

Rachel studied the photo without comment, then without looking up at Dana, she asked, "How old was G-Dan then?"

"About twenty-two."

She studied the photo another moment before she looked up, her eyes misty. "How old was she?"

"A year older." Dana held her breath, unsure of what Rachel thought.

"I look like her, don't I? G-Dan's wife...your mother. What's her name?"

"Mae Elizabeth. Her maiden name was Harris."

"What happened to her?"

Dana caught her breath. "I...I don't know the whole story, Rachel. She left when I was little...maybe four. I have few memories of her, and Dad has always been...it's a taboo subject with him. I'd like to know more. Hopefully someday I'll find some answers. I did an initial internet search, but only came up with her name. I think it's her anyway...in Havre, Montana."

Rachel was thoughtful for a moment, her dark eyebrows and mouth showing her puzzlement. "It seems like you've had a lot of pain in your life, Dana. I hope you find some answers."

She changed topics quickly, "I've wondered about G-Dan's story. He hasn't said much to me, even when I've hinted about his romantic life, so I thought there must be something in his history. He was a cutie, wasn't he?"

Dana was fascinated to think of her father through her daughter's hero-worship perspective. She recalled that at one time, she too, thought of him as handsome and bigger than life. Right now he seemed emotionally stunted and self-centered, but she didn't allow her face to reveal those thoughts.

"Thanks, Dana, for this picture. I'll treasure it.

"Thank you both—for the perfect bracelet—perfect lunch. And...celebrating my twenty-first with me."

Chapter Thirteen

SINCE GENIE AND RUTH had made a guarded peace with each other a few weeks prior, the comfort level among all the women had increased. Dialogue during sessions about present concerns and relationships was becoming more authentic. As a result, the women were showing signs of trust and openness.

Prior to the group's arrival, Dana pulled each woman's chart to evaluate her progress. Looking at Susan's first, Dana thought about how consistently she was attentive to the other women and the discussions, yet emotionally, she remained blunted. Her passion about students was obvious because of her dedication to them, as well as her determination to get advanced education, but even when she spoke about them, it was without enthusiasm. *Her anxiety seems acceptable to her as long as it is moderately controlled. She probably has some Asperger Syndrome, but... Am I pushing for something that is beyond her, or does she just need a break-through?* Dana had hoped this group would motivate Susan to strive for other goals — perhaps address the enmeshment with her parents, or develop some friendships and outside interests. *What am I missing? Is she getting lost in the process?*

The next chart on the stack was Brandi's, *the princess.* Dana smiled at the moniker assigned by Genie. It did fit. Brandi was one of those rare women with a *Cover Girl* face and figure. Her silky blonde hair framed flawless skin. She was pert, pleasant — intriguing, really, just to look at. Her facial expressions were deliberate and camera-perfect. Controlled. *Hmm...like she needs to perform. I wonder who is the authentic Brandi?*

Sheryl. The redheaded spitfire in braces who moves like a gangly teenager and bubbles over with ever-present laughter. Dana noted that her laughter is lower pitched now, and she acknowledges what changes she needs to make to get her stress under control. *I need to monitor her symptoms more closely, though, to know the real progress. It's too easy for her to hide truth behind laughter and deny the reality of her aggravation.*

Ruth. There's a vulnerability about Ruth in spite of her bravado. It's more than her daughter's rebellion. Her acquiescence to Genie is positive, but she's avoiding something. It's got to be a safe place before she'll have a break-through, but how can she feel safe when Genie is so...so volatile?

Genie. She's warming to this group just a little. That tough-girl persona keeps her from moving faster, but she seems more attentive to the other women's plights, exposing just a bit more of her softer self.

Dana straightened the stack of charts and slipped them into the top drawer of her desk. Before long, the women arrived at about the same time, hanging wet jackets and slipping off boots and shoes. Dana noticed they all entered the circle in stockinged feet — the second week running. *Hmm...connection or weather?*

As they settled in their usual chairs, Dana checked the mood and demeanor of each woman. Susan was stoic as usual, but observant of others. Something was going on with Genie — she looked more spirited. Brandi avoided eye-contact.

When the chitchat about the weather and shorter days quieted, Dana began. "Okay, let's get started. Good to see you all. Let's do check-ins, then I have a topic for us. Who'd like to start?"

The routine was familiar now, so there was little hesitation to speak, but it was a first to have Genie start.

"I'll go." Genie's voice would not be considered enthusiastic, but it was cordial. "I got my one year token this week. It's been a trip! I haven't had a year clean and sober since I was six years old, so it means a lot to me." She held her chin up, clearly not finished with her turn. "And I found a place where I can play pool.

"That's my gig, but the bars are off limits to me, so it's been hurtin' my game. I hooked up with a guy this week whose got a professional table at his place. He doesn't allow any drinkin' or smoking inside, so it works for me. There's quite a few players that hang out there, so I've got someone to compete with. The place is small, but better than nothin.'

"That's about it. Everything's good."

Congratulations were offered all around.

Dana shook her head once, "Great. That is quite an achievement." Her raised eyebrows signaled for someone else to speak. Sheryl's laughter announced her intention.

"I'm lookin' forward to Thanksgiving break, I tell ya! I don't know if it's winter coming on or what, but the *inmates* are riled!" Sheryl wiped her brow, letting her chuckle run down. "*Oy vey,* what one doesn't think of, two more will. One of those little buggars loosened the receiver for my mouse...on my computer? So while I'm banging around cussing under my breath at the system, trying to figure out how to go forward without the electronics, the class is getting out of hand. Finally, one of the sixteen-year olds took pity on me. It's a good thing, the little stink...or I'da come up with extra homework for them all!

"But I'm doing okay. Still upright."

Dana couldn't help but smile at her humor. "Sheryl, how is it going with others wanting to impose on you?"

Sheryl's eyes widened with surprise. "It's working! That one gal I mentioned hasn't been bumming rides since I told her I could be there for an emergency, but I didn't want to make it routine. I still can't believe that one...it seemed so...I guess I just made it harder than it was. She looked hurt at first, but she's talking to me."

"That's great. And how's your sleep?"

She sat back in her chair as if to think about it. "Better some — as much as the hot flashes allow anyway. I'm really mad at Eve for how she got us cursed, and power surges are a part of it!"

As the women laughed, Dana decided to push it one step further. "And how about your ability to focus and remember things? Are you noticing any difference yet?"

"I guess. I can't remember."

With the resulting laughter, Dana had to let it go. "Okay. Brandi, you're awfully quiet."

Brandi's hand dabbed a tissue at the corner of her eye, as if to erase an invisible smudge. Her head dropped as she spoke to her hands open in her lap. "I uh...I told my husband to leave the house. I need some time to decide if...if he should come back at all."

She took a deep breath, her lips pulsing as she exhaled. She looked up at the other women, her face unmasked. The room was so still, her quiet voice seemed loud. "Goodell has been having an affair with a co-worker. I suspected something was going on, but I didn't think it had gone this far. She has been in my home before. I know who she is. She and her husband came to a barbeque we hosted last spring. I would never have guessed, but her husband blew the whistle on them." Her eyes were misty, but no tears bypassed her careful dabbing.

"I don't know if I want him back. He said it would never happen again, but I can't trust him. It isn't the first time. But the children..." She adjusted her perfect hair. "So...I'm going to take my time. I changed my schedule to days so I can be home when the children get there.

"That's what's going on."

The impact of Brandi's story settled on the room like a cold canvas tarp. The sympathetic responses were gentle and quietly spoken. Ruth added, "You're certainly justified to divorce him...for adultery. And Brandi, I'll give you my phone number—if you get in a bind, just holler. I can bring a meal, or play taxi."

Brandi's gratitude was obvious when she flashed her perfect smile in response.

Genie's furrowed brows studied Brandi, but her lips remained clamped shut.

Dana asked, "How can we help as you work through this, Brandi?"

She shook her head and sat back in the chair, slumping slightly. "Just do what you're doing—hearing me without judgment. I've got to work through it myself. But I'm glad I've got you all here with me.

"That's all I want to say."

Dana felt her heart squeeze and eyes water at the thought of Brandi's predicament— little children to raise with a cheating husband. Her mind crested on the cross slopes of sympathy for Brandi and the need to keep this group moving in the right direction. "It's a really tough spot to be in, Brandi, but you've got a lot going for you. And we're here for you.

"Susan, how are you doing?"

Judy Hudson

Her response was immediate and without emotion. "I'm okay. I feel bad for Brandi."

Dana nudged for Susan to expand on other aspects of her life, but she simply nodded that everything was okay.

Dana's body language signaled a change of subject. "I hope tonight's topic is timely...I thought we might explore how we develop the *idea* of who we are—our identities. How do you see yourself and why? What are the events...people...ideas...or personal characteristics that have influenced your identity as a woman?"

The silent shift of eyes, subtle grimaces, and changes in posture told Dana that the topic was indeed thought-provoking. She out-waited the silence.

Sheryl held her receding chin high, uncharacteristically serious. "I always knew I wanted to be a teacher. Even before grade school. Maybe I got it from Sunday school...I dunno...but I used to daydream by the hour about being in front of a blackboard with little faces anxiously waiting for my pearls of wisdom."

She slapped her knee and guffawed. "Boy was that ever a fantasy! If I see my students looking at me intently, I know something is about to come down...or I've got my shirt on wrong-side-out!"

Sheryl looked around as her chuckle lost its vigor. "But it's who I am—my identity. I can't imagine *not* being a teacher."

Ruth shifted in her chair, her wrists back-to-back as her hands grasped her knees. "In Small Town, South Dakota, when you grow up on a chicken farm with mom and dad and siblings, everyone has a job to do. It's pretty clear who you are and what's expected of you. You learn to be strong, reliable, because if you're not, things fall apart. Animals die, or people suffer." Ruth hesitated, her eyes focused at the space in front of her. When she resumed, her voice was more contemplative.

"I was the one in my family who made sure things got done...organized. There was a lot of love...and community. It was a good life—people watched out for each other; had fun together. We didn't worry much about drugs, and kids getting caught up in sex slavery. Most people went to church. We were the Benedict family—that said who we were.

"I learned early on that I was stronger than...others. More efficient. So, I guess it's natural that I combined my love for cooking with my organizational skills to develop a catering business. I don't mean to brag...I just know I'm gifted that way. There are things I can't do, but...I'm good at homemaking. And helping others."

Dana asked, "Who are your heroes, Ruth? Is there someone who influenced you as a woman?"

Ruth's eyes ratcheted diagonally as her mind considered the possibilities. "Eleanor Roosevelt. She served our nation tirelessly, being the legs for her husband, advocating for the underdog. She was the first lady, and yet she was humble and self-sacrificing. She advocated for African Americans even before the civil rights movement. I did a portrayal of her in drama class, in high school. We had to study about our characters before we performed, and she was an amazing woman." Ruth sat up straighter.

Dana's head tilted as she responded. "Hmm. It sounds like you have a lot of Eleanor in you, Ruth. I would love to see you bring her to life for an audience today!" Her eyes lingered on Ruth as that thought settled.

"Who would like to go next...what are the influences that defined who you are?"

Brandi spoke, her face masking her pain as she mimicked a haughty woman. "My mother taught me well: Women must keep up appearances at all cost. Take care of yourself and your family. Accommodate your husband's needs. Make him look good so he will be successful."

Her chin trembled, her façade crumbling as she pushed out the last words. "That's who I am...and it's not working. It's a lie. It was a lie then, and it is a lie now. My father cheated on my mother too."

Dana's quiet words were soothing, "That's not who you are, Brandi. How the men in your life behave is not a reflection of who you are. You are precious and intelligent and lovely. And you'll work through this time of trouble."

The room was again quiet for a long moment before Genie spoke, her voice raspy at first. "You count too much on your men! They're all scum. Everyone of 'em will cheat if you give 'em a chance. It doesn't matter how beautiful you are, princess, they're gonna do it. You don't need 'em. You've got everything goin' for ya. You oughta kick him to the curb."

Genie smirked and looked away from the group, mumbling, "Sorry if I cross-talked again, but that's how I see it."

Dana knew Genie's tough exterior was thinning, her fragility moving closer to the surface. She needed to release some of the rage without crumbling like Humpty Dumpty, never to be put together again.

She quietly asked, "Genie, what has been influential on your self-concept...your identity?"

Her response was explosive. "Scumbag men, starting with my father! Using me like a sex toy before I knew what it was. They used me all the time while their ladies were raisin' their kids, keepin' their houses, and workin' their asses off FOR THEM! Like what you good ladies are doin' for your husbands!" She looked directly at Ruth and Brandi. "I won't let no guy do that to me again...ever!" She sat back in the chair, her arms wrapped around her body, her over-shirt vibrating from the intensity of her anger, even though her face was set hard and eyes dry.

Every fiber in Dana's being wanted to reach out to the damaged little girl inside Genie, but she knew sympathy might send her over the edge. She needed empathy and perspective--a good balance of what her heart was telling her and what her mind should be telling her. "I'm so sorry that happened to you, Genie. You didn't deserve that. You deserved goodness and protection. You were harmed by their actions, but that does not define who you are...unless you let it. You are courageous and strong. You are precious, Genie."

After a deliberate pause, Dana asked her, "How did you survive? What kept you going in spite of it all?" Dana continued to prod as she watched Genie battle for control of the raw emotion surfacing within her, her body still quivering. "In spite of horrendous circumstances, you didn't give up. You developed into the strong, capable woman you are today, Genie. You're determined. You've overcome tremendous obstacles. What is it within you that kept you going?"

The silence in the room was dense. All motion had ceased; ten eyes intent on Genie. The clock counted the moments as Dana prayed for wisdom to handle whatever might spew forth.

Finally, Genie's body began to quiet, her deep sigh ending with a ragged exhale. Her voice was just above a whisper as she spoke to the corner she faced. "I couldn't let them win. My mother couldn't survive without me. I had to stay for her."

Dana searched for the words to affirm Genie, not knowing what the circumstances were for this abused child to feel responsible for her parent. Finally, she simply restated Genie's words. "You survived to protect your mother."

Genie slowly nodded, turning her face to Dana, her eyebrows more relaxed. She waved her hand across her front, motioning for Dana to move on.

Acknowledging the gesture, Dana broke the silence. "Thank you for sharing that with us, Genie. You're very courageous. In fact, I think courage is a big part of who you are."

It was hard to move on from such an emotional disclosure, but Dana couldn't leave Susan out of the process. Her personality encouraged that kind of inattention, and Dana was determined to not reinforce that neglect. "Susan, how about you? How do you see yourself, and what influenced you to be the person you are?"

Susan looked intently at Dana, her words measured as if rehearsed. "I'm a quiet person. I need a lot of time to myself …to prepare. So that I can do my work. My students need the kind of tutoring I know I can give, as long as I have quiet time to recharge.

"My family is a lot like me, so I suppose my parents have been the greatest influence on who I am. They encourage what I do."

Dana's nod belied her internal struggle with trying to understand Susan and her perspective. Was she truly content with this simple life, living quietly with her parents, devoid of friends and social engagement? Or was the anxiety keeping her from stretching…wanting more?

She decided to accept it at face value for now and move on. "Thank you, Susan. You do important work, and I suspect your tutoring is life-changing for many of your students, and their families. Thank you."

Dana wrapped up the evening by acknowledging the depth of what was shared, the enormity of the challenges, and the courage of each woman present. She announced plans for them to do a fun project the following week on the topic of identity, and closed the session with a guided imagery intended to increase awareness of how emotions are held in the body.

Sitting in the circle after the women left, Dana realized how utterly drained she was herself. Ruth had revealed so much of her upbringing. *I hope she'll be able to see her strengths with some objectivity.* Dana's cheeks were wet with tears as she thought about Brandi's situation and the probable effects on her children. She marveled at the crack in Genie's armor and prayed for wisdom to see her through the dismantling of the fear and shame that holds her captive. *Lord, help me be wise and insightful with each of these women*

Chapter Fourteen

THE WOOD FIRE BURNED down to small embers, dropping the temperature in the room. Dana had been so focused on her internet search, she didn't realize how cold her fingers and nose had become. One look out the window told her the storm had not let up. The wind blowing off Lynn Canal drove the heavy rain toward the house, creating rivulets on the deck, but there was no way of getting around it — she would have to step out for more firewood.

The dogs perked up when she reached for her hooded rain coat, but they didn't venture from their position next to the wood stove. "You wimps! Stay." They immediately dropped their heads back to the floor.

Dana made quick work of replenishing the day's supply of logs, and coaxing a blaze in the stove. Her movements were automatic, a task she had done hundreds of times before, but her gratitude for its warmth and beauty was lost this afternoon. She had searched every data base she could think of and found nothing on her mother — no address, arrests, announcements of civic activities, or death notice. It angered her to think that her father probably had some clue of where to search, but she had to do this on her own.

Looking at the dreary day out the window, her mind didn't register the white capped water roiling in the canal. *Why do I feel guilty — disloyal — for wanting more information about my own mother?* She stopped in front of the picture of the *Adelaide* hanging on the wall, her childhood home on the water. *What if I find the answers and it's ugly?*

Crossing her arms, she continued to stare at the picture as her memory flitted over the years spent aboard the fishing vessel. The image presented calm seas on a sunny day, the tackle and gear stored orderly, the vessel freshly painted. She stood next to her father with his arm around her shoulders. She had waved at the photographer. Remembering the yacht, she now wondered how they got the photograph back to her father. *Had he known them?*

She spoke aloud, "Why is he so close-mouthed? What is he hiding?" The more she thought of how emotionally stunted Dan was, the angrier she got. *He probably treated her just like he's treating me now... judging me without understanding.*

The tears slipped down her cheeks as she sorted through her motherless childhood, dwelling on the moments when she was acutely aware of her mother's absence — her embarrassment when her doctor had to explain her menses and options for self care; the move from Ketchikan as a high schooler bereft of friends; her first thoughts of love for the boy with compelling blue-gray eyes that turned dopey when she smiled at him.

"Damnit!" With no further thought, Dana grabbed her handbag and slicker, slipped her wool stockinged feet into her rubber boots, and headed outside. She backed her Subaru out of the garage and headed toward Mendenhall Loop Road. Indignation fueled her anger at the man who had an opinion about everything that came his way; a kind word for everyone in the community; who could share a good-hearted laugh with virtual strangers, yet had nothing for his own daughter.

Dana hit the steering wheel. "Damn him!" Without a plan or thought of how to start a dialogue about the secrets of their lives, Dana arrived at her dad's apartment complex. She noticed his pickup parked under the carport, and was thankful Rachel's Jeep was not there. She pushed down the apprehension that surfaced as she opened the car door, determined she would not let her father treat her like a little girl — it was time for an adult conversation about taboos.

She leaned on the doorbell, unaware of her disheveled appearance or rain-drenched slicker. The astonished look on Dan's face when he opened the door caused her to hesitate just a moment.

"Dana, what's wrong?"

Somewhere in her brain it registered that her father was concerned about her well-being, but she couldn't hold that thought and maintain the determination she had mustered to get answers about her mother.

Her dad pulled her through the door, all the while searching her face. He pushed her hood back from her face and put his hands on her shoulders. "Dana, what's happened?"

Dana stepped to the side, breaking the connection of his familiar touch. If she allowed herself to cry, she would slip into that child-like role with him and cave-in.

"Dad, I need some answers! I want to know what happened to my mother! I know this is not comfortable for you, but I need to know!"

Dan turned swiftly away from her, running his hand over the top of his head. Turning back, he bellowed. "Is that what this is about? You show up at my place looking like a ship wreck, scaring the daylights out of me, and that's what you want?"

It registered with Dana that she had scared her dad, but she was determined to push through. "We're family, Dad. I know you were hurt, but I was too. I've been looking for her and I can't find anything about her."

Registering that his body had become still, his jaws set and eyes widened, she spoke louder. "I've spent my whole life with this...void. With this big question about my life, but with absolute certainty it was not okay to talk about it. What is the big secret? Was she a pervert? What?"

Her father stared at her, his rage barely contained. His response was loud, "No, she was not a pervert."

"Then what? Why did she leave me?"

Dan snarled, "She didn't leave you! She left me! And this discussion is over. I won't dredge up sludge because you're on some tangent and show up at my doorstep like...like somebody died!"

They glared at each other with furrowed brows—two opponents sizing each other up. Dana's mind raced, debating the next step. He was madder than she had ever seen him, but she couldn't back down. It had taken forty years to come to this point, and she needed to know truth. What would cause a mother to leave her only child behind?

"Then what did happen, Dad? Why did she leave?"

Dan's angry voice was deep. Controlled. He spoke between clenched teeth. "That's all I have to say, Dana."

Feeling her resolve starting to slip, she spoke the words she knew would get back at him. "Well, if you treated her like you're treating me, I don't blame her for leaving!"

Dana whirled around and burst out the door, jogging to her SUV before he could see her break down. Lurching out of the parking lot, she turned toward the glacier to avoid cross traffic. Her anguish filled the dank car as she tried to see through the fogged windshield, wiping it with her open hand.

The incessant rain blocked the winter sun. It was hard to see on this stretch of road with no street lights. Dana finally pulled over to the side of the road, aware she could not see well enough to drive safely in this state of mind. She sat with the engine running, allowing her anguish to pour out, feeling the pain of the little girl abandoned by a mother whose image was just a picture hidden away in the bed cupboard of her home on the water. She grieved for never having a whole family — either as a child or as a woman with the man she loved so dearly. And now that her daughter was found, the remnants of her relationship with her father were breaking. How could she have made such a mess of everything — the devastating decision twenty-one years ago, and now she was losing her dad. *Oh God, help me.*

Chapter Fifteen

PHYLLIS' OFFICE WAS TUCKED away in an inconspicuous corner of her church building. Dana came to the outside entrance, waiting for her colleague and mentor to signal before she clomped from the car to the door held open for her.

Dana's spirits mirrored the bleak weather. Her rounded shoulders and slow movements as she removed her rain jacket and wool cap showed her sense of defeat. When Phyllis wrapped her in a comforting hug, Dana melded into her shoulder and wept like a child, her body shaking with the sobs.

Phyllis seemed to know just what she needed, holding her until the angst had subsided. Dana sighed, feeling like a comforted child and loving Phyllis for her generous love.

Neither spoke as they settled into their accustomed chairs across from each other. Phyllis' ample size filled the rose colored arm chair completely. Her thick blonde hair curved around her radiant face, with not-so-subtle eye shadow drawing attention to her thick black eyelashes. She was a generous-sized, beautiful woman.

Dana's expressive hands lay limp in her lap. "I've really screwed it up this time, Phyllis. I don't know that I've ever been this low...even when I grieved over Rachel."

Through sighs and a monotone account, Dana told Phyllis about the disastrous confrontation with Dan over the secrecy of her mother. Given some distance from the event, she could see clearly that she approached it all wrong. At the time, she needed anger to propel her assertiveness, but in hindsight, it was aggressive. Of course Dan would respond defensively. And being the blusterous person he was, he defended himself vigorously. She knew the accusation of running her mother off cut him to the core, whether it was true or not. She was also certain that Dan would never forgive her. He was a person who held a grudge a long time.

When she told Hub about the incident, he was gentle but clear that she had crossed the line and didn't blame Dan for his reaction. It might have been her imagination, she told Phyllis, but it seemed that Hub was avoiding her. "He said it was my deal and I'll have to figure it out. He thinks it'll blow over, but I know it won't, Phyllis. I've seen how stubborn my dad is, and he won't back down.

"So, not only have I gotten nowhere on the search for my mother's story, I've lost my dad." Her eyes teared up, her voice faltering. "I know better than to let anger control my actions...but I just couldn't stop myself. It was like all the years of suppressed longing over-rode my common sense. It's embarrassing...I'm supposed to have some level of insight to human behavior, for crying out loud, but I acted like an out-of-control fish wife.

"I've destroyed every relationship important to me – my dad, who was my whole world at one time; my husband is hurt by all this, and I don't know how that'll work out; and I've lost the opportunity to parent the most precious daughter a woman could ever want."

After Dana honked her nose in a tissue, Phyllis asked, "How is it going with your daughter – Rachel, isn't it?"

"Pretty good, considering...although I can't trust my own judgment right now...maybe not. She seems to accept me a little more. We celebrated her birthday at the Twisted Fish, and that went well. We've talked a few times on the phone...nothing deep, but pleasant. I gave her a picture of my family when I was a two-year old – the only picture I have with my parents. She got kind of choked up, so I think there's some interest in a relationship. That is if my father doesn't turn her away from me."

"Is he the kind of person who would do that, Dana? Is that his character?"

Dana's face puzzled as she considered the question. "Not really. He's always been a man of principle. But who knows...he's oblivious to my grief, and how he could have helped the reunification with Rachel. He's just so self-centered!

"He and Rachel spend a lot of time together. They do things he never did with me – he joined the athletic club! It's so out-of-character for him. I'm glad he's doing it for his own health, but...I don't know. It's just different. I understand it—he finally gets to be a grandfather, and she is adorable."

Phyllis lifted her feet to a footstool, sinking into her chair more comfortably. "So, your father is exploring this new part of himself as a grandfather...making up time with your precious daughter. And of course it's an adjustment for all of you...you're not the only apple of his eye, and he is behaving like a new grandfather. Men do that, you know—there is a transformation that takes place when a father becomes a grandfather that is more profound than any other milestone in human development. It is astounding, but usually it's to see them speak gibberish and perform unbelievable antics to get smiles from an infant. It sounds like your father is doing the same thing, only it's geared to a twenty-year old child."

Dana affirmed her conclusion with a nod.

"So, Dana, what instigated the questions about your mother? Why now? You had a certain resolve about it before."

The question pushed Dana deeper into her chair. "I've asked myself that a hundred times since yesterday, and I really don't know, Phyllis. I guess...on some level, there's always been an interest in my heritage—how am I like her? Did I get her bad genes? How did she look when she was my age—that sort of thing, although it's not been a huge thing. I guess...maybe it's my dad's animosity toward me. It makes me question everything I believed to be true.

"I don't know that he's ever said it in so many words, but I've always understood there was something fundamentally wrong with my mother. She left him—a good man, and me. Just disappeared." She groaned. "If that's true! Now I wonder. I was so little I don't remember much about her, but it devastated him—literally. It was a hard time in my life too. I remember him being drunk a lot, and it seemed he wasn't there for me, although I was safe. Well fed. Naturally, as a little girl, I blamed her—he had become my whole world. It was years before he got through the depression. By then, I was nearly a teenager and growing away from him. I just accepted the fact that my mother was a taboo subject.

"I guess it didn't register how emotionally shut down he was until this...crossroad, if you will, of Rachel showing up in our lives. I knew it would be an adjustment, but I didn't think he would turn his back on me. He simply will not let me tell him the whole story. Unless Rachel told him, he doesn't even know I was raped, and he has no idea of the anguish I've lived with — before her birth and for twenty-one years since.

"It made me look at him differently. I pretty much had him on a pedestal before — before there were any real tests of his character, I guess. He's not who I thought he was. And maybe what I believed all my life is...not true.

"That's a long way to answer your question, Phyllis, but I think that's why it has become an issue with me now. I want some answers, and I can't trust him to give me...unbridled truth. I might have to hire a detective to find out what happened with my mother, although I hate to do that. It would cost a fortune, and what if they don't find anything, or...it's really bad? "

The two women were silent as they considered this juncture. "Dana, do you remember Marla suggesting you consider doing some twelve-step work? I'm not saying your dad is or was an alcoholic, but it seems that some of your family dynamics mirror the typical *elephant in the living room* functioning — a huge event, or reality controls the interactions, but you don't talk about it. It controls how you interact with each other, and ultimately influences your self-concept and how you problem-solve. The *secret* still controls you."

The thought of doing her own recovery work at this stage of her life was a tough pill to swallow. Dana had done graduate school, individual counseling, workshops and conferences galore. She'd read a ton of books, all with an eye toward how she could help her clients, and figure herself out along the way. She felt she had good insight into human behavior, and was quite successful at counseling others. Yet on some level, what Phyllis suggested made sense.

She sighed in resignation. "I know you're right. I could learn something from it. I just can't imagine going to a twelve-step group and spilling my guts along side my clients."

"No, no...that wouldn't work at all, but there are other options, Dana. What if you do a workbook or journal about it, and then supplement that with some sessions with me? There are some good tools out there...*The Twelve Steps for Everyone*, Janet Woitiz' *Adult Children of Alcoholics*. Or you could do some on-line groups. It's something to think about."

"I will. I'll look at the book Marla gave me, and some of these other options. Thanks, Phyllis."

"Your demeanor tells me we've not hit the mark yet, Dana."

"No...no...this has helped. I do feel some hope; it's just...hard. You've redirected me to something I can actually control instead of flapping in the wind wishing my father would be different."

Phyllis stood in the doorway while Dana dashed to her Subaru a little more straight shouldered.

Chapter Sixteen

BRANDI REMOVED HER HOOD and outer coat, giving full attention to each slow movement as she unwrapped a long knitted scarf, her head pivoting as the scarf spiraled up like a hangman's noose. Hooking her coat on the rack, she removed a thick fabric from her pocket and dropped it at her feet. She stepped on the fabric to dry the soles of her knee-high boots before trudging over to her customary chair. She glanced sideways at her companions without acknowledging anyone.

Dana sent a prayer missile heavenward for wisdom as her heart ached for Brandi. She looked around at the other four women, assessing body language. The mood overall was a good match to the dark and rainy weather.

Her voice was gentle as she searched for a starting place. "It's a dreary night, and I appreciate that each of you are here in spite of it. Our magnificent eco-system is definitely being replenished this month, isn't it?"

She faltered at the minimal response from her comment. "Well, let's see what we can do to tackle some of that gloom. Brandi, you're hurting. Let us share some of your load."

Brandi studied the floor, her hands shaking as they sought repose. "I'm sorry. I don't mean to be a downer, but it's been a pretty rough week. My children are sick, and I haven't been getting much sleep. Goodell acts like it's too much trouble to help out with his own children. I had to hire a babysitter for tonight because he can't be bothered."

She looked up as she rubbed her forehead with splayed fingers. "I didn't expect him to just walk away from everything—his children; friends. He didn't go to his Friday night poker game. I don't know what he's doing with his time, but I don't think he's with her. Her husband said they are trying to work things out."

Looking at the group, the whites of Brandi's eyes showed all around her irises. "I'm afraid he won't help out with the bills willingly. I might have to proceed legally to make sure he pays child support."

Sighs of empathy hung in the silence. Dana wondered which direction to take. Her mind flashed through the sad statistics about divorce in America, showing the wife usually worse off economically, and the children harmed emotionally and developmentally.

The silence was broken when Genie looked over her crossed arms resting on her crossed knees, her foot tapping a silent beat. "You want me to take care of 'im, princess? I know people. He deserves a little *ther-a-py*." Her invariable furrowed brow suggested sincerity, but her mouth revealed the slightest grin.

Brandi looked at her as if trying to decipher a foreign language, then the irony exploded before she could form a proper response. She guffaw-hiccupped, covering her mouth as if to deny such an inelegant outburst. There was an extended hesitation as she tried to regain control, then she lost all composure.

The others watched in wonder as their picture-perfect friend decomposed into laughter and tears, her body shaking uncontrollably as her mascara left smudges where she swiped with the pads of her hands. There was nothing to do but to join in the laughter that escalated out of control. Even Genie couldn't contain a half-smirk.

It took several minutes for the humor to have full vent, as if the jigger valve of a pressure cooker had been lifted, and moments were required to wait for full release.

The women waited for Brandi to speak first. She shook her head, framing her face with opened hands. "I can't believe I just did that."

Her eyes flashed, her expression nonplussed. "I can't believe it. But it felt so good...to laugh so hard. To...to be out of control.

"Thank you, Genie. Your offer is...generous, but probably not..." She dissolved into a milder fit of laughter before she could continue. "Oh dear. Genie, I have this image of him tied to a chair with you badgering him about his behavior, making him spell *in-teg-rity* over and over.

"I know, I know...that's not the approach you would likely take, but it struck me as funny. Obviously."

She sighed deeply before she concluded, "I couldn't have asked for a better solution than that. Thank you. The laughter is healing. I know you all can't change things for me, but it helps immensely to know you want to help. In spite of my unladylike behavior."

Dana smiled, "It was wonderful to see you release some of that pent up stress, Brandi. Yes, laughter *is* good for the soul.

"Is there anything we can do for you?"

Brandi shook her head. "Thank you, but no. I just need to...see it through. I hope he'll come to his senses – the children need him."

Unsure of how to transition the group after such an intense engagement, Dana looked for cues from the other women of what their needs might be. The mood had changed from the earlier gloom. "I have a project for us this evening, or we can continue with check-ins first..." She looked questioningly at each person and received signals to move on. "Okay then, as a follow up to last week's discussion about identity, I'd like you to create a collage that says something about you."

Dana gave instructions to the group, offering a stack of magazines, scissors, glue sticks and card stock. Very quickly, the women settled into the process – tearing out pages that contained images or words that intrigued them. They worked quietly until each had a stack of a dozen or so images. Then, as instructed, they cut out the images or words and arranged them on the card stock. After thirty minutes, Dana interrupted their concentration.

"I can see you're not all done, and that's fine. You can finish them at home, but I would like each of you to share just a little bit about your collage, and what it says about you."

"I'll start." Susan held up a full magazine page showing an austere den Dana recognized as a promotion for an investment broker. Susan had overlaid the image of a black and white cat almost covering the bright window, and a drawing of large eye glasses lying on the desk. "You can't see it, but the wall behind here is floor to ceiling book shelves. And they're filled with all my favorite books. So, this is about me...I love to read, and I have a cat that looks just about like this one, except she has orange on her. This would be a very peaceful place for me when I'm not with my students." Susan hesitated before concluding, "It's quiet and uncluttered."

The non-verbal nods and smiles from the group showed support for Susan as the attention shifted to Sheryl, who was next in the circle. She held up a fan of images showing a quilt with a vase of flowers, yarn and scissors. "I didn't get everything glued on it yet, but I like to sew and do crafts — anything creative." She chuckled before she continued, "This room is way too tidy to represent my surroundings, but I would fill it up in no time. I do tend to collect things. Okay, some might consider it hoarding."

She studied her images as if lost in thought, so Dana asked, "And what does it say about you, Sheryl?"

"Oh yeah. That I like variety and boldness. I'm not fussy...and I'll try anything once!" Her self-deprecating laughter was soft.

Genie was next in the circle. She pushed her collage along the chair arm, her lower jaw prominent, her eyes hooded as she looked at Dana. Her card stock was covered with images of babies, children at play, cartoon characters and puppies. She spoke as if the words were being pulled from her mouth. "I like things unspoiled. Natural. Before they get worn out or ugly. I like to watch little kids and how they're so straight. They don't dress up their words — they say it like it is...no put-ons.

"This little kid reminds me of my brother. They took him away when he was five. Maybe he got a better life."

Dana whispered *thank you* and nodded for Ruth to go next. She held up a picture of a family at the dinner table. She drew a cross on the wall, and glued pictures of flowers all around the bottom. Cutouts of African children were on the sides. "I uh...I value my family and my church. I appreciate beauty, and colorful décor. And I've always wanted to go to a third world country to help the children. Someday."

The silence in between the presentations seemed to honor the intimacy that was deepening among the women as they exposed more of themselves.

Brandi huffed, sitting up straighter. She held up her card stock with the single image of a huge ponderosa pine tree, surrounded by several seedlings. "I am the adult in my family, and I am rooted. Strong. I will do whatever I have to do to take care of my children."

* * *

Dana was thoughtful after the group ended. The interactions among the women were subdued as they left, each appearing more settled in some way. Doing collages was a good idea. It suddenly occurred to Dana to do one herself. She retrieved a stack of magazines — National Geographic, fashion, and sports magazines. Settling in to a quiet perusal of the images, she let herself be led by intrigue rather than purpose.

After collecting a stack of fifteen images and cutting them out, she checked the clock and was surprised to see that forty-five minutes had passed. After a quick text to Hub that she would be another hour, she sat back, pushing the cutouts around at different angles. Tears slipped down her cheeks as she could see truth so plainly.

Sand and blue water peeked through all the emblems of tenderness — intertwined bare feet, alluring eyes, the broad-shoulder of a poised archer, two teenage girls huddled together on the grass, a gold locket draped over an aging hand, an outcropping of rocks and boulders that called for exploration. Almost lost amidst the display was a solitary male figure in shadows. Dana moved it to the center of the collage. She smirked at the glaring truth before her — Hub, her soul mate and lover, her rock — was getting lost in the shuffle. *And I miss him so much. I need him. How could I have let so much get in the way of our togetherness?*

She set the collage materials aside, and gathered her coat and bag, anxious to find her man, to tell him how sorry she was for letting her angst about Rachel and the dispute with her father interfere with her most important relationship.

Chapter Seventeen

NOW RETURNING HOME, DANA thought about how she and Hub had blended in with most of the families taking advantage of the Thanksgiving holiday to locate blue sky and sunshine. Pale faces had beamed from layers of vests and jackets over shorts and tank tops that were uncovered at touchdown in Hawaii. The return flight now was subdued with tired suntanned faces anxious to end the punishing six-hour flight.

Dana had found a bungalow near Honaunau Bay where they snorkeled with the dolphins, walked along the bay in the evenings, and enjoyed the delights of relaxed love-making. Reminiscent of their first honeymoon, they were playful and attentive, but with the flavor of maturity and intimacy that sweetened their togetherness.

Dana had left the angst about her father and daughter in Juneau when they left. Even now, as she neared home and started the mental transition of getting back to the routine, it looked different. Perhaps it wasn't as hopeless as it seemed just six days ago. She promised herself she wouldn't get so worked up again. After all, they were family. Her father had raised her. They loved each other. Somehow, they would build bridges.

She wondered how he had spent Thanksgiving — if he and Rachel had celebrated the holiday together. Almost every year since graduate school, her dad had spent Thanksgiving with her and Hub. She had told herself their tension wasn't the deciding factor of their trip to Hawaii, but it sure helped to avoid the possibility of a family gathering with stilted conversation and denial of grudges. Or worse — that her dad might reject her again by declining their traditional gathering.

She sighed involuntarily. *I guess I made a pre-emptive strike by leaving. Maybe he was relieved too.*

She studied Hub's face as he dozed, leaning against the window. She touched his arm and thanked God for blessing her with this incredible man. *My life could never have been complete without him.*

* * *

Getting back into the routine was harder than Dana thought it would be. Her body had adjusted to the peaceful rhythms of Hawaii, and she wanted to continue at that pace — mentally and physically. She wanted to connect with Hub, at least with a languid phone call, but her tight schedule made it hard to coalesce with his. *This is what you've been doing to yourself, Dana — you created this crazy pace! Remember Hawaii and keep it simpler in the future!*

She took some deep breaths and pulled the stack of group charts nearer. Remembering Brandi's predicament tugged at Dana's heart, but the image of her tree analogy was encouraging. Hopefully that self-awareness will carry her through the tough times.

The group, as a whole, is moving in the right direction. More openness. Trust. Just thinking of their progress moved Dana to a higher gear. She could feel the energy in her body rev up a notch as she thought of the importance of her work.

When she entered the group room, all were present except Genie. Brandi was talking about her retail finds on Black Friday while Susan, Sheryl and Ruth listened. Dana could feel the release of her tension, knowing that Brandi was holding up at least.

Just as the women settled into their chairs, Genie edged in the front door sideways, her face hidden from the group. She quietly hung her coat on the rack, then turned squarely to the group.

Mouths dropped and all small talk ceased as she took a few steps closer to the group. It was hard to read her expression as she looked cock-eyed at the circle. The edge to her typically defiant pose was softer, but the set of her jaw signaled to *approach at your own risk.*

Dana's heart squeezed, tears instantly filling her eyes as she studied Genie's battered face. Clean short stitches in her left eyebrow showed where she had often worn a silver ring. Yellow discoloration around her cheek bone attested to a nasty week-old bruise. When she sat down, Dana noticed a hesitation in her movements, suggesting pain avoidance.

Before Dana could speak, Genie responded to the astounded five faces. "You should see the other guy." Her one-sided grin protected the healing split in her upper lip. "Sorry, ladies. I wanted to protect you from seeing this side of life, but my PO wouldn't cut me slack." She winced as she pushed her body deeper into the chair.

Weighing sympathy against objectivity, Dana's slight smile acknowledged Genie's humor and bravado.

Brandi's loving concern spoke for all of them. "Are you okay? What happened?"

Genie's eye movement suggested smugness but was contradicted by the slight muscle contraction around her mouth. She hesitated before she spoke, as if sizing up the group's potential response. Lifting her chin in resolve, she told her story. "Wrong place at the wrong time. Bastard hooked up with the wrong chick, though, and now he's coolin' his heals waitin' for arraignment."

She took a deep breath and seemed to collect herself before she continued. "I shoulda seen it comin.' The dude with the pool table. He set up a phony match. No one showed up but me." Her look of derision spoke of her self-blame.

"Tried to take what I wasn't willing to give, but he got more than he bargained for. He messed with the wrong chick. He told the cops I wanted rough sex, then tried to bilk him.

"He forgot the texts he'd sent me about the match. Cops kept my phone for evidence, but didn't PV me. So, I got stitched up. Took a couple days off. I'm fine."

Sadness permeated the room, suppressing words of comfort. Finally, Dana spoke, her voice hoarse. "It hurts to think about you being harmed, Genie. I vacillate from relief that you survived the ordeal...to anger that someone would do this to you.

"Good for you for calling the police! I assume you did anyway."

Genie nodded. "Yeah, well...the neighbor did. I've not always had the best luck with the cops. But this cop was...different."

"So...how are your spirits, Genie? You've been through a huge trauma. You were assaulted. Manipulated into getting there in the first place. You must be hurting on many levels."

Dana knew she was pushing the line to suggest vulnerability with Genie, but hoped that stating the obvious would allow it.

Genie's flash of defensiveness turned to a glare at Dana. "Wasn't nothin' new."

Dana's voice was a whisper. "Nothing new?"

Ruth's words spewed forth accusingly. "You talk like it was nothing, Genie...and we see you with bruises and stitches, and you're hurt...yet you say it was nothing. It wasn't *nothing*, Genie! It hurts me to see you like this. You could have been killed!" As her anger turned to anguish, she mumbled, "You could be one of my daughters." Her head shook imperceptibly, her eyes closed.

Dana pushed back in her chair, searching for understanding and words that would move recovery forward. Genie's face was unreadable, but she did not react to Ruth's outburst.

"It hurts to think about Genie being harmed. I think we all share that concern, not just for Genie, but for Brandi...for each of you at different times and in different ways. And it hits close to home especially for you, Ruth, because you have daughters who...could be harmed."

Ruth nodded without making eye contact.

Dana waited. She thought the earlier antagonism between Genie and Ruth had improved—they were more invested in the group and the process now—but a confrontation could be healing for both, or create more contention.

Finally, Ruth spoke quietly. "I'm sorry if that was cross talk. It's just...hard."

Genie shifted away from the group, her words almost swallowed, "It doesn't matter."

Ruth reacted immediately with a noisy intake of breath and abrupt straightening in her chair. She glowered at Genie, who maintained an aloof posture but looked back at her sideways.

Ruth's body shook as she spoke evenly. "It does matter, Genie. We disagree a lot, but wrong is wrong, and what happened to you was evil. I hope you won't make that mistake again...and he rots in hell!"

The only sign of acknowledgment was Genie's eyes shifting back in line with her face turned away from the group.

"Okay." Dana spoke tentatively, as if her thoughts were barely ahead of her words. "Thank you for sharing your heart, Ruth...and yours, Genie. It seems that what we are talking about is control...the fears and frustrations we have about things beyond our control. And recognizing when we have control, and when we don't. I have to say, it's something I struggle with personally, yet it's all important if we are to navigate our own ships." She pushed her hands to her chest as she spoke earnestly, "To live our lives according to our own paths rather than other people's expectations or agendas."

She looked around the circle, making eye contact with each as she asked, "Might that be a topic worth exploring tonight? We can intersperse that topic with check-ins."

Brandi jumped right in. "I know it's germane to me." She tilted her head to readjust the huge alligator clip holding her blond tresses on top of her head, her movements slow and deliberate. "I've been all over the board this last month trying to control things in my world. Trying to keep Goodell from being stupid. To make him *want* to stay with us...to be a responsible father. And husband. To keep from losing my home.

"I've cried. I've threatened. I've made promises to myself and broken them. I've stayed away from him. I've followed him and tried to catch him doing whatever he does, but it's crazy. It wore me out and didn't do any good."

Her eyelids touch-closed as she reached for resolve, gripping her hands as she spoke. "I swore I would never let my children witness what I did as a kid. My mother was frantic about my father's whereabouts. She dragged us kids out of bed to go with her—driving all over town looking for his Audi. She made us call him or pretend we were sick to gain his sympathy. It was...I was embarrassed for her. She's so pretty, so talented...and she let him treat her like she was...unimportant. It's not a whole lot different now, but he doesn't cheat any more. I don't think, anyway."

She looked up at Dana, "That's all about control, isn't it? My mother spent her life trying to control my father. I don't want to do that. I won't do that."

Dana asked the unanswered question when it wasn't forthcoming. "Brandi, what do you have control over…under your present circumstances?"

"That's harder to see, isn't it?" Her perfectly shaped eyebrows dimpled; her lower jaw protruded. "He's been making overtures…paying attention to our children. He says he made a mistake and is sorry. So far I haven't given him any encouragement, but the children are glad to see their father more. And he did pay his share of the bills this month. I refuse to chase him again."

"Have you thought about what change would look like, Brandi? What you would need to see happen before you could recommit to him? You mentioned he has cheated before, and you must have worked through that…or at least buried it. What would be different this time? What would real change look like?"

Brandi's face showed the internal debate, but her posture remained straight. "I don't know that I want him back. But he would have to go to counseling. He would have to prove that he's not messing around."

When Brandi didn't continue, Dana suggested, "It might be worth doing a little research about the qualities of a healthy relationship…what does trust and intimacy look like? I've got a handout for you all on that, and we'll talk about it more in group. But spend some time writing out what you would need to see…over time…to feel like trust could be regained.

"Sometimes disrespectful behavior becomes so familiar, we think it's normal. Then when someone comes along who treats us special, it closes the door to reconciliation before we can really figure out how to tell deception from truth. I suspect you're vulnerable to someone else's attention right now, Brandi, just because it is such a struggle. So often we repeat the same patterns because we haven't figured out what is our own baggage and what are reasonable expectations. Does that make sense?"

Brandi's head shook as she continued to look deep in thought. "I don't want another man, I just want… You're right. I need to figure out what I do want. Thanks, Dana."

Scanning the circle with raised eyebrows, Dana's eyes settled on Sheryl.

"Sometimes I think the only real control I have is between an *A* and *B*, a *C* and a *D*. With twenty hormonal teenagers every hour, it's a wonder they learn anything about trigonometry basics." A chuckle escaped as she contemplated. "Really, I think I'm doing okay with control right now. Since I put my foot down with that other teacher, it's been different for me. I've been bossier, I guess. But my life is pretty good right now. Had a good Thanksgiving with some friends. My son got to come home for four days. I'm getting ready for Christmas…things are good."

Dana shook her head to affirm what she heard from Sheryl.

Ruth's voice was firm but calm. "I know I can't control my daughter's choices…or Genie's." She half-smiled toward Genie. "I just want them to be…safe. I know I have no control…I just don't know what to do with that. How do I ignore all the pain around me and do nothing? How do I watch my girls walk into the lion's den and do nothing?"

Dana's deep sigh and scrunched mouth preceded her response. "I don't know, Ruth. I think it's something we each need to figure out for ourselves, and I admit, I'm still working on the answers for myself.

"Some things you might want to consider: The *Boundaries* book by Cloud and Townsend is a great reference on the topic. And there are some options with twelve-step recovery programs for co-dependent issues. I think there's even a group in town that meets weekly — I can give you the contact information after group.

"It's helpful to write about it — just take a piece of paper and put a line down the middle On one side, list what you can't control; on the other, list what you can. It's a good first step to figuring it out."

"Thanks, I will."

Susan's eyes were rounded, looking surprised. She pushed her glasses against her face, signaling she was ready to talk. "I can't control my compulsions…or the urge to…check things. I pick my cuticles sometimes. But I can control my sugar intake. Taking my meds. Sometimes I can force myself to go for a walk even when I don't want to. These are things that help, and I can control them a lot of the time, even if the urges are there." She looked around at the other women before she sat back, returning her attention to her folded hands.

Dana had learned that was Susan's signal she was finished talking. She squinted at Genie, the last person in the circle to speak.

Genie's mouth moved like she was working up to a response, her body fidgeting. "I try to stay out of other people's business. They're gonna do what they're gonna do." Her knees flexed rhythmically. "In NA, I learned to give up my will to Higher Power cuz' I can't stay away from drugs on my own. So me and Higher Power hang out a lot. We avoid what we can't control. I shouldn't a gone to that dude's place to play pool. He's just like all the others."

"*All* the others, Genie? Is there no man in your history...ever...that you could trust?"

Genie's eyes moved as she sifted through the chapters of her life. "The janitor at my grade school. The only time I went to the same school two years in a row...Elko, Nevada. He talked to me. Told me I was smart. Said I should talk to the principle if things was bad at home. But I never did."

"I'm so glad he was there for you, Genie. How about men in recovery? Your work?"

"No. Maybe one. My boss is a good guy. We joke around a lot. He's more like a grandpa. And there's a guy in NA that seems harmless. I'd trust him some."

"Genie, what are the indicators to you that someone is trustworthy? Sometimes it's easier to see the flaws than it is to see character...the integrity in a person."

"I guess I'm not so good at seeing that." Her demeanor changed to haughty. "If there are guys out there with *in-teg-ri-ty*, they must not travel in my circle."

"Okay. It's too late in the day to start, but next week I'll be prepared to share a handout on trusting relationships. But I'd encourage you to do some writing about it...what does integrity look like to you? What are the qualities in a person that make you think they can be trusted?"

Dana ended the group with a relaxation exercise intended to increase self-awareness of physical reactions to distress.

Chapter Eighteen

"IT LOOKS LIKE A perfect night to see the northern lights. Shall we save our walk for later?"

Hub looked out the window as if assessing weather conditions. "Yeah, that'd be nice. Think the dogs will let us defer?"

Dana chuckled as she tried to settle Mica and Nikki vying for Hub's attention while he removed his boots. "I took them out earlier for a short one."

It was Friday evening—the end of Hub's workweek, and Dana had big plans for his time. She had retrieved the Christmas decorations from storage and spent the day transforming their log home into a showcase of holiday memories from the last eighteen years. An open space for the Christmas tree was half-circled with boxes of lights and tree ornaments. The fragrance of cinnamon spices simmering on the woodstove made the house even more festive.

Hub encircled Dana in his arms as he looked around at her handiwork. "Looks nice. You've been busy today, I see."

Their quiet embrace lingered before he continued. "I saw Rachel at the coffee shop. She said she is going to Minneapolis for Christmas, but would like to get with us before she leaves. Said you've been talking by phone."

Dana stayed in Hub's arms, nodding her head slowly. Finally, she pulled away to see his face as she spoke. "We have. Nothing deep—just chit chat. But she said she would think about coming here before she leaves. I told her it was okay if she wanted to meet at a restaurant. Maybe take a tour of Christmas lights—the Governor's mansion is beautiful this year."

"Well, she talked like it was a plan. I mighta' got it wrong, but that's the impression I got."

Dana squealed like a child. Coming to the house was one more indication that Rachel was warming up to her, letting down the barriers. Throughout the day, as Dana had pondered Christmas memories while she set out the assortment of decorations and the treasured nativity scene, she daydreamed about how Rachel might respond to them. She envisioned Rachel asking about the mementos of her and Hub's years together. She thought of traditions they might develop together—putting up the Christmas village, sharing favorite music, decorating cookies. And now it looked more like it could actually happen.

Her excitement pulled a laughing Hub into a makeshift dance around the living room. "That's just the best news ever. I can't wait to get the tree up. I've got so much to do. It'll be perfect!"

Their supper of stew and cornbread muffins was unnoticed as Dana chattered about the details of wrapping up her work schedule within two weeks, finding the perfect variegated yarn to knit socks for Rachel, adding more lights to the deck railing, and planning the dinner menu. Hub's attention waned, but he grunted at the right times.

As they walked the dogs along the road later, wrapped in coats and Dana with a knit scarf circling her head, Hub approached the topic. "What about Dad? Are you going to invite him?"

Dana's response was immediate. "No! He would ruin everything. It would be...I'd have to dance around his mood...his judgment, and I don't want him to spoil it. Hub, it's the first big breakthrough where *she* is taking the steps to draw closer to *me*. It's such a huge deal...I...are you suggesting I *should* ask him?"

Hub's response came after his typical thoughtful pause followed by an intake of breath. It irritated Dana at times when she thought his circumspection was a ploy to state an obvious truth, as if she were a child who couldn't see it for herself. She felt her shoulders tense before he said a word. She was ready for bear.

"Well, he *is* family. He usually joins us for Christmas. And he and Rachel are ahead of us in...connecting. Don't you think she might feel awkward if he isn't part of it?"

Dana's steps stiffened to a stomp, her shoulders hunched as she leaned into the walk. Her mind darted to all the possibilities. What Hub said might be true, but she refused to cater to her dad's childish temper tantrum. It was his typical way to avoid any topic that might create unpleasantness. Just like he avoided the topic of her mother — she'd have to pretend disinterest, and she could not do that with Rachel.

"I don't care, Hub. I can't go there. He's going to have to make some concessions before I can open my heart to him again. I just can't."

* * *

By Sunday, all the Christmas decorations were in place, although Dana's enthusiasm was ramped down considerably. She stewed over options and possible scenarios if her father came for the dinner, or his obvious absence if he didn't. She thought about discussing the dilemma with Rachel in advance, but didn't want to impose the conflict with her father onto Rachel.

As she worried her lip, trying to focus on the heel of the sock she was knitting, the preacher's message from this morning's sermon nagged her. *If anyone has a grudge against his brother, he should leave his gift at the alter and go make amends.*

Make amends. Her eyes were drawn to the twelve-step reference Marla had given her a month ago. It sat there, untouched since she brought it home. Throughout all the hullabaloo of decorating, she had left the book out on the side table. Somehow, it seemed sacrosanct and she couldn't tuck it away. Besides, she didn't want to forget it — Marla or Phyllis would surely ask about it. She stared at it a moment, before she pushed it away in her mind — maybe she'd save it for a New Year's resolution.

Chapter Nineteen

SNOW BLANKETED THE BOROUGH, promising to stay for the season. Blue skies appeared with the sun about ten o'clock, reminding Juneauites to appreciate Alaska's magnificence while they could see it in these short winter days. Dana noticed that some kind soul had shoveled the office steps for her. Before removing her coat inside, she went through her routine of opening the office — window blinds up, lights on, thermostat up, faux fireplace turned on, and diffuser filled with a cinnamon oil mixture.

As she waited for the hot water to boil, she appraised the group room and kitchenette for last minute housekeeping details. She had hung a few Christmas lights the week before, and set out her snowman assortment — pretty sparse decorations compared to prior years. With the extra classes she taught this fall and the distress with her father, her motivation for extras was limited.

Dipping her tea bag in the cup of hot water, she realized how she'd been counting the days left before she closed the office for Christmas break. It was startling to realize how weary she felt in spite of a tranquil week on the Big Island. Mentally, she sifted through possible causes: sleep — no; nutrition — it's good; hydration — good. She crossed her arms. *Dad. Admit it, Dana, this conflict has you frogged. And he's probably oblivious! This should be the greatest celebration ever — Rachel has been found…and it's killin' me, Lord. Would you fix him? Would you help him see how wrong he is?*

Standing up abruptly, she pushed her contention to the back of her mind and began a mental list of goals for the day. She had a light schedule, so she would start some of the end-of-year jobs — closing out charts, reconciling accounts, and gathering tax information.

The dreary afternoon turned into a productive day, even though two clients had cancelled, not uncommon with this weather. By the time her group began to arrive—all five bundled up against the weather—Dana was reenergized.

"I'm so glad you all made it on such a wintry evening. I hope the roads will stay clear." Dana was affirmed by each woman as she made eye contact around the circle. "With check-ins, I'd like to hear any thoughts about the last discussion. We spoke about control—what we can and can't control, and healthy vs. unhealthy relationships. Genie, would you like to start?"

The surprise in Genie's eyes was quickly masked by her street-wise tough girl demeanor. Dana chastised herself for breaking her own rule. "Genie, that was unfair. I put you on the spot, and I apologize. If you don't want to start, that's fine."

Dana accepted Genie's glare, but could see a softening around her eyes that still showed a hint of yellow bruising.

She leaned her forearms on her wide-spread knees, her body reaching toward Dana, staring. "You said you wouldn't do that. It seems as though the shrink needs a little of that *in-teg-rity*."

Dana half-smiled as she returned the stare, clearly seeing how thin the brittle layer of Genie's façade had become.

After controlling the silence for a long moment, Genie responded in a raspy voice. "I'll let it pass…this time."

She shifted in her chair, then continued. "I did a lot of thinkin' about last week. Not the control thing—I try to live the Serenity Prayer." At a few questioning looks around the circle, Genie recited it.

> *"God, grant me the serenity*
> *To accept the things I cannot change,*
> *To change the things I can,*
> *And the wisdom to know the difference.*

"It's my mainstay. But I been cogitatin' on what the church lady said." She glanced at Ruth. "I know you were thinkin' about yer girls, and I hope they never experience what I did. Any of the stuff I done. But you said it mattered…that I was beat up."

Genie adjusted her body again, crossing her legs and arms. She swallowed several times, rubbing the tattoo of tears dripping from the knuckles on her left hand. "I know that's true about your girls—it matters if they get beat up or not. Or my mom—it matters if she...is safe or not. Or the kids across the way where I live. Or the princess. But it's a stretch to think it matters about me."

She huffed before she continued haltingly. "It's been worse—much worse. It's happened a lot. So I tell myself it don't matter. But you're right, church lady. It sorta does. Matter.

"That's all I got to say. 'Cept you'd better go to confession, church lady...about that rot-in-hell stuff."

Dana hesitated, her chin resting on clasped hands as she tried to not be diverted by Genie's humor. "Thank you for sharing that, Genie. That's a boatload of insight. And...not only do you matter, you're important."

The import of Genie's personal revelation held the silence a moment. Ruth had listened intently to Genie, her face unreadable except for the pink appearing on her forehead. She broke the silence. "Thank you, Genie, for saying that about my girls. But I did mean it to include you too. I do care what happens to you...in spite of your nickname for me, which...probably fits."

Ruth's deference broke the suspense that held the group's breath, but her tone turned serious again as she continued. "Last week was thought-provoking for me, too." She glanced at Genie, "And thanks for the Serenity Prayer. I've heard it before, but it resonates tonight.

"I made that list...actually several of them, trying to figure out where I have some control and where I have none. The *none* side is filled to the brim. I have control over very little—my personal choices, the efficiency of my business. My attitude...giving, or not. I choose to serve and try to do God's will for me, but I know I get side-tracked at times trying to tell him how to do his business. Even with my husband...I try to get him to do the right thing...what I think is the right thing, but in reality—he makes his own choices."

Resignedly, she added, "I got that Boundaries book... Maybe after Christmas."

When Dana asked about her daughter, Ruth sighed. "A little better, I guess. We're not fighting anyway. I just don't know what will happen when she graduates."

"I think you'll get a lot from the Boundaries book before spring arrives."

Brandi spoke next. "I made another collage this week. I really like what we did in group last week, Dana. This one, though, was on what I need from my husband. At first, it showed all the things Goodell isn't—appreciative; helpful with the children and household chores; honest; trustworthy; genuine. I could have said the very same things about what my father lacked.

"Then I did some search on the internet about relationships—what is respectful in a marriage. I tried to not think of Goodell, but to just think in terms of a good relationship. It kept me from focusing only on his...flaws. And it was a little more balanced, because he isn't all bad—he's a good provider. He's romantic at times, and good with the children when he's...focused. I just can't count on him—he's not consistent. And when he *is* trying, I'm waiting for the other shoe to drop, so he gets impatient with my suspicion and we argue, bringing up all the things from the past. I don't know...I'm still thinking it through."

"Good for you. We'll talk some more tonight about trust and intimacy—maybe that will give you some more ideas."

When Dana's eyes settled on Sheryl, she burst out laughing. "I did the homework, Ms. Dana, honest...but the dog ate it!" Her cheeks flushed and her body shook until her humor had emptied out. "*Oy vey*...you'd think I could come up with a better excuse after hearing them for twenty years. Sorry, Dana, but I...just...didn't...do it. Put me down for an incomplete, and I'll behave better next week."

Dana shook her head, smirking. "I bet you have heard some doozies as a teacher. Well, I promise not to send you down the hall. Is there anything else you'd like to share?"

Sheryl shook her head. "No...I'm good."

"Susan, how are you doing, and is there something from our last session that stands out with you?"

"Nothing that hasn't already been said. It was nice to have some time off. I read a lot."

Dana's head nodded as she evaluated Susan's demeanor. Flat affect. Comfortable posture. Plain but neatly groomed. Hands resting quietly.

"Alright then, let's talk about relationships and intimacy." Dana passed around a handout that showed four concentric circles with descriptors within each circle. The women divided their attention between the sheet of paper and Dana's explanation. "Okay. The center circle represents you. Notice the heavy line around it that denotes a boundary—no one belongs in that circle except you. It represents your identity, your choices, values, priorities, goals, privacy, and perspectives."

Brandi held the handout with both hands, both feet planted solidly on the floor. She reminded Dana of a college student anticipating an exam. Suppressing a smile, Dana continued. "The small circle immediately surrounding the *you circle* represents your closest relationships—perhaps only a few, or a handful of people, belong in this group because it has such a high level of trust. With this relationship, you can be yourself, make mistakes, explore ideas, and have deep disclosure with each other because you accept each other without judgment. There's unconditional acceptance. And because of the high level of trust, there is generally a lot of sharing with all kinds of emotions, thinking and events, including difficult times.

"Another important aspect with this closest relationship is that it is reciprocal. In other words, you give and receive from each other. It isn't a matter of one of you being the rescuer and the other being dependent, or one of you is an open book and the other closed and unavailable—there's mutuality to it. Giving and receiving. And you trust they won't use anything you've said against you at a later time, and *vice versa*. We might call this the *intimacy circle*."

Dana's voice tripped over the word *intimacy*, feeling a sense of shame for pretending expertise on the topic. She had struggled most of her life with emotional transparency, and it felt deceptive to proclaim the importance of intimacy now. Pushing back the emotion, she reminded herself, *this is not about me!*

Checking how the concept was settling with the group, she could tell they were receptive. Even Genie studied the handout intently. "Now the next circle out represents relationships that are important, but for whatever reason, there is not the high level of trust as described in the *intimate circle*. Here, these people may be family or friends, coworkers…sometimes even spouses. It's an important relationship—but trust is conditional. You might trust them with your vehicle or to cover your work station, but you wouldn't allow your children to spend the night with them, or loan them money. So in this relationship circle, you're more guarded with personal information, or feelings that you hold close to your heart. You might enjoy a lot of time or activities together…be tight in some aspects, but that *lack of trust* makes you cautious, and you don't share the negative emotions or more private thoughts. We might call this the *friendship circle*.

"Now the outside circle represents people in your life who you simply cannot trust, so your interactions are superficial — the weather, the news, the exchange of factual information. These people may be associated with your work; sometimes it's family…but you've either learned you can't trust them, or you don't know them well enough to know if they're trustworthy. Let's call this the *guarded circle*.

"Ideally, when we meet someone, we begin the relationship with them being outside all the circles, and as we get to know them over time, we let them in the closer circles. As they prove their trustworthiness under different circumstances and stressors, we let them get closer, and so on. But sometimes," Dana held her hand with splayed fingers over the handout, "relationships are imposed on us, like a family system. We are born into a family with a domineering, self-serving relative, for example. Or we jump into a relationship too quickly and allow them into our intimate circle before we realize they can't be trusted. Then we're distressed as we try to reclaim our own space or self-direction."

Dana pronounced the word *self direction* slowly as she looked around the circle to assess the reactions to the concepts. Clearly, it was thought-provoking as the women began to shift their attention from the handout to her with thoughtful expressions on their faces.

"So when you think of relationships in this way, and the need for different boundaries with different people under different circumstances, what rings true with you?"

Dana didn't need to prompt anyone to start the discussion—several faces showed readiness to share opinions. Brandi started, "My husband is clear out in the outer circle! I don't believe what he says. I can't trust him. And I can't tell him I made a mistake, because he'll use it against me. I regret telling him anything about my life before I married him, because he throws it in my face when we argue. That's pretty sad."

"Is there anyone in your inner circle, Brandi?"

She studied the paper before responding. "My sister, maybe. Not my mother. And certainly not my father. My children...but they're pretty little."

The pause left an opening for Ruth to step in. "I would put my husband in that inner circle. He's my best friend...and lover, but right now...my girls would be in the middle circle. I can't say much to them without it being misunderstood, and...they get defensive. I have one sister who is close to the inner circle. We don't get to talk uninterrupted very often, but when we do, we can say anything. We're close."

Sheryl's eyebrows furrowed as she spoke without looking up from the paper. "I have several friends I would put in the inner circle. Even though we seldom see each other, we went to school together; got married and had kids about the same time. And the curmudgeon..." She looked up at the group, pronouncing *curmudgeon* with some difficulty around her braces, "I'd put him smack dab in the inner circle. He knows all my warts and I know his. We put up with each other." Her wide eyes were rounded at she looked at Dana and chuckled with her closing remark. "I guess that's as intimate as I can get."

Dana raised her eyebrows in question at Susan. "My mom is in my inner circle. Everybody else is in the outer circle. This group might be in the middle circle. I trust the group for the reasons we're here."

"I like how you clarified the context with the group, Susan...we share a lot of personal information in this group—we go pretty deep, yet it's within a context, isn't it? We trust within the group, but outside of this forum, your relationships would be untried. You would need time and experience together to determine if there was a closer friendship."

Turning to Genie, Dana asked quietly, "Genie, what are your thoughts?"

The muscles around Genie's mouth tightened, her eyes furtive. She growled, "My mom is in the inner circle. Everybody else is off the chart. I don't let nobody get too close. I just like it that way."

"Genie, what about your sponsor? Or your boss? Is your trust level or interaction different from someone like…a regular customer or a new neighbor?"

Her hooded eyes searched for answers. "I tell my sponsor some stuff. I have to tell my boss some stuff, like where I live. He knows my mom lives in Utah. In case of emergency. I guess he'd be in that outer circle—we talk about sports. He shoots pool, too."

Dana acknowledged Genie's perspective and sat back in her chair. Signaling a shift in topic, she asked the group, "So, how does thinking about relationships in this way help, or cause problems for you?"

Brandi sighed heavily. "My husband should be in my intimate circle. I should be able to trust him with everything, but obviously, I can't even trust him to be faithful, or to be where he says he will be. I…I guess I've set the bar pretty low for a number of years."

"What if you raise the bar…expect more…might he rise to the occasion? I'm a big advocate of *tough love* and have seen some remarkable turnarounds in relationships when the issues are confronted head-on."

Seeing how Brandi's eyes moved as she sorted through her thoughts, Dana continued. "*Love Must Be Tough* by Dr. Dobson is a good reference. There are some others there on the bookshelf—you're welcome to borrow any of them. I could give you some names of counselors for him, or you both…to work through the issues if that's what you decide to do."

Brandi nodded without comment, the dimple above her brow showing her internal concentration.

Dana turned to the other women, "Other thoughts…how do the boundary circles help or cause problems in thinking about relationships?"

Ruth grimaced. "I'm sorry for what you're going through, Brandi. I wish I could help in some way.

"I guess…for me…the concept makes me appreciate my husband a little more. I take him for granted a lot. We've had our struggles over the years, but I know I can count on him. I get irritated at times, but…he's my best friend. I just hope someday my girls will be in that inner circle."

The group waited as Ruth sought words, her face showing conflicted emotions. When she finally spoke, her voice was soft. "I know I come across as judgmental at times, and that keeps me out of their inner circle. I…I want to change that."

"Good insight, Ruth… it's often hard to see it from the other person's perspective."

Dana's voice faltered as her words spoke so directly to the conflict with her father, but she pushed the thought to the back of her mind. Her eyes settled on Sheryl, inviting her to go next.

"The reciprocal quality of that inner circle reminds me that I get in one-way relationship sometimes. And that's usually when I get stressed out—it's not just the other teacher who expects rides all the time—it's my neighbors. Even my family. I get sucked into commitments that are too costly or time-consuming, and then I avoid the person because they expect too much. I'm good right now, but that's probably because I've been avoiding people."

When she didn't continue, Dana asked, "Is that problematic…avoiding connection?"

Sheryl squirmed a bit before responding. "Some. It gets sort of…lonely at times. But dull is better than hanging from the curtains!" Sheryl's humor generated chuckles among the other women. After it faded, she added, "Maybe there's a happy medium in there somewhere. I'll find it!"

When Dana's eyes rested on Genie, she scowled back. Her voice was haughty when she finally responded. "I don't do relationships—too much drama. I don't need anybody in my circles."

A debate launched in Dana's mind—*Is now the time to state the obvious? Is she too fragile to face the truth of her isolation? Can she handle deeper reflection within the group setting?*

Dana held Genie's stare, hoping her eyes showed the empathy she felt. "I understand, Genie. And sometimes that's what we have to do to feel safe—keep everybody out. But at some point, you may feel differently. Our protective walls keep the bad stuff out…but they also keep the good stuff out."

The conflict with Dan again threatened to chastise Dana, but she refused to entertain the thought right now. "I think of Rapunzel in this tall stone tower—she's safe from the wicked witch...but isolated from everyone else as well. It can be a very lonely place. We all need people, Genie...safe people...who we can lean on at times, and who can lean on us."

Genie's face revealed no expression, although Dana could see the slightest movement of her nostrils as she continued to stare. Finally, Genie broke the standoff with a flick of her chin and looked away, clearly expressing the end of her dialogue.

Dana let the silence hold for a moment before turning to Susan. "Okay. Susan, what are your thoughts about the boundary circles?"

Susan shrugged one shoulder before she spoke. "I'm a little like Genie. I don't like the drama, so it's easier to keep to myself. It works better for me that way."

Her confirmation of Genie's position was perplexing. Dana began to question her belief that human beings need intimacy. *Was Susan's dearth of relationships normal, yet Genie's not? But Genie's behavior was maladaptive, where Susan seemed comparably stable. Susan's need for isolation was likely related to brain functioning, whereas Genie was reacting to years of abuse and neglect. But that affects the brain too. Maybe I'm imposing my values onto them.*

She tried to conclude the session without impinging on anyone. "Understood. Relationships are complex—life is complex. And we each get to decide what works for us."

Chapter Twenty

"DAD'S GOING TO HAINES for Christmas."

Dana stared at Hub as if he had announced he would run for mayor. Her thoughts whirled as her astonishment intensified her rounded brown eyes. That would certainly solve her dilemma, but he never missed Christmas with them. *He's making a preemptive strike…running off to avoid any possible confrontation! Darn his hide!*

As much as she tried to be neutral about it, her voice was accusing. "He must have talked to you."

Hub took a deep breath, his eyes looking away from Dana momentarily. His condescending tone revealed his frustration. "Yes, Dana, we talk. You're the one that's riled. He and I don't have a problem, Dana. He's still dad to me. I just thought you'd want to know since you've been stewing about it."

She knew before she spoke that he was right, but the thought of them talking about her was infuriating. She imagined their smug jokes about how emotional women can get, especially the one in their lives. She shouted, "I'm not stewing about it! I just don't want to see him until he can…he can share some truth!"

Dana turned toward the window overlooking Lynn Canal, her arms crossed. She wanted Hub to comfort her, tell her it would all work out; that her dad loved her and would eventually get around to talking to her; that he missed her, but probably didn't know how to approach the situation. Instead, she heard Hub put on his coat and quietly shut the side door.

She stood clenching her teeth, not perceiving the northbound ferry inching behind Aaron Island. She knew it was unreasonable to expect Hub and her dad to be in discord just because she harbored this resentment.

Resentment! What the heck does this have to do with boundaries? The thought jerked Dana's swirling thoughts into focus. How many times had she told her clients that resentment is often an indicator of a problem with boundaries…saying *yes* when you wanted to say *no*, or vise versa. The emotion generally implied personal responsibility — not the other person's behavior.

I do resent him…but it's because he's clammed up — not me! As she traced the concepts of boundary-setting applied to the conflict with her father, Lionel rubbed against her leg. Automatically, she picked him up, but continued to focus internally about the interactions with her father.

I have a right to know what happened with my mother, whether it's hard for him or not. My rape and decision to adopt Rachel out wasn't any of his business! Tears escaped as Dana couldn't deny the truth that her decisions about Rachel did affect Dan, especially if there was any possibility she might enter their lives.

She slumped down on the couch, lifting her feet to rest on the coffee table, her foot pushing the book aside — *Perfect Daughters: Adult Daughters of Alcoholics.*

Damnit!

* * *

Rachel had asked if she could bring a friend for dinner. As Dana fussed over the table-settings before their arrival, she wondered if the friend was male or female. She was prepared this time to respond to questions about their relationship. She smiled at the memory of how she panicked when Rachel's last friend had asked if she and Hub had children.

In the last several weeks, Dana and Rachel had found a more comfortable level of polite interaction. It was progress, but Dana longed for the day she could put her arms around her daughter — to feel the closeness of her own flesh and blood. *Maybe today will provide an opening.*

Dana and Hub were still cool to each other, or rather, Dana was cool to Hub. She knew he was right, but she wasn't ready to *eat humble pie.* She needed more time to sort things out in her own mind.

Hub's aftershave announced his presence before she noticed he had joined her in the open kitchen. She glanced at him, immediately attracted to his rugged good looks. The dusty blue dress shirt that matched his eyes perfectly was tucked nicely into creased Wranglers. His strong forearms rippled as he rubbed his hands together, looking at her expectantly.

The temptation to meld into his arms was overwhelming — to be comforted by his strength and reassurance, but the internal conflict held her back. She asked tentatively, "Truce?"

He continued to hold her gaze with a penetrating look. Dana studied the vertical lines defining the muscles around his generous mouth that, at this moment, revealed nothing of his thinking or feelings. He didn't respond to her feeble attempt to establish warmth.

Dana dropped her head, unable to defy his noble character. Huffing, she grabbed the back of the chair. "I love you, Hub, and I'm sorry you're in the middle of this. I know you love my dad. Of course you see him and talk to him. I'm actually glad about that...it would be hard to not know how he's doing. But I've got to sort it all out. And I will. Can we be okay anyway? While I'm wrestling with it?"

The muscles around his mouth twitched slightly as he considered his response. "I understand it takes you time to sort things through, Dana, but I thought we had moved forward...being honest about what was going on with each other."

Dana gritted her teeth at the reference to the walls she had built around her heart the last several years that kept him at arm's length. Her tendency had been to grapple with emotional distress alone, letting him suffer with the uncertainty and distancing. She had resolved to overcome that habit, but knew she had slipped right back into it. "Hub, I'm sorry. Let's just...let's talk after Rachel and her friend leave."

It wasn't long before they heard the crunch of gravel, and the excited dogs pranced for release to greet company.

Rachel and a strikingly handsome young man came through the mudroom, stomping the snow off their boots before they stepped inside. Dana tried to calm the dogs as she welcomed them.

Rachel introduced Justin Williams simply as her friend, although Dana could see that her radiant smile suggested more. As they shed coats, scarves and boots, Dana accepted Justin's gift of an elegant box of chocolate covered strawberries. The small logo of the Princess Cruise line was in the lower corner of the box.

"Why thank you, Justin, what a lovely gift."

"It's a little something my company gives out to service providers. I hope you're okay with it being from Princess Cruises. I had some extras."

While Dana got wine for Justin and mulled cider for Rachel, Hub showed the young people around the house, naming the islands seen from their living room window, "Aaron, Bird, Gull, and then Shelter is the bigger island. That's the Chilkat Mountain Range in the distance."

Dana studied Justin and his interactions with Rachel as they and Hub conversed. He was certainly good looking – thick dark hair, athletic build, taller than Rachel by about six inches. He appeared very confident; socially graceful. He conversed with Hub as if they were old friends, yet he included Rachel in the conversation.

Her daughter was radiant. The sage green slacks and simple cream colored blouse accentuated her long neck and olive skin. Thick curly locks swept away from her face, then loosed down her back from an elegant gold clip. *She's beautiful – the best from Mario and me.*

The foursome visited comfortably throughout the afternoon, Rachel and Justin sharing tales of Juneau adventures. Justin lived in southern California, but traveled to Alaska frequently to attend to service contracts for the Princess Cruises. He was an avid outdoor sportsman and seemed to find plenty of time to ski, rock climb, and scuba dive in the many destinations his company sent him. Rachel spoke of her trips to scuba dive and ski with her father when she was still a teenager. Dana could see where their athleticism and adventurous spirits were a strong part of their attraction to each other.

Dana was content to coast, watching Hub direct the conversation to their guests' passions of travel and sports. She found herself again studying Rachel covertly, memorizing every expression, inflection and nuance about her. These precious moments with her daughter were plugging holes in her heart.

The affinity between Hub and Rachel was obvious. They interspersed stories about personalities and happenings at the coffee shop, revealing a shared experience with the Auke Bay coffee community. As their conspiratorial dialogue became more humorous, Justin quietly followed their volleys with a grin on his face. Like Dana, he seemed content to simply observe the rich connection between Rachel and Hub.

After a while, Rachel noticed that Justin had slipped out of the conversation, and she made an obvious attempt to broaden it. Leaning closer to him, she pointed out the window. "Once, I was fishing with Hub and G-Dan way out there...past the tip of Shelter Island, when we had engine trouble. Dana rescued us. She came out in her little boat, then joined us for awhile. G-Dan says she knows more about these waters and where to fish than any man he knows." Laughing, she turned to Hub, "except maybe him and Hub. And she's a psychotherapist, so you'd better be careful, Justin...she might read between your lines!"

Dana's face flushed at Rachel's attention, but was gratified that her recall of their initial meeting seemed positive. She remembered that first encounter as disastrous.

Rachel's eyes darted between Justin and Dana as she introduced more of Dana to him. "She grew up on the water around here." Turning to Dana, "G-Dan said you were home-schooled a lot of years while you lived on the boat, and you were way ahead of your grade. The way he tells it, you could have taught the teachers! You knew more about Alaska than the cheechakos."

Laughing, Rachel shrugged her shoulders. "He calls me his little cheechako."

Dana smiled at the obvious affection Rachel had for her grandfather. Jealously warred with gratefulness inside her. She was conflicted to hear that her father spoke about her with pride, considering he had avoided her since learning that Rachel was his granddaughter. It also sounds like he glamorized their life on the boat, especially the schooling part. It had been hard for Dana to adjust to public school once Dan moved them to land, and just now, Dana realized she resented him for that too.

"What is the biggest fish you ever caught, Dana?" Rachel's natural enthusiasm escaped from her earlier veneer of sophistication.

"Probably halibut ...I've caught a number of hundred-pounders over the years, so that would be the biggest. The biggest king salmon weighed in the fifty pound range...several of which were pretty memorable. They weren't record-breakers by any means, but exciting for me."

Rachel held Dana's gaze a moment before she spoke. "Maybe next summer we could...uh...maybe do some fishing."

"I would love that." Dana could see there was something more on Rachel's mind, but she had glanced away, leaving an awkward moment before Justin and Hub took up the conversation.

As the afternoon progressed and the meal enjoyed, Dana basked in the presence of her family. *Family. It feels...normal to have Rachel here, part of me, even tentatively.* The sense of normality had eluded Dana in her earlier years, always guessing at how *regular* families interacted — families with two parents and the security of a home place, but this felt like the beginning of wholeness.

Rachel was delighted with the socks Dana had knit for her, and Justin seemed pleased with the jar of blueberry jam proffered. Hub inquired about Rachel's pending trip to Minneapolis to visit her mother. She took a deep breath before diving in, her beautiful eyes and mouth bracing as if facing into a foray. "I leave Thursday for a whole week."

She glanced at Justin, then briefly at Dana to include them in the conversation. "This is a big deal. I am deliberately entering the lion's den." Chuckling, her expression turned to exaggerated resolve. "Not really. It's different now, and I hope we can keep it positive.

"My mom is a worrier. She frets about everything until she makes herself sick...and me crazy. But...she's different now. I hope. Before she left, we squared off, and apologized for the past. She's trying hard to not hover, but it doesn't come easy for her. We've managed okay by phone, but this will be the real test — a whole week in each others' presence. I might need to run the trails while I'm there — snow or no snow!"

In the lull that followed, Dana's mind quickly replayed her impressions of Rachel's adopted mother, Ellen. She had been her client the previous year, struggling with indecision and an obstinate daughter who, it turned out, was the daughter Dana had given up at birth. Ellen had found some resolve and moved to Minneapolis before their common tie to Rachel was revealed, so Ellen and Dana's alliance was yet tentative. Their professional relationship had ended, but their new relationship was yet to be established.

"Please give her our regards...from Hub and me. Could we take you to the airport?"

"Got it covered. Justin's going to drop me off, and G-Dan said he'd pick me up, but thanks anyway."

Reminded of her relative importance to Rachel, Dana pasted a smile on her face as gratitude was expressed for the afternoon and coats were donned. Hub and Justin locked in a brief conversation about how the Oregon Ducks might fare at the Rose Bowl, leaving an unguarded moment for Rachel and Dana.

Rachel's fingers interlocked her hands together, but her body language indicated she had more to say. "Uh...thank you again...for the socks—I love them. And having us over. It was nice. Maybe we could do coffee sometime."

Standing this close to any friend, Dana thought they typically would have embraced, but Rachel's demeanor neither invited nor disdained a hug. Dana refrained, hoping that one day her affection would be invited.

After the kids had gone, Hub stoked the fire while Dana cleaned up the kitchen. When Hub reached for his coat to take the dogs for a walk, he studied Dana as if testing the waters. "Do you want to go with us?"

"Do you want me to?"

Hub shrugged, "I asked, didn't I?"

It felt like a rejection to Dana. She turned back to the sink without answering. Hub left with the dogs.

By the time they returned, bringing the crisp outdoors with them, Dana had settled in front of the picture window with a cup of tea. She wanted to settle the *cold war*, but it was so hard to be humble and still maintain her ground.

Hub sat in the chair angled from the couch. "Okay, I'm ready."

This was not the opening she had hoped for. No sympathy for her feelings. No encouragement that, whatever the differences, they would work it out together. For a moment, she tamped her eyetooth over her lower lip while she searched for words that would gain his alliance.

"It should be the happiest time of my life with Rachel finally here and opening up to me just a bit, but I feel like I'm the *odd-man-out*. She's my daughter, yet you and Dad find intimate times with her. You, you...tease with her like you've had a lifetime of knowing each other. You refer to events...and, and joke about things I'm not privy to. I don't even get the chance to take her to the airport, or chop wood together because you've already got it taken care of. It makes me wonder what you and Dad say about me when I'm not around.

Hub released his breath in frustration. "We don't talk about you, Dana...not like you're insinuating. Yes, we see Rachel more often because we get coffee when she's on duty, or she stops by the shop. It's just...we work out here and come across her more often than you do in town."

Dana's voice was hoarse. "She stops by the shop? She just drops in to see you? You never mentioned that."

Hub's head bounced forward, his frustration undisguised. "Dana, yes, she and your dad stop by. I generally don't mention it because I never know how you're going to react. You're...you're obsessed with trying to make them fit into your timing. Can't you just let things be, Dana? Let things unfold as they will? Your dad knows you want to know more about your mom. Rachel knows you want to be in her life. Maybe they have to respond in their own way...when they're ready."

The volume in her voice increased. "You make it sound like I'm being unreasonable! That I shouldn't be so upset that Dad keeps secrets about my own mother! He can't even...it's been my whole life, Hub! He has lied to me about why she left and what he knew about her afterwards. And then he is outraged that I kept Rachel's existence from him. That's just not fair!"

As tears slipped down Dana's cheeks, Hub rubbed his hands together, looking for words. Opening his hands in resignation, he grimaced. "I don't mean to say you're unreasonable, Dana. It's just that...there are three people involved in this...this conflict: You, Dad, and Rachel. So it seems to me there are three very competent, determined skippers on the water, each with their own speed and vessel. Hopefully you're all three headed for the same destination, and I get to be part of it, but I'm back on shore for this deal."

The two studied each other, separated by the wave of Dana's stubbornness. Her chin trembled as she moved to her knees in front of Hub, wrapping her arms around him. "I'm sorry, Hub. It does affect you, as much as it does me. This is your family too. I don't mean to make it worse for you. I just don't know how to do it."

Hub kissed her temple, his strong arms pulling her onto his lap. They sat quietly entwined in each others' arms a moment before he whispered, "We've come a long way, Dana. A year ago you were just praying to know where she was — that she was okay somewhere in the world. And here she was in our home today. I don't think God's gonna leave us midstream."

It made so much sense, Dana wanted to believe it

Chapter Twenty One

THE CHRISTMAS BREAK OFFERED Dana two full weeks with very few commitments. Dan was in Haines. Rachel was en route to Minneapolis. Holiday preparations were as complete as they were going to get. She was good with Hub. Dana was jazzed.

Nikki and Mica pranced when Dana reached for their leashes. The morning was still cold, but the blue sky and full sun beckoned to Dana. "Come on girls…we need a run while we've got such a gorgeous day."

The fresh air was exhilarating, and Dana soon found herself shedding gloves and face mask to cool down as she jogged along Lena Loop Road. Few cars passed, and no people. Off leash, the dogs explored the ditch, but stayed close to their master.

As her steps and breathing became rhythmic, Dana began her dialogue with God, thanking Him for the blessings in her life—the afternoon spent with Rachel, the resolution with Hub; her trust they would construct some kind of a family connection. She thanked God for her clients, praying for each one as she considered their individual journeys. She was so grateful for the uncluttered days before her—a quiet time for just her and Hub.

And Lord, would you please have your way with my dad? Will you help him see my needs? I need to know about my mother. I know I didn't make the best decision regarding Rachel, but I thought I was protecting her and him. That was part of it, anyway. Would you make him see that?

Dana's long legs jarred to a fast walk. She took deep gulping breaths as her heart rate adjusted to the slower pace. Although she didn't hear God's words responding to her silent prayer, something was off kilter. She traced her thoughts back in her mind and was dismayed at what she was asking of God. "Oh…okay. I get it."

Her pace slowed as she focused inwardly. The dogs continued to sniff in circles, yet alert to cues from Dana.

She chuckled, silently communing with God that she got it. *Back to the control issue.* It was so clear to her when she counseled her clients, helping them to find peace with those people or events over which they had no control. This seemed different, yet it wasn't—it was just personal. And difficult. *Okay, God, I give up. I'll read the dang book!*

Later, with hot tea in hand and the dogs settled by the wood stove, Dana picked up the book her colleague had loaned her. *Perfect Daughters: Adult Daughters of Alcoholics.* Dana didn't consider herself in that category since her father had quit drinking when she was ten or so. Yet Dana knew that dysfunction in families was similar in many ways, whether it was an addiction that controlled the family system, a mental illness, anger, or chaos. *Or a father who is emotionally stifled.*

As she read the opening chapters, Dana had to continually remind herself to read it from the perspective of self-help rather than a therapist. The book reinforced much of what she already knew. It was a good reference, but seemed to have limited applicability to her.

- Feeling different from other girls. *Well, yes, but I felt privileged to grow up on the water, especially when Dad adored me.*
- A sense of unresolved issues or something is missing. *Not really. What's unresolved is Dad withholding important information from me. Of course, I missed my mom. But that is just a reality.*
- Competent in some areas of my life, yet vulnerable in others. *Yeah ...that's true to some extent.*
- Relationship issues; attracted to the wrong people. *No. Hub is a rock. Thank God! And my close friends are solid.*
- Secretly trys to hide low self-esteem. *Not too much.*

Dana refreshed her tea and walked around the living room, thinking about what she had read thus far. It seemed odd that Marla would recommend this particular book to her, but she was determined to finish reading it. It was a good resource — certainly she could glean something helpful for her clients.

Coming to the discussion on problems of intimacy gave Dana pause. She recognized her struggle in that aspect. *Okay, we're getting closer to home here.* Then a statement on the very next page made her heart pound, *...one of the most frequently mentioned problems of adult daughters relates to the concern about their ability to be healthy parents.*

"Oh-kay. I did not know that!" The dogs laid their heads back down when Dana said nothing further to them. Her attention returned to the book with new focus.

The author claimed that the most critical developmental task of children of alcoholics is to establish emotional intimacy. *The most critical! No wonder it's been so tough for me!*

A corner of Dana's heart tugged until tears began to slip down her cheeks. She remembered her angst of twenty-one years ago so clearly. She felt so inadequate at the prospect of being a parent—terrified that she might be responsible for ruining a precious child. She chastised herself for her inadequacy, certain that she was uniquely flawed to handle such a universal role as a parent. But, to think now that it is a common response to growing up in a dysfunctional family system, was simply overwhelming.

Dana set the book aside and stood up. She picked up a log to add to the fire, then closed the door realizing it was not needed. Dropping to the couch again, she reached for Lionel, who rejected her interest. Her mind jerked from one disjointed thought to another. It was exciting on one hand to think that her distorted thinking was...predictable—a common response for women who grew up in similar circumstances. *But does it really have application to me?* Dana had to think about the concepts with respect to her thought patterns and ways of coping. She needed time to think.

The following days turned into the most quiet, and yet most frenzied time Dana could recall since graduate school. Freed from her hectic schedule, she stepped back into the familiar role of a student, researching every resource she could find on the topic of adult children of alcoholics and family dynamics. It was an empowering quest—she was certain if she could understand it, she could conquer it.

* * *

Hub took Dana to a concert, then to dinner at the Hanger. They walked hand in hand along the indoors board walk, perusing the old pictures of Juneau's history. Subdued all evening, she enjoyed the quiet pace with her best friend and lover.

Without having to voice it, they signaled to each other their readiness to head home, and walked through the dark to Dana's SUV. While Hub drove, Dana sunk into the passenger's side, enjoying the comfort of his lead.

She looked over at him, studying his familiar profile. The glasses for night driving was a recent change, as well as the silver mixed in his sideburns.

He glanced at her. "What?"

Dana's languid response held the mood. "I'm just so blessed. I'm married to the sexiest man in all of Alaska, we live in the most incredible place in the world. I have a warm and comfortable home I wouldn't trade for a mansion. And we can count on three critters that will be excited to see us no matter our mood. I'd say that is just about as good as it gets."

Hub smiled and squeezed her hand as he attended to the road.

"Hub, we don't have intimacy problems now, do we? I mean…since I figured out how the blips in my childhood kept me from totally trusting myself with you, and we talked that through…we're tight, aren't we? I don't think I could feel any closer to you than I am now."

As was his character, Hub was thoughtful before he responded. "I'm not sure where you're going with this, Dana. We're married. We're lovers. Best friends. I don't see any problems."

It was another mile before Dana continued. "Well, I've been reading about daughters of alcoholics, and the typical dynamics of families — ways of interacting. It's not new material for me, but one of my colleagues, Marla, loaned me a book on the topic. It's making me look at things a little different. Maybe I'm not such an anomaly after all."

"You think your dad is an alcoholic?"

"Not really. He had some serious drinking years when I was little, but obviously, he got past that part. In some ways, though, he may as well have been an alcoholic — the way he behaves. We behave.

"I'm still sorting it out, but...some of the trouble I've had with trust...it goes way back. And even the fears I had about my ability to be a good mother. I felt so inadequate when I had Rachel, I was afraid I would ruin her. As it turns out, that's a common fear of women who come from alcoholic homes."

"But you said your dad isn't an alcoholic."

"Yeah, but...his years of drinking when I was little, plus the disappearance of my mom, set me on a path of trying to control my world. I loved him so fiercely, I think I had to ignore a lot to keep him on that pedestal. And now that I see his selfishness...the real Dan Jordon, it makes me question my whole history. My beliefs. Even the validity of my memories."

Hub looked at her sideways with a questioning brow, but said nothing.

Dana shook herself. "Anyway, I don't want it to spoil our evening. It's just...I wanted you to know that I'm trying to understand myself better, and Dad."

Hub shrugged. "Okay. I trust you'll figure it out. I appreciate that you're talking about it...not doing your isolation thing."

Dana noticed the heater wasn't keeping up with the cold, and pulled her coat tighter around her shoulders. She stared ahead as she questioned the advisability of talking about it before she had time to fully understand it. What if she couldn't mend the rift with her father? What would that do to Hub...and her budding relationship with Rachel?

Chapter Twenty Two

CITY WORKERS WERE TAKING down the last of the holiday decorations as Dana arrived at her office after the Christmas and New Year's break. It was still dark when she arrived early for her ten o'clock appointment. Her office felt cold, and she was anxious to create a welcoming ambiance, starting with the faux fire place and essential oils in the diffuser.

Determined to start the new year at a more measured pace, she promised herself she would not take on extra commitments. *I need to allow space to continue my personal growth.*

Journaling had become part of Dana's routine the last few weeks, revealing a deeper array of emotions than the anger and resentment she had been nurturing toward her father. She had to admit she missed him and their prior camaraderie. The chasm saddened her, and if she allowed herself to dwell on the loss, she could feel the edge of anxiety pressing against her heart.

The routine of opening her office made Dana think about how different she was from just two weeks before when she closed it down. *The routine is the same. My clients are mostly the same people, yet I feel like I'm different...less naïve maybe? Something.* She took a deep breath, and pushed it to the back of her mind so she could be present for her clients.

By five o'clock, her therapy group had arrived, each seated in their familiar place in the circle. Dana's enthusiasm at seeing them again was infectious.

Check-ins were newsy and cursory as each woman reported on her holiday and present status. Prompting deeper dialogue, Dana suggested they follow up on the boundaries topic and explore how to be assertive about them.

"You might think about some of the interactions you've had with important people in your lives over the last few weeks, and how you asserted yourself...or wished you had. How you represented your desires or preferences...or how you wished you would have."

The shift from a reunion atmosphere to therapeutic mode was discernible. Brandi let out a deep breath, her shoulders dropping measurably. "Well, like I said earlier, we had a pretty good Christmas. Goodell was on his best behavior for the most part. He wanted to stay over Christmas Eve...for the children, of course, but he...I let him in my bedroom. And we did have a good day as a family. He fixed breakfast, and played with the children a lot. But by the next day, you could tell he was getting edgy. I knew it was too good to be true, and sure enough, he said he was going after beer and snacks, and didn't come back that night. I'm so mad at myself for letting my guard down!"

Genie crossed her arms, leveling her gaze at Brandi. "Sounds like addiction to me, princess. Says he's gotta do something, but disappears. Been there done that."

Brandi made a tent with her hands, her steepled fingers rubbing her chin. "But he doesn't drink that much. He doesn't really get drunk, he just...has to leave. And I don't think he would take drugs—he's too vain about his body to pollute it."

Before responding, Genie glanced away. "There's lots of addictions. Drugs, sex. Porn. I'm just sayin'...it fits the behavior."

Brandi sat back in her chair, crestfallen. Nodding her head, she added, "He has done porn. That would make sense. He can't get on my laptop because I set up a pass code. It was part of the cheating the last time I left him. He swore he would never do that again because I hated it so."

"Sorry, princess. Could be wrong."

Dana interjected quietly. "If it is a porn addiction, Brandi, it can be every bit as controlling as street drugs. In fact, the same part of the brain is stimulated with pornography as it is with heroin. And with Internet availability, addiction to porn can be rapid and intense. It's very difficult to overcome.

After watching Brandi's head nod slowly, her mouth clenched, Dana continued. "You may want to check out *Every Man's Battle* by Stephen Arterburn, or *Battlefield of the Mind* by Joyce Meyer. They will give you insight about the addiction and some ideas on how to set boundaries, if that's what it is. It could be something else...but his inability to keep his word and need to disappear is suggestive of something, isn't it?"

Brandi's messy bun had come loose and one thick tendril hung at the side of her face, emphasizing her look of defeat. "I guess I didn't want to believe it, but you're right. That's a very strong possibility. Thank you for tapping on my thick skull—I needed that."

Ruth hesitated. "I'm sorry, Brandi. I hope it turns out to be something...manageable." Her eyes searched around to her left, her lips pursed in uncertainty. "Two of my daughters were with us for Christmas. I decided I would not say *anything* that could cause dissension—I just wanted to have a peaceful time with my girls. I put a smile on my face, but inside I was very sad. It felt so fake. It *was* fake."

Sighing heavily, she continued. "But it was peaceful. Truth be told, I think my girls preferred it that way, because they seemed content with that surface interaction. I wanted to say a lot of things, like how our being together meant so much, and how times like this knit families together, but I promised myself I would say nothing unless they instigated it. And they never did. It was so...flat. I don't know what I could have said that would have been welcomed by my girls."

Dana asked, "Did you and your husband discuss it, Ruth? Did he pick up on anything?"

Ruth scrunched her mouth. "He thought it was fine...that they enjoyed themselves and there wasn't a lot of tension."

"Are you able to tolerate *superficial* for awhile, Ruth? I would think, over time, your girls will tire of shallow interaction. Maybe when they see your restraint, they'll want to test the waters. Is the Boundaries book helpful?"

Her voice was despondent. "Yeah. I'm the poster child for a *Boundary Buster*. I can see clearly where my boundaries are, but it's harder to honor my children's edges. I guess I cast too big a circle and need to pull it in tighter."

Dana's gaze held Ruth's eye contact for a long pause. "You'll get there. Don't give up.

"Who would like to go next?"

Susan pushed her glasses up further on her nose. "I had a quiet break. No drama. It was nice." She shrugged her shoulders. "I didn't really need to assert myself."

"Okay. How about Sheryl or Genie?"

Sheryl's chuckle percolated. "You might have created a monster, Dana. We had dinner on the wharf Christmas Eve. I ordered a glass of sweet wine, but it was pretty sour to me. I actually sent it back, and another one as well before I got what was acceptable. I have never done that in my life! The curmudgeon was beside himself, wanting to apologize for my behavior, but I wouldn't let him.

"I can't say it felt good. I felt guilty, actually, but I kept telling myself it was okay to ask for what I really wanted." Her laughter spilled out before she concluded. "I'm either gonna play the connoisseur...or avoid going out in public."

"Good for you. The unfamiliar often feels wrong only because it's unfamiliar — not wrong.

"Genie, how about you — did you have some *aha* moments over the break?"

Her serious face swept around, stopping with her chin jutted out toward Dana. "Actually, I did." Genie let the clock tick a full ten beats before continuing. "You said way back when that I wasn't good at boundaries with myself. Well, I've done a lot of cogitatin' about that. And you might be right...a tiny bit. So. My sponsor invited me to Christmas dinner. Normally I would say *no* without a second thought. But Dana was in my head, and I decided *why not*? So, I said *no* to my *no*."

Dana blinked a few times, her mouth opened, then shook her head decisively. "I get it. You pushed out of your comfort zone. And how was it?"

"Not bad. They have a pool table and a kid who wants to go to the championships. He knows all about tournaments and who wins 'em. He was actually pretty good, but I taught him a few shots."

"All right. And how was it being outside of your comfort zone?"

Genie let out a deep breath before continuing. "Uncomfortable. But tolerable. They didn't have too many forks to choose from, so I didn't show my ignorance. They had some Champaign glasses, but it was only sparkly juice." Holding up an imaginary goblet, she added, "I even made a toast — to a nice family facing a new year full of good things."

Brandi bragged, "I'm proud of you, Genie. I never know what to do with formal settings either. And you're not ignorant!"

Dana added, "I'm proud of you too...all of you. You're all stretching in different ways.

"So, let's talk about asserting ourselves a bit more. That's how we represent ourselves, and set boundaries with others...with our words and body language. Think of a situation, or a person, where it's hard for you to set boundaries...someone in your personal life, a family member, a co-worker, someone in authority? Then look at the phrases on this handout I'm giving you, and see if any of them might work for you the next time you need to say set a limit."

It took a moment for each person to review the list of ten or so statements.

Genie harrumphed. "Yeah, right. *Thank-you-for-your-kindness-but-I-have-to-decline*? Who talks like that? Just say *no*!"

Dana couldn't help but chuckle at Genie's frankness. "That phrase might be a stretch even for me. But this isn't a script...they're only suggestions. Think in terms of what might work for you. Modify them, or identify your own. What you want to do is speak directly, clearly — assertively. You don't have to get mad or be aggressive. You don't need to explain yourself. Just let your *yes* be *yes*, your *no* be *no*."

Sheryl spoke out. "It's always hard for me to say *no* to my bosses unless I have a clear conflict — like I plan to be in the hospital that day with a concussion! Even then, the Girl Scouts can get to me for cookies."

As they all laughed, Brandi teased, "Oh, who could turn down a Girl Scout?"

Sheryl continued. "Okay, this one — *I'm sorry, it just won't work for me*. I think I could say that. Now, if I can bite my tongue and not follow up with a *be-cause* — that's what gets me into trouble."

Susan looked at the other women before claiming her turn. "*I'd prefer not to* is a phrase I could use when people at work ask me to join in various causes. I always feel uncomfortable with saying *no*, but it would be worse to get involved in something that is not my thing."

Brandi frowned, "You know...with my husband, I wish I could say, *I guess we see it differently,* and have him let go of it, because sometimes I do just see it differently. But he will not let it be. He badgers me until I give in just to keep the peace." She pursed her lips, scrunching her eyebrows before she continued. "However, I think it will be different in the future. He has lost all credibility with me."

Dana said, "Sometimes we have to sound like a broken record — if they don't accept what we're saying, we can simply repeat the same statement. Even a bully will get tired of hearing the same response.

"Ruth, do you see something here that will help you?"

"Yes. *This is hard for me to say.* I feel so defeated right now, it really is true — everything is hard for me to say with my daughters. It seems to soften what might follow, though...so my girls might not get so defensive."

"Good.

"Genie...can you think of something you want to add to your *definite no?*"

She jerked her head once, the set of her mouth clearly signaling her negative response.

Dana chuckled, "You're good at being definite, aren't you, Genie?"

Her raised eyebrows and smug look was her only response.

"So tell me, what *is* challenging for you, Genie? What would make your life better if you could just...?"

Genie stared at Dana for a moment before she growled, "A tighter plug. For the bottle." At Dana's questioning look, she added lyrically. "The magical bottle that holds the magical genie and all her secrets." She then shifted in her chair, her shoulder facing the group

Dana and Genie held eye contact as Dana's thoughts raced. She'd picked at the scab covering Genie's wounds, and the slightest hint of its enormity oozed out. Oh how she longed for Genie to find freedom from her past, but it would only happen if she confronted it. Dana questioned herself — *she's here because she was court-ordered; is she invested enough for her own healing? Should I push a bit harder?* The risks were high — Genie could throw up her walls, or disappear from group; perhaps relapse. *But she could have a break through too.*

Dana's voice was gentle as she probed. "Would you like to release just a little bit of the pressure from that bottle, Genie?"

Giving the briefest glance at Dana, she declared, "No!"

"Alright. Mm-kay." Dana paused, signaling a shift to a lower gear, starting with a deep breath. "Let's end tonight's session with a body-awareness exercise. A lot has surfaced this evening; we've touched on some painful spots. And you each have challenges before you this week. So I'd like you to sit back in your chairs, take some deep breaths, close your eyes if you'd like."

Dana's voice was soothing as she invited the women to notice how their bodies moved with each breath, repeatedly bringing their attention back to their breaths. After a few moments, she suggested they allow all their worries to be locked up for safe keeping while they released the tensions held in their bodies, remembering what it is like to return to *neutral*...a natural state of being — a natural level of stress hormone, blood pressure, and adrenaline. As they appeared more relaxed, she directed their awareness to their physical boundaries — where their bodies touched their chairs, and what they felt — hard or soft, warm or cool, smooth or textured.

As she continued to direct their attention and watch their reactions, she could see that Genie's shoulders dropped noticeably, although her lowered eyes were open. The change in Sheryl and Brandi was dramatic as they slumped in their chairs.

The session ended with a few acknowledgements of how relaxing the exercise was. Conversation was subdued as the five women left.

Dana locked the door and picked up the office, moving by rote, her mind reviewing the interactions of each woman. Brandi's life was likely to be rocky for awhile yet. *Lord, give her wisdom and discernment. Please be so present in her life that she can see you clearly. And Genie...Lord, hold that girl in the palm of your hand. She's so wounded.*

Chapter Twenty Three

DANA JUGGLED A BAKERY box and her tote as she pulled the heavy glass door open to Lisen's clinic. Friendly chatter could be heard coming from the inner office where her peers had gathered for their first meeting this year. She held up the box of assorted muffins as they turned to welcome her. "If you've not already broken every New Year's resolution, these might do the trick!"

The feel of reunion stepped up to a higher gear as these colleague-friends reconnected. Their meetings had been sparse throughout the Thanksgiving and Christmas holidays, so there was great anticipation at seeing each other again.

When they turned to the business of professional challenges, Marla shared her frustration about the number of relapses over the holidays. "I don't know why I let it surprise me every year—it always happens! Holidays are hard for addicts. The little guy I mentioned last time...Dyl? He did great through Christmas and New Years, then bolted the first day back at school. I don't know where that kid is. I'm hopin' he'll get picked up and have probationary supervision before he hurts himself. The dad is about to blow a gasket; mom's beside herself. Maybe they'll be amenable to counseling now. Phyllis, you'd be a good fit for them if you could take on a distraught mom and an overbearing dad."

Phyllis nodded. "Sure. Give them my number."

Marla quickly finished her turn, mentioning a Family Systems workshop she was trying to bring to Juneau.

Leaning toward Marla, Phyllis looked intently at her. "And how are you doing yourself, Marla. Yes, holidays are hard on people—including therapists. Are you taking care of your own needs?"

Marla sighed, momentarily showing exhaustion. "Yeah. Mmm, maybe not." Her eyes danced around as she searched for an answer. "I guess not really. It's been awhile since I've been to a meeting for me, and I'm waking up at nights—can't go back to sleep. I guess that's telling, isn't it? Okay…I will take some steps."

"Exactly what steps do you intend to take, and when, might I ask?"

The women chuckled at Phyllis' loving persistence about the self-care of each one of them. They knew she would not relent until she was satisfied that Marla had a specific plan to avoid burnout. "Okay…I will…schedule an extra few days off. Hop a ferry to Sitka to spend some time with my buddy there who makes me laugh. She's medicine for the soul."

Sitting back in her chair, Phyllis snickered, "Good. I'll expect to see pictures next time…or a note from your friend."

Ami, her short hair perfectly spiked, a silver ring piercing her left eyebrow, leaned in toward Marla. "My kids are reactive too—over-the-top drama. I got two late-night calls from girls whose boyfriends broke up by texting them, a frantic parent whose son ran off, and I don't know how many other minor emergencies. My number was supposed to be used for emergencies only, but I should have expected it—chaotic families have a different gage for crisis. And it's hard for teens to see that their drama might not be the end of the world. Yet that's what I worry about—sometimes they think suicide when it's just drama."

Looking around the circle when a pause invited, Dana asked, "Do any of you have a recommendation for a possible male porn addiction? One of my client's has a husband showing signs. I suspect she'll confront it soon, and I'd like to provide a referral if you know of someone who does sexual addictions." Seeing the head shakes around the group, she added, "What would you suggest? Has anyone had some training?"

Marla offered, "We do have a guy at the clinic who's had some training. He doesn't have a group, but I know he's got some porn addicts on his caseload. It's such a huge problem, but we've not responded well in the community yet. I'd give him Steven's name, though, 'cause he's developing some skills in that arena."

The women continued sharing minor aspects of their therapy practices, but no one had specific cases to process this day. Finally, Phyllis asked, "Dana, how's the journey with that new daughter? We're all anxious to hear how things are unfolding."

Dana beamed. "She is so beautiful...inside and out. I want to bore you with pictures like any new parent, but I will refrain. However...here is a shot I took when she and a friend came to a pre-Christmas dinner."

Passing her phone around the circle, Dana accepted accolades about what a beauty Rachel was and how she took after Dana, as well as questions about the cute guy she was with. After the comments died down, Dana continued, her eyes lingering on the picture of her daughter. "Thank you. She's still skittish, but we've had a couple very pleasant connections, and each time she seems warmer to me. I'm hopeful it'll all work out.

"I uh...I'm learning some things about me, though. Marla, thank you for lending me that book a few months ago. I finally cracked it open over the Christmas break, and it's created a lot of questions for me. More questions than answers, but I was surprised to learn that it's common for adult children...of alcoholics, or whatever...to be fearful of their own parenting abilities. I thought it was just me...back when I gave her up for adoption...because I didn't have a mom growing up. Apparently it's a common response when there's an *elephant in the room*."

She sighed deeply before continuing. "I thought I'd dealt with all this stuff years ago, but I'm seeing it differently now. The questions about my mom really nag me — why she left; what Dad knew beforehand, and after she disappeared. I always thought there was something fundamentally wrong with her because...the subject was so forbidden, but the more I think objectively about my dad, the more I wonder. He's ignoring me — punishing me for keeping the secret of Rachel from him. He refuses to talk it through." Dana studied her hands as she continued tentatively. "And if he treated my mom like that...maybe she couldn't handle it either.

"Of course…she left me too, so I don't know what that says about her. I might have to hire a private investigator to find the answers, because so far I've only found dead ends."

When the encouraging murmurs from her colleagues ebbed, Marla said, "Dana, I'm proud of you. You cracked open more than the book. It's not easy to examine the core of who we are as adults…and that's what you're doing. Good for you!"

"Thanks—I think. It is painful. But it's painful to *not* face it too. It's complicated. I don't want to lose what I had with my dad, but I'm not sure I can go back to ignoring the *elephant in the living room*. I can't lose Rachel because of my conflict with Dad, though—I'd live with a herd of elephants to protect our relationship. She is more than I ever dreamed she might be."

Chapter Twenty Four

STANDING AT THE WINDOW of her office, Dana frowned at the remaining ridges of dirty snow on the street. The wind whipped the insidious rain against the building, pushing the cold through her energy-efficient windows. Juneau definitely lost its allure as February marked the tail end of the dreary winter.

Two clients had cancelled their appointments for today, not surprising since people often hunkered down this time of year. Depression, addictions, relationship tensions ran high.

It was a bit of relief to have a lighter day, yet Dana couldn't shake the doldrums. *What is bugging me? Yes, it's gloomy February, but I know the brilliance of spring is around the corner. That's not it.*

She and her father were still estranged, but she had resolved to let that lie until she worked through the twelve-step concepts. It wasn't about Rachel — their phone calls were more frequent and friendly. In fact, they had made a luncheon date for the following Friday — just the two of them.

She and Hub were good.

Her fingers tapped the sofa table as she searched for the source of her agitation. *I'm ready for the group – they're all moving in the right direction.* Brandi found evidence that her husband is addicted to porn, and their finances were dire as a result, *but she's coping. Ruth is progressing, even though discouraged with the slow journey. Sheryl is fine – her humorous take on life will see her through the rough spots. Susan. Not tremendous growth, yet she seems satisfied to be where she is. Genie. Genie is like the little Dutch boy holding his finger in the dyke. There is a crack in the dam. I hope I can handle it wisely when her vulnerability breaks through.*

She turned from the window. *Why am I gritting my teeth?* Ticking through her mental list of self-care needs, nothing stood out. *Wait. Maybe it's the lack of* exercise. *Hub's been running the dogs with this weather, and I've been a slacker.* She again considered workouts at the gym, but the possibility of running into her father squelched that idea.

Her exasperation broke the silence, "Why am I letting him control my actions? Darn it." As soon as she asked herself the question, Dana was prompted to reconsider whose choice it was. *Of course, I'm doing it to myself…making a decision in anticipation of how I think he might react – just like I have done my whole life.*

Aware of this step forward in her self-discovery, Dana resolved to make a change.

By the time the group arrived, darkness had settled and the light rain seemed endless. The smell of wool emanated from the coat rack and the cold languished from the door being opened several times. Brandi rubbed her hands together, putting her warm palms on her cheeks. "I'll be so glad when spring gets here. I'm sick of the darkness!"

A comparison of winter woes followed for several minutes before the dialogue trickled to quiet, signaling a readiness to focus on their purpose. Dana began, "It is a tough time of year…a dreary stretch before spring. It's important to be aware of its effect on us.

"Let's do check-ins, then we'll get on topic. Who would like to start?"

Brandi's body language announced her readiness. Her head tilted and fists shook toward her tightened jaw. "I'm…so…angry. I think I'm madder at myself than Goodell because I ignored all the signs. I wanted my marriage to work so badly. I didn't want my children to have a broken home, and now we might not even have a home."

As her friends sighed, their bodies deflating at her latest news, Brandi continued in a quieter voice. "I found out he borrowed money from one of those title loan places, but he's only been paying interest, so now it's so high, he'll lose his car and still owe them money. His credit's shot…"

She faltered, her lower lip trembling before she went on. "I know he won't make the house payments, and I don't make enough money, so we'll have to sell."

"I should have paid closer attention – he always has to have the best. I knew he played poker, but he's also into on-line gambling. I didn't realize how much money an addict can spend...or how conniving he could be to hide things from me.

"I can't stand to even look at him. He took our children for a couple hours Saturday, and I had a friend come over so I wouldn't have to see him."

Dana prompted, "Do you have an attorney or financial advisor to help you through this?"

"Yes, I've got an attorney. I have to protect myself financially. Everything he does while we're married obligates me, so I could end up paying for his stupidity."

Genie's expression was smug as she looked out from hooded eyes. "The offer still stands, princess. You want him taken out?"

The four who had learned to appreciate Genie's humor chuckled before Brandi responded, "Thank you, Genie, but no...it's probably not a good idea to wipe out my children's father. But I admit...it is very tempting!"

Check-ins continued around the room without major developments. Attention returned to Dana in anticipation of the topic. "Okay, I'd like us to explore the concept of self-direction tonight. We've talked about boundaries and assertiveness... what shaped our sense of who we are. To build on that, I thought it would be good to consider what is the underlying motivation for you in making decisions? How often do you make choices based on your personal values, dreams, goals, preferences, energy, priorities...things important to you...rather than what others expect, demand, prefer...or how they might react?"

Brandi's pending divorce was an obvious start. "I would prefer to keep my family intact...to be able to trust my husband and create a future together. But I have to think of my children." Her voice faltered. "I need to divorce Goodell to survive and be able to provide for them. It doesn't matter what I prefer, or even my values. My morals are to honor my marriage vows, but I can't. I have to take these steps."

Dana's voice was compassionate. "Understood, Brandi. A very tough situation. You're doing what you have to do. I don't want to put you on the spot, but it might be helpful to think about *prior* choices since the present situation is so intense. You mentioned you were angry at yourself for ignoring the *red flags*.

Were you making choices then, do you think, based on other factors?"

She hesitated for a moment before deciding how to respond. "I don't like to admit that things aren't okay...so I covered for his self-centeredness. I knew he bought a lot of things—a whole workout center in the bonus room that doesn't even get used, but I didn't look at receipts! I accepted his bizarre excuses...and lies! Even with the children...I minimized his neglect of them...made excuses for his absence. And sexually..." Brandi closed her eyes, her emotions running high. "He was so...demanding." Her voice was but a whisper. "I ignored so much."

After collecting herself a moment, she continued. "I didn't want others to know we weren't all we appeared to be, you know? We had a good life in spite of friction—friends; family time; vacations. We had fun a lot of the time. My co-workers—they looked up to me in some ways. It's hard to admit it was all a *house of cards*."

"So it was easier to ignore the *red flags* than to confront the suspicions."

"That and to keep the peace! Every time I did try to get answers, Goodell would rant and rave around the house. It was miserable for us all." Brandi studied her fingernails a moment, then flicked her hand to signal she was through talking.

Dana's heart was so heavy for Brandi, it was hard to move on. "Thank you, Brandi. Ruth, you look like you're ready to go next."

Ruth scrunched her eyebrows like she was studying the answer. "I've always thought I was pretty clear about my purpose. I know what my God-given talents are, and how he wants me to use them. I'm alert for opportunities to use them to help people. But..." She squared her arms, clasping her elbows, before continuing. "That Boundaries book talks about motivation...doing the right thing for the right reason, and while I start out with the best of intentions, sometimes it's not appreciated, and then it bothers me. If I'm truly doing it for the Lord, then it shouldn't bother me if someone doesn't appreciate it. It feels like rejection—especially from my family. Then I get my feelings hurt and back away from them. So, it's a quandary between doing what I think is right, and how it is received."

There was a stretch of silence before Genie snickered, "If a person wants ice cream, your broccoli is no gift."

Ruth's head jerked as she looked directly at Genie. "What? What do you mean?"

The adrenaline dump in Dana's gut was instant, but she felt so weighed down by Brandi's pain, she couldn't intervene before Genie responded.

Genie shrugged and raised her eyebrows, "You talk about helping people, but maybe what you want to give is not what they want. Just sayin.'" She turned her head away from Ruth.

The group watched as Ruth collected herself, her face reflecting the roller coaster of potential responses. Finally, she took a deep breath and stumbled through a response. "I...want to think you're wrong...about that. But I will think about it...some more."

Dana's kind voice was soft. "You're a very caring person, Ruth, and this is hard. I applaud your openness to consider a different possibility."

At seeing Ruth's nod and meager smile, Dana turned to Sheryl. "How often do you make choices based on your values and personal goals versus others' opinions, Sheryl?"

Starting with a deep sigh, Sheryl plunged forward. "It's getting better. I don't know — after the wine incident, my husband's scared to take me out in public, so maybe it's not!" Her characteristic laugh was subdued.

"I think I'm more aware. I still choose, generally, to *go with the flow*, but I'm okay with that. I don't need to lead, unless it's in the classroom. But I'm more thoughtful about...about having permission to say *no* or set limits. I'm in a good spot."

With all eyes on her, Susan started to push her glasses up on her nose, then self-consciously touched the temple to adjust them instead. "Maybe my balance is different than others. Sometimes I think too much about what my preferences are rather than what other people think. I attend to my...anxiety first, most of the time. But if I do, then I can do more...think of others too. It works for me."

Nodding, Dana commented, "That's a good gage, I'd say...it works for you.

"Genie? What are your thoughts?"

Genie huffed in response. "I drive my own rig! I don't care what other people think...except my probation officer for two more years, and then I won't give a damn what she thinks." She turned in her chair, looking back at Dana over her shoulder.

Dana was thoughtful a moment, before lifting her chin. "Okay. Then what factors do you consider in making a decision...for example, when you encounter an injustice...say a vulnerable woman in an abusive relationship?"

Genie's face flushed immediately, her foot began to tap, pulsing her whole body. "I know what you're trying to do, Freud." She glared, her voice gaining volume as she continued. "I see things. I know things other people don't know. So that's what *fac-tors* into my decision-making. I wouldn't stand by and just let some jerk beat a woman!"

Dana's voice was soft as she stretched a cupped hand toward Genie. "I've touched on a raw nerve, Genie. Let us walk with you here...it's such a painful spot. Can you manage it? Take some deep breaths?"

Genie's glare never wavered, her body thrummed. Dana watched her take deeper breaths, her eyes following scenes known only to Genie. Dana nodded slowly, willing Genie to face her pain. "Those factors...sometimes they're internal. And they control our choices until we face them down." She took exaggerated deep breaths to prompt Genie to continue.

"It's unimaginable...some of the things you've lived through. You don't need to say what it is unless you want to, Genie...just be aware of what's happening at the thought of a woman being violated. Inside your body...where you feel the pain. Notice the images that go along with it. When you hold all that together...allow it to break through...what do you believe to be true about yourself?"

Genie's rounded eyes were riveted on Dana, her deep breaths intense, her face flushed. Her whole body shook as her words came out staccato, "I...can't...stop...him! No one can save me." Her breathing changed to deep gulping breaths, pushing her body with each one.

"We're here with you, Genie. You're safe now. Just notice how the images move...tap your feet back and forth with me. That's it. Let the images pass by."

Moments passed as Dana's breathing mirrored the intensity of Genie's energy and movements. Dana's soft reassurances interspersed, "You're safe now. It's over. They can't hurt you anymore. You're okay. You survived."

Genie's breathing finally slowed, her body convulsed a moment, then she slumped back in her chair, still holding eye contact with Dana. Her habitually furrowed brows softened.

Dana continued to tap her feet back and forth slowly, her breathing deep and slow. Genie followed suit, appearing more relaxed with each breath.

Her soft voice dominated the room. "That's good, Genie. Just continue to breathe...let all the tension drain out your toes as you relax even more. Take the things I'm going to say that work for you, and discard the rest.

"Genie, you survived some terrible things. You didn't choose them. You needed help ...you didn't have the protection you deserved as a little girl, but you survived. You are safe now. You've learned how to protect yourself. You're powerful. And you're learning more and more how to cope in positive ways. You are amazing."

Genie's breathing became deeper and slower. She finally broke eye contact and sighed.

"You are so precious—uniquely you. You're important and capable, and you have great purpose in this world. The ugliness of the past doesn't define who you are. You're steady and responsible. You have good work and people who care about you. You're bright and talented. You're important."

Dana's breathing continued to mirror Genie's.

After a stretch of silence, Dana said, "When you're ready, Genie, you might want to move your feet. Feel how you're grounded. Solid." She watched as Genie responded, her body seeming to come awake. "And when you're ready, you can look around. We care about you and we applaud your courage. You don't have to say anything if you don't want to, just know we are here for you. We're honored to have walked alongside you for these moments."

Genie blinked, her eyes focusing on her immediate surroundings. She glanced around the circle without looking at faces, then held eye contact with Dana again. Quietly, Dana asked, "What are you feeling right now, Genie? Notice your body and what you feel in your body. Share with us if you'd like to."

Her feet shuffled. She looked away and sighed again.

Dana waited out the silence, wanting to give Genie the opportunity to process if she would, yet not compel her. Finally, Genie spoke, her words coming from a dusty voice. "Well, that was a ride."

She studied Dana a moment, her face unreadable. Sighing, she continued, "I guess that's what you call a break through, huh Freud? Can't say it was fun."

No one moved as they all watched Genie's eyes follow her internal journey. Then she focused back on the group and the present, her body settling like a seagull coming to rest on the water. "I'm okay."

Brandi was the first to break the silence. "I am so proud of you, Genie. And honored to be here with you. You're very brave. I knew I would learn a lot from you."

Genie managed a half smirk and self-conscious glance at Brandi in response.

Dana sensed Genie had reached her capacity to handle *center stage*, so she led the group in a relaxation exercise. Her emphasis was on awareness of immediate physical boundaries — where their bodies connected with their chairs and the floor, the inside of their socks. As she spoke, she gently reminded the women of their strength, beauty, and courage; of their journey of self-discovery and goals of living self-directed lives.

As the subdued women were departing, Dana queried Genie's state of mind and if she might be able to come in for an individual session. Genie's brows returned to the familiar half-scowl. Her abrupt response was, "I'm good. See you next week."

Chapter Twenty Five

FRIDAY COULDN'T COME SOON enough. Dana's excitement was palpable as she drove toward Mi Casa's where she and Rachel had agreed to meet for lunch. Nine months. Dana laughed out loud at the irony. It had been nine months since she knew for sure that Rachel was her daughter. *How symbolic...birthing a new relationship.*

Dana had envisioned a dozen possible outcomes for this first private outing with her daughter—what similar interests they might find, physical similarities, shared aversions, disclosure of personal histories. She realized she needed to calm down, so she checked her driving speed and began to breathe deeply. Before she could reach a count of ten, though, her mind was swirling again. *Oh, dear Lord, please calm me down. And have your way these next few hours. You know the desires of my heart.*

Arriving early, she waited in her vehicle until she saw Rachel's Jeep turn in to the parking lot. The two women greeted each other, then walked toward the entrance of the restaurant together. Their strides matched, as well as so much else. Without a close look at the fine wrinkles beginning to show at the corners of Dana's eyes and mouth, anyone would guess they were sisters. Both wore straight leg blue jeans that stretched neatly to their hiking shoes. Both carried themselves with purpose and confidence, oblivious to any eyes that might follow their movements.

Settling into a booth, Rachel removed her cap to allow her thick chestnut hair to fall loose over her shoulders.

"You've changed your hair. I like it."

Rachel laughed, scrunching the mass that had been packed under her cap. "Yeah, I decided it's too much trouble to keep up, so I'm letting it go back to natural. This is pretty close to my natural color. And Justin likes it down, so I'm trying out...*girlish*, I guess."

"Well, it's lovely. Are you and Justin getting to be more of an item?"

Rachel shrugged, but color tinted her cheeks. "Somewhat. He travels so much, it forces us to go slow, and I like that. We have a lot of fun when we're together—he likes adventure. Doesn't take life too seriously, and I'm into that. But I've got a lot on my plate, so a relationship is not my priority right now."

Interrupted by the server, the two women returned to their conversation. Rachel started, "Your hair...I like your hair, Dana. Do you have to straighten it?"

"Not really. It's has very little curl in it. You got your hair... Uh, I don't think you got your hair from me."

When Rachel looked away, Dana felt chastised for venturing too close to dangerous waters. "Well, how's school? You're well into the new semester, I take it."

The neutral topic sparked a new direction and the two women launched into light conversation. Throughout lunch, Dana and Rachel found humor and common ground regarding classes, skiing, hiking trails, winter doldrums, and updates on Rachel's adoptive mom, as well as Hub's loveable personality. Their banter and enthusiasm created a comfortable rhythm between them, the unapproachable topics easily left aside.

With lunch finished and thirst satiated, their dialogue wound down, but neither seemed in a hurry to part. After a comfortable silence, Rachel started tentatively, "I've really enjoyed this afternoon, Dana. Thank you for lunch. I'm...sorry I've been so...resistant—you're a good person. I...I like you." Shaking her head, she added, "Maybe someday I'll be able to sort out why it's so hard for me to...accept that you gave me away. I guess I should thank you for not aborting me."

She let out a deep breath. "I'm not angry anymore. It's like...I don't know what to do with it. I have a mom—and she's more than I can handle!

"Just kidding. You're so much younger than she is...you could have been a sister to me really. I...always wanted a sister or brother...maybe that's where we'll land." She looked out the window, appearing uncomfortable with what she had disclosed.

Dana tried to keep the emotion from her voice, knowing this was a big concession for Rachel. "I'll be very honored, Rachel, to be in your life in any way that works for you. I've always wanted a sister too. So...maybe that's a good place to start."

Rachel turned swiftly back to Dana, spunk returned to her demeanor. "G-Dan just doesn't have the goods—I keep asking him questions he can't answer! I notice we wear the same kind of shoes...even the same size—nine? I can't wear a lot of shoes because of my stupid bunion."

"I have one too...right foot?" With Rachel's nod, and a quick glance around the restaurant to see who might be watching, Dana reached to untie her right shoe. Rachel followed suit. The two women laughed as they held their feet next to each other, then both removed their socks to marvel at the likeness of their feet. Not only were their feet and ankles shaped the same, they both wore emerald nail polish. Rachel slipped Dana's shoe on, and stared in amazement. "We're exactly the same...it feels like my own shoe."

Neither woman spoke as they considered the significance of the similarities and put their shoes and socks back on. Sitting back up across from each other, Rachel was the first to speak. "Wow. That blows my mind. I've never...I mean, I see we're built a like, but..." She blew out her breath. "This is a lot to take in. Dana, do you hate asparagus?"

They both laughed as they launched a new direction in their discovery of similar likes and dislikes, ranging from food to brands of makeup to sleeping idiosyncrasies. They laughed at their mutual challenge to find dress slacks long enough for their legs and generous enough for their curves. By the time they walked to their vehicles, the afternoon sun was going down. They made promises to repeat the afternoon soon.

Dana was so full of gratitude, she didn't think she could fit anymore joy into her heart. Then Rachel reached out to her tentatively, embracing her in a hug. She whispered, "Thank you again, Dana. This has been sweet."

Forcing herself to move, Dana folded her body into her Subaru, still watching Rachel as she jogged to her Jeep. They waved goodbye once more before Rachel pulled out of the parking lot. Dana sat there, unable to contain the joy. The afternoon was more than she could have dreamed...the connection with her daughter more than she could have hoped for. Her tears overflowed, her heart repeating, *Thank you, Lord, thank you. Thank you, Lord, thank you.*

Chapter Twenty Six

IN SPITE OF THE *mountain top experience* that lingered after meeting with Rachel, Dana couldn't shake her worries about Genie. A break through like Genie had the last session could be the beginning of deep healing, or it could trigger overwhelming memories — memories that could drive her to old ways of coping. Returning to drugs. Sexual exploits. Who knows the possibilities?

Dana had called Marla, Genie's addictions therapist, who was in a better position to intervene, but she had learned nothing more. As the time drew near for group to begin, Dana prayed more earnestly for wisdom to handle whatever comes next and grace to cover her mistakes. *Darn, I hope I didn't push her too fast.*

Genie was the first to arrive, with Susan and Brandi immediately behind, which precluded individual interaction. Dana could see by her furrowed brow and posture that Genie was in a foul mood.

As the group settled in their respective chairs, conversation was stilted. Genie was the *elephant in the living room* — everyone was concerned about her, aware that something was going on, yet the message her body signaled was crystal clear: *Don't mess with me!* The heavy makeup did not completely cover the bruising on the side of her right brow, or distract from the broken blood vessel in her eye.

Dana's voice was tentative. "I'm glad you're all here."

Genie refused to look at anyone.

After a moment's hesitation, Dana continued. "Genie, it was a..."

Genie immediately interrupted Dana, gesturing with her hand to stop. Pointedly, she never looked at Dana, but the set of her lower jaw made it clear that she did not want Dana's attention.

Dana sat back in her chair, contemplating how to handle the situation. "Okay. We'll...start elsewhere. And hopefully we can come back to you, Genie. We want to know how you're doing. That's important to us...because we care about you.

"Alright...who would like to start check-ins?" She surveyed the other four women. Brandi was somber, but gave no indication she wanted to start.

Ruth lifted her hands, then let them drop in her lap. "I'll go.

"I don't even know where to start. I'm worried about you, Genie, but I respect your choice to not say anything. I...I hope you'll change your mind.

"I finished the boundaries book — twice. I bought three more copies, one for each of my girls, and then realized that was exactly the problem — I want it to help them like it helped me, but right now they would see that as pushy."

She smirked at Genie before continuing, "They want ice cream and I want to give them broccoli. So they're sitting on the book case...the books...in case my daughters ever happen to ask me for a book on healthy boundaries! Or broccoli." Ruth's playful observation of herself elicited chuckles around the room.

"It...it is changing me. And it's making a difference in my family. It's embarrassing to admit this, but I think my husband and daughters are more relaxed around me. I hate to think that my love...my caring...makes it harder for the people I love the most, but that really is the truth. My...self-centered perspective has kept me from clearly seeing their hearts."

Her lips fluttered with an exhale before she continued. "So...I'm on a quest. To know their hearts. To learn their perspectives — without judgment." She reached into a tote bag next to her chair, bringing out a leather binder, and fanned the pages displaying a variety of photographs and messages. "This is the first one — I'm doing a *baby-book-scrapbook-journal* sort of thing, gathering pictures and stories, and *interviewing* my girls about their memories and dreams — that sort of thing, and putting it all together. Then I plan to write letters and intersperse my thoughts, and...apologies. It's a way of honoring them, and hopefully a way of saying how proud I am of who they are, even when their choices are different from mine."

Ruth shrugged her shoulders, signaling she was finished.

"Wow. What a creative way of pulling it all together, Ruth. And it is changing you, isn't it? You look more..." Dana's eyebrows furrowed, searching for the right word, "*settled*."

"I am. That's a good description. Settled."

Sheryl asked, "When you say you're interviewing your family, have you begun that process? I guess I'm wondering about your oldest daughter especially, the one who has been estranged."

"I'm leaving her 'til last. She'll be the hardest because of distance and...the history. But since Christmas we have been building some bridges. Bridges of straw, mind you, but we're talking—superficially, but it's a start."

"Good good. Thank you, Ruth. I admire your humbleness. It's very hard, for me anyway, to ask for forgiveness." Dana looked around at the others. Genie was still folded away from the circle. Brandi's sadness was unmistakable. Dana raised her eyebrows, inquiring if she was ready to go next.

Brandi nodded, but hesitated before starting, her voice monotone. "Well, it looks like I'm going to have to move. So now I have to decide...do I simply get an apartment, or do I move south. Back home. And Goodell will fight me on that. He said he wants the children half-time—joint custody, but that's not going to happen. My attorney said she will fight dirty if it comes to that—using his addictions against him. He would be mortified for people to know, so I think he'll acquiesce.

"Anyway, it's a mess. I finally told my parents, and my mother is coming up in a few weeks. They were better about it than I expected. She'll help get the house ready for sale."

Ruth and Sheryl offered sympathy. Dana asked, "How are your children doing?"

"Pretty good. They miss their father in the mornings mainly, since that's when he interacted with them most, but I'm home in the mornings now, so it isn't too bad. And he gets them Saturday."

"How are you holding up?"

"I'm...tired. Lonely. A lot of *our* friends were from *his* circle of friends, so I'm left out. And I miss him...the good times, anyway. It's hard to have no one."

"Is there any chance of reconciliation? Is he open to rehab?"

"I don't think so. He makes promises, but I don't' see any real change in his behavior. No therapy, no financial accountability. He's not taking care of the house maintenance, or really looking after our needs. It's all talk."

Ruth interjected, "I'm so sorry Brandi. I don't want to be pushy—please tell me if I am, but I would love to fix you a dinner and bring it over so you don't have to cook one night after work."

"That would be sweet, Ruth. I would truly appreciate that. How about Thursday night?"

"That would work just fine. I'll get your address after group."

Dana asked, "Is there something you can do just for you, Brandi? I know it's difficult for a solo working mom to find time, but if we don't recharge, our batteries go dead. A bubble bath? Workout? Girl time?"

Brandi chuckled at the analogy of the cell phone. "Maybe. I am hiking with a friend Saturday if this blasted rain lets up. It's supposed to be nice for the weekend."

"Good. We'll keep hoping for the best even if you don't know what that looks like right now.

"Susan, how are you?"

"Not real well. I got accepted for the summer semester at Stanford, so the worrier voice in my head went into overtime about things that could go wrong—the plane might go down, or I might get on the wrong shuttle, or have a roommate who's a serial killer."

She tapped her head. "I know it's unlikely, but *The Worrier* is not convinced. I'm not sleeping well, so it's hard to get going in the mornings. I'm afraid the next four months will be...difficult."

Dana studied Susan a moment before she spoke. "No...no, that would be awful—four months of worry. Let's do what we can to manage that.

"Susan, it seems to me that you've made a shift regarding your OCD—you called it *The Worrier*. You have separated *it* from *you* in your mind—it's something you have, not who you are. Am I reading it right?"

Susan nodded, but made no comment.

"Does that seem significant to you?"

Before responding, Susan dipped her head, pushing her glasses up tighter against her face. "Yes. It feels different. I don't feel as embarrassed about it. It's more annoying, than embarrassing. And I just hope I can...manage it."

"Good. Good. And do you have an idea of what you need to do to manage it better?"

Her head dipped again. "I know I should walk, but it's still dark when I get home from school, and the weather is so bitter. I guess I could walk in the halls before I leave the school. Some of the other teachers do. I would like to come in for some extra sessions with you, if you could see me after school."

"That will work. Let's get you on my schedule before you leave this evening. Thank you, Susan.

"Sheryl, are you ready to check-in?"

"Sure. Although I don't have a lot to say. The changes are subtle, but I'm not as stressed as I was this time last year. We just ended another quarter, grading and all that stuff. Typically, I'd be flappin' my wings and screeching like a banty rooster, but this time I'm just nesting." Her laughter exploded and took a minute to settle. "I guess roosters don't nest, but...that would be like me to get my metaphors mixed up!"

As Sheryl's humor was spent, the distractions also dissipated, leaving the heavy question of how Genie would participate. Her posture had remained stiff, poised away from the circle of women. She had refrained from showing any emotional connection as the other women spoke. Dana's gut clenched. *Lord, how do I break through to her? Please guide me.*

Finally, she began tentatively. "Genie, my heart is hurting for you. I'm not sure where you're at right now, but I'm hoping you will let us walk this path with you."

There was no discernible change in Genie, but Dana waited. The pendulum of the old Regulator clock on the wall sounded like a time bomb ticking away. The group continued to wait.

Without changing her posture, Genie's hoarse voice began quietly, "I blamed you for what happened this week. I told my PO I couldn't come back here."

She turned her face abruptly, glaring at Dana. "But she wouldn't cut me any slack. So I'm here." Her right foot began to bounce rhythmically.

Dana's heart clenched as she read the sorrow in Genie's face and knew that she must have caused that anguish. She remembered the last session and how she had pushed Genie to crack open the barriers that protected her heart from pain. And after Genie allowed herself to be vulnerable, sharing some of her pain with the group, Dana hadn't done a good enough job of helping her close the barrier back up—preparing her for what might happen in the days following.

She felt the stirring of panic and nausea as she realized she had failed Genie. Perhaps harmed her. The internal accusations of incompetence threatened to overwhelm Dana. Perhaps she had failed the whole group. Why didn't she realize she might be putting Genie at risk—driving her away from healing? She should have consulted with her peers before prodding deeper…waited until she was further along in recovery.

The two women stared at each other, neither revealing their internal dialogue. Finally, Dana broke the deadlock. "I'm sorry, Genie, if I…put you on the spot. If last week was too much. We can move on to topic. I…"

"It wasn't too much." Genie's harsh voice was accusatory.

Dana realized her choice of words might have offended Genie's sense of control. She shifted in her chair, nodding once to acquiesce the point.

Finally, Genie exhaled and looked down. "You didn't push too hard. It's what I'm here for, right?" She appeared to fold within herself, excluding the others as she began her monotone narration. "I remember more. A lot more." She snarled, "I was just a little kid—like those kids across the street from me. Playin.' 'Cept I had to protect my mom."

She gasped involuntarily, yet did not look up as she continued with a trembling jaw. "He would stop beating her if…I…got his attention. He would be sorry…say that he was mad—crazy…that I could…soothe him. That I was magical and could make him sane."

Genie looked up at Dana, her face deadpan. "I didn't sleep. The nightmares…the memories. I needed a hit. Just one…to keep my sanity. I found my supplier."

Her lovely hands shook as she covered the tattoos on her left hand. Her eyes seemed to look through Dana as she struggled to go on. "He...he... His smug face when he took my money...he was like him. My father."

The glower to her eyebrows returned along with the snarl. "I wasn't going to let him get away with it this time. I...attacked him."

For a moment, Genie sat there, the muscles in her jaws working. Finally, she said quietly, "I could have killed him—he isn't that big. I could have gone to prison, and he wasn't the one that deserved it. He's just a dealer."

Finally, she lifted her chin and sighed, her face void of all emotion. "But, I didn't relapse. I didn't kill the guy. Now I'm trying to do the next best thing, as we say in NA."

"Genie, I am so sorry. I should have prepared you better for the possibility of more memories...the vulnerability you might experience after opening that door."

Dana's apology hung in midair while Genie shook her head. "It wasn't you that made the choice. And the guy will live—he's no worse for the wear. And I'm...I'm gonna be okay. I didn't relapse. Or kill anyone. I know it'll get better one day at a time...if I keep on keeping on."

Dana sensed Genie was spent. Her own emotion kept her from speaking above a whisper, "How can we help you, Genie? How can I...what would be helpful?"

Genie's voice was strong again, "Don't do your voodoo on me, Freud. Just keep your probe out'a my mind. Here, anyway." She shifted in her chair, but did not appear to have finished. "Maybe I'll come in sometime for a *lobotomy*." Her smirk signaled to the group that their friend was back. The change in mood was palpable.

While the women affirmed Genie's courage, Dana privately collected herself, so thankful that Genie had worked through it with limited harm. She made a mental note to process it later with a peer and figure out how to avoid repeating the same mistake in the future.

The session time was nearly spent. "I think instead of beginning a new topic, I'd like to close out tonight with a visualization exercise, and I want to read you a poem by Portia Nelson, from her book, *There's a Hole in my Sidewalk: The Romance of Self-Discovery*. It speaks to me, and I hope it will to you too.

"She calls it an autobiography in five short chapters."

Chapter One
I walk down the street.
There is a deep hole in the sidewalk
I fall in.
I am lost.
I am hopeless.
It isn't my fault.
It takes forever to find a way out.

Chapter Two
I walk down the same street.
There is a deep hole in the sidewalk.
I pretend I don't see it.
I fall in again.
I can't believe I'm in the same place.
But it isn't my fault.
It still takes a long time to get out.

Chapter Three
I walk down the same street.
There is a deep hole in the sidewalk.
I see it is there.
I still fall in...it's a habit
My eyes are open; I know where I am;
It is my fault.
I get out immediately.

Chapter Four
I walk down the same street.
There is a deep hole in the sidewalk.
I walk around it.

Chapter Five
I walk down another street.

Group ended quietly after the visualization. Dana was emotionally drained, and physically exhausted. She sat in the dark long after the group left, mentally reviewing the interactions and progress of each person over the last seven months.   *Thank you, Lord, for your grace, cuz sometimes I sure get it wrong!*

Chapter Twenty Seven

DANA HAD BEEN SURPRISED to hear from Genie the day following group saying she was ready for that *lobotomy*. Even though her schedule was tight, Dana managed to shift some appointments to see Genie in the evening.

Sitting before her now, Dana was elated. This remarkable, complicated woman had endured unimaginable horrors, yet she was confronting her past like a bulldog.

"You know I must trust you a lot, Freud. There are no witnesses here." Genie's smirk said so much—*I am opening myself to you, but don't make a wrong move. I'm tough, but this is scary. Don't forget I'm in control here, but don't hurt me.*

Sitting with her arms crossed and a smirk on her face, Dana reflected on Genie's unspoken message. "You are an amazing person, Genie. Very brave. And I'm honored that you are letting me walk along side you as *you* discover answers for yourself. Did you get a chance to read the brochure on EMDR therapy…Eye Movement Desensitization and Reprocessing?"

At Genie's nod, Dana continued. "Truly, you are in control. EMDR is like having one foot in the present and one foot in the past as you allow your brain to reprocess traumatic memories or events that interfere with your life. You're always aware; always in control. My job is to help you process memories in a way that allows you to experience, or become conscious of how those memories are affecting you in the present—physically, emotionally, mentally. And I'll monitor the intensity of your reactions as you process the memories so that it's neither overwhelming nor ineffective."

Genie's head nodded perceptibly, her lower lip moving nervously.

Dana explained how each person processes memories uniquely—there's no right or wrong way to do it. She suggested

Genie trust her wonderful mind to remember what is important, and she should simply notice what images or memories surface. "Don't try to hold on to the images—just let them *go by* like you're on a fast moving train. Your brain will make sense of it all in a more adaptive way—connecting the problem-solving part of your brain and your wisdom of today to resolve the past."

After more discussion to prepare Genie for the process, Dana led her in a visualization exercise to start from a relaxed state of being, and had her experience shifting back and forth from a relaxed state to an agitated state. Genie's shoulders had dropped perceptibly, the muscles in her face softened, her brows were more relaxed. Dana noticed how young and vulnerable she appeared in contrast to her typically hyper-vigilant state. Dana alternately tapped the back of her hands as Genie looked down, a part of the EMDR process that serves to stimulate both hemispheres of the brain.

"Okay, Genie, I want you to bring to mind the worst of the nightmares you've been having, and nod when you have that in mind. You can share as little or as much with me as you want."

Seeing her choose to just nod, Dana continued. "Okay, now focus on the worst part of that image, and tell me what you believe to be true about yourself. I'm...what?"

Genie's jaw movements indicated the increase in her agitation. "I'm bad."

Dana had automatically shifted into her therapeutic voice, intended to reassure and comfort. "And what is the emotion that goes with *I'm bad*?"

"Anger."

"Is there an emotion beneath the anger...like fear, shame...?"

Genie's eyebrows danced as she looked at possibilities. "Shame."

"And where is that shame in your body?"

"Right here." Genie motioned to her center.

"And, Genie, what is the intensity of that emotion on a scale of one to ten?"

"Eight."

"Okay. I want you to take some deep breaths...belly breathe. That's right. Let the tension release with the out-breath. Good." Dana watched as Genie's body relaxed. She again approached the troublesome image with Genie, but the tension in her body immediately increased to a level that was too high to continue.

Helping Genie return to a relaxed state, Dana suggested she take someone with her in her mind...someone like her adult self, a trusted person, an angel, or anything would make it safer for her. "Let me know when you have that in mind."

Genie gave a firm nod. "Got it. Me in my leathers."

This time, Genie was able to bring the image to her mind while Dana tapped the backs of her hands. She told Dana it was intense, but not too much to handle. Dana watched Genie intently, and frequently stopped to check her level of distress and desire to share what was happening. Genie said little, but wanted to continue with the process.

Over the next thirty minutes, Dana watched as Genie courageously faced the horrors of her past. Her deep sighs, followed by the subtle movements of her body, told of the internal battle being won. As the minutes flew by, Dana could see that Genie's distress was diminished.

Finally, Genie took a deep breath and slowly exhaled, slumping into her chair. Her eyes were directed toward Dana, but she appeared to still be focused on an internal scene for a moment.

Dana simply breathed slowly to signal calm, matching Genie's breaths.

Genie's brows remained soft, making her eyebrow ring look heavy and severe. Her voice was soft. "I'm tired. But...lighter. I feel like I just dumped a whole boatload of garbage.

"That voodoo is really something, Freud."

"You did some hard work, Genie—of course you're tired. What's your distress level?" Genie simply shook her head and turned her mouth down to indicate that it was nothing.

"Okay, this is a good place to stop if you'll come back again to finish the process—to see what else comes up and to *install* the positive cognition about this memory—that's the process of connecting the images to an adaptive belief about yourself. And to check for physical reactions." Genie nodded.

"Let's talk about what's happened here, and what might come up for you this week because you did open some of those closets." Dana waited for Genie's lead for the next step.

"I want to talk about it, Dana.

"Somewhere in the fog, I think you mentioned a train. That's a good description...a big ole' black train with an engine that could mow down anything in its path...that just kept slammin' down the tracks regardless of what was ahead. Funny how it helped to have me in my leathers—holding on. Almost like Superwoman." She grinned as she seemed to consider the analogy.

"The nightmare was about a...beast. Coming after me. I was little. I couldn't cry out. There was no one to help me. Then I remembered standing in the kitchen. My father had...used me, and afterwards, my mother was in the kitchen, trying to make Jell-O for me. She was talking real fast...frantic about getting the Jell-O to set. I couldn't tell her what just happened. I wanted her to see me, to help me, but she wouldn't look at me. She just kept fussin' with that damned Jell-O. I can't eat the stuff to this day."

Genie rubbed her eyes with the palms of her hands, then sighed. "I don't know how she kept from goin' crazy. She had to have known. She was...is mentally ill, I know that now. He beat her down so bad, she still barely functions."

Dana sensed that Genie's energy was spent. "What do you believe now...rather than I'm bad?"

She harrumphed and shrugged instantly. "I was just a little girl. An innocent little girl."

Letting the truth of that hang in the air, Dana rejoiced internally at the steps Genie had taken. There would be more mountains to climb, but she had conquered the biggest one. Dana was humbled and grateful to have been able to witness Genie confronting this challenge.

She spoke about the possibility of other memories surfacing, or Genie experiencing unusual sensations, urges or moodiness. They identified some possible ways of coping, and Genie promised she would contact Dana or Marla, her addictions therapist, or her sponsor if things got rough. Genie's bearing as she left the office conveyed victory and hope.

Chapter Twenty Eight

AS DANA WAS WRAPPING up the last individual counseling session of the day, her mind began to stretch toward her five o'clock group. Checking her focus, she disciplined herself to stay present with the client before her—Catherine, a State worker who came in periodically to *test her perspective*. She was a conscientious supervisor and very thoughtful about her subordinates. Dana was unsure how helpful her counseling was, but Catherine needed to process, so Dana accepted her own value of simply being a *sounding board*.

After Catherine left, Dana allowed herself to return to mental preparations for her therapy group. Admittedly, she favored this group over her other work. It was gratifying to see how the women interacted with each other in such a supportive way, drawing strength from each other to face their challenges. It seemed that personal growth, for the most part, was rapid now, especially with Genie. Since her breakthrough in the last few weeks, her *bad girl* energy was subdued. She made more eye-contact with the group; her remarks were softer, moving from tolerance to empathy. She still used the nicknames for everyone, but now more as a tribute to their character rather than sarcasm. She and Ruth had settled into a respectful tolerance.

After check-ins, Dana introduced the topic for the evening. "I'd like you to look in your rearview mirrors tonight. You know, sometimes we need to do that to see how far we've come. Sort of along the philosophy of Søren Kierkegaard, *Life can only be understood backwards; but it must be lived forwards.* I think change is often so subtle, we forget—we forget how we are doing things differently, coping differently, thinking differently. And when we can acknowledge those changes, it helps reinforce them.

"So, take a few minutes to grab some card stock over there and any art materials you want to use. Try to capture some of your journey these last weeks and months – perhaps some of the obstacles you've encountered; things you've left along the road; distance you've traveled."

Dana refreshed her tea, trying to not distract the contemplative women as they rummaged through the baskets of markers and craft materials. After ten minutes, all five were settled in their chairs again and appeared ready for discussion.

"It looks like we're ready. Who would like to start?"

Susan held up her card, surprising Dana at her initiative. It showed two sets of seven squares. The first set was of equal size and shaded in a gray. In the second set of squares, six were blank and of equal size. Only the last one, doubled in size, was darkened. "This is the difference between *before* and *now*. I still have OCD, but it's more contained. I used to attend to it every day, but more and more, I can wait. Like now I can wait 'til Saturday to check all the fluids in my car, air in the tires, and not be late for work during the week. I take all the time I want on Saturdays, and it seems to help. Not always, but it's better. That's what's changed for me. That's all."

"Very nice. And Susan, what helps you resist the temptation to tend to your car during the week?"

Her eyebrows moved as she sought an answer. "I think it's because I gave myself permission to do it thoroughly on Saturdays. It's my choice. I feel more in control."

"Nice. Who's next?"

Ruth sighed heavily. She waved her card in front of her, which showed a long highway with battered boxes and boulders along either side. "I guess this is what my journey looks like. I feel like I'm making the miles…progress, leaving behind a lot. The rocks represent the load I try to carry when…it's not mine to carry.

"In that boundaries book, Henry Cloud makes a neat distinction between carrying a knapsack, which is an individual's own responsibility, and a boulder, which is when someone's load is too big and they might need your help. I haven't made that distinction before, and I see where I try to help when it's better for the person to do it for themselves. It comes across as controlling, when that is not my intent."

Ruth sounded weary. "The boxes are...I don't know...habits? But I'm afraid there might be treasures in those boxes, and I might lose something important, or someone very dear to me. I'm driving further and further away, and I don't know that it will be better where I'm going. Especially with my girls, maybe I'm throwing away any chance there is to build bridges. I feel so out-of-control. I'm not even sure who I am anymore."

"You're a mama bear!" Genie's gruff voice ratcheted all eyes toward her. The muscles around her mouth showed her search for the right words. "You want to protect your cubs, but they're yearlings, and need to take some chances. You're right behind 'em, though, so they won't get in too much trouble."

Ruth studied Genie, open mouthed.

Genie dropped eye contact, her voice barely audible. "You're just doing what mama bears do...even for cubs that are orphaned. Like me. It ain't wrong...it just annoys the cubs."

Genie turned to the side, retreating within her chair. Ruth blinked a few times before saying, "Thank you. I think."

Dana considered what had just transpired between Genie and Ruth. It seemed positive, but she felt it would be intrusive to try to expand on it. Shifting attention back to the topic, she asked, "Okay, who will go next?"

Sheryl spoke up. "I will." Laughing, she showed a drawing of progressively large stick figures with squiggly red hair. The last figure was large and dressed in a Wonder Woman costume. "I'm not gonna show this to my husband — he's already nervous that I've become brazen." Sheryl's laughter exploded, then trickled to a chuckle. "Oh Dana, what have you done? I told my principal this week I won't be available for summer school this year, and left it at that. I didn't explain myself or try to justify it...I simply said I won't be available. And the thing is...I'm not sure what I'll be doing — I just wanted some flexibility this summer."

Sheryl wiped her eyes, containing her laughter. "The thing is...it wasn't the end of the world. My gut was churning, and it took everything I have to not add *but-if-you-really-need-me-I'll-change-my-life-around-for-the-benefit-of-the-summer-program.* He did look perplexed, but I let it be. And I have every confidence that by tonight, and a glass of wine, my stomach will tell me it's okay."

"Good for you!"

Brandi held up her drawing of a single road leading to a Y. Before the Y, the road was lined with neatly spaced trees with branches only on the side that faced the road. After the Y, the road was dotted with blank traffic signs. "I guess when I look back a few months, I see an illusion...like a movie set. On the surface, it looks fine, but it's really a façade. A cardboard front. And that's what I'm leaving behind...the façade. I won't pretend anymore. The road ahead is uncertain. I never wanted to be a single mom; I don't know how I can make it financially; I worry about how it will affect my children; but I feel I don't have a choice.

"I know I'm stronger now. Just a few months ago, I let my husband bully me. I feel so stupid for letting him do that—when all the time he was destroying our family. I...I...*think* differently. Before, I took things at face value. Now, I'm more suspicious. Maybe even hardened."

Genie guffawed. "You're about as hard as a soft pillow, princess, pardon-my-cross-talk."

Laughing, Brandi teased back, "But you're my trainer, Genie. I'm getting tougher." After the chuckling ceased, she added, "It's frightening, but I have hope. He's no longer seeking custody of the children, so that's good."

"Thank you, Brandi. How about you, Genie? What do you see when you look back over the last weeks or months?"

Genie appeared to brace herself as she lifted her card. The drawing showed indistinguishable marks completely covering the lower half; the top half showed one large boot print. Pointing to the lower half, "That's my life before the program...when I still used. It was insane." Pointing to the upper half, "This is where I am today. I take it one day at a time—one step at a time, and it works for me." She looked away from the group but continued to hold her card up, her elbow resting on her knee.

After a moment, she continued in a quiet voice, "You girls help too...if only to know I'm not the only one that's screwed up." The resulting laughter evoked a grin from Genie. Even Ruth seemed to appreciate the humor.

Dana basked in the warmth of the group a moment. "Wow. You gals are amazing. You inspire me. Thank you."

Before ending the session, Dana led the group in a visualization of themselves at their best. She invited them to pay close attention to their bodies' *felt* sense, a physical awareness of how it feels to be strong, erect, confident, alert yet relaxed, centered. "Notice your breathing…the energy — the incredible beauty and design of how you are uniquely you."

Dana watched as her rhythmic voice orchestrated the discernible changes in these five lovely women, knowing that little by little, their wounds were healing; they were gaining insight and determination to live their lives untethered from trauma, distortion and shame.

Chapter Twenty Nine

AS THE LONG DARK nights of winter gave way to the promise of spring, Dana began to notice the changes within herself — separate, but in close step with her therapy group. She was inspired by Genie, the street wise child-woman with the bulldog mask who was overcoming, one step at time.

Steps. That was the key for Dana now in so many ways. Her personal reflections as she worked the twelve steps as an *Adult Child* was removing the edges of anger toward her father. In some ways it was freeing, yet like Ruth, she had some fear about letting go of *perceived control*. Realizing she truly wasn't responsible for his moods or well-being, and never had been — even as his cherished little girl — was freeing. It wasn't because she wasn't good enough...insightful enough...attentive enough. He had his own issues and ways of coping, and he was, in fact, in charge of his own life. She knew that professionally — had used that concept with her clients for years, but somehow it had been distorted internally. Seeing it now resulted in a change...a release of worry. Anxiousness.

Yet, if she didn't have that kind of power...influence over her cherished father, then who was she? What was the truth? What was their relationship...their love; their common history? She journaled daily, exploring the different perspectives, trying to make sense of her history and why she thought the way she did. At times, she processed concepts with her addictions colleague, Marla. Other times, she tried to explore her journey with Hub. While he was patient and tried to follow her emotional dredging, he couldn't relate to the depth of how she questioned what had shaped her. So, Dana took her typical approach of delving into the research, studying resource materials, and exploring its meaning privately.

She worked out twice a week now, often joining Rachel for her routine. Their preferences and agility were so similar, they were amazed by each new discovery. They both chuckled at the occasional question from others, *are you two sisters?*

Infrequently, her dad's gym routine overlapped hers. They were cordial to each other, their superficial communication expanding, but the rift between them was clearly present. She could read *sadness* in his face, and her inclination was to console him, but Dana had determined she would not approach the subject until prompted by God and her twelve-step journey.

Overall, Dana felt like she was in a good place. Peaceful. More in tune with the present. Content with the pace of her personal growth, and especially, the deepening relationship with Rachel.

The office was quiet; Dana was engrossed in preparing the end-of-the-quarter reports for her accountant, when she heard the familiar groan of the old door opening to the outer office. Looking through her private office window, she could see a tall, well dressed man turning back to close the door behind him. She thought he must be a salesman, although for Juneau, he still seemed out of place.

Closing her laptop, she stepped around her desk and had entered the reception area before she could see him clearly. He stood just inside the door, his right hand opened in supplication.

Suddenly, Dana couldn't breathe or move. Her surroundings become surreal, time suspended. She couldn't make sense of what she was seeing or what time frame to approach the image. She stood there a moment with her head cocked, studying this stranger, before her body began to shake.

"Hello, Dana."

The sound of his voice removed the fog and thrust reality to this Monday afternoon in her quaint Juneau office, one thousand miles from their history, half a globe away from where he should be. Dana touched the chair back to steady her body that was settling like lead weight over her stockinged feet. Once she was able to validate the scene before her, her mind began to swirl. Her thought of danger was fleeting — his expression was humble, questioning.

He'd aged slightly. Gray hair touched his temples, his crimped russet hair tamed in a short tapered cut that enhanced his sophistication. The sage green casual shirt hung from his broad shoulders, which now suggested linage rather than a young man's weight lifting routine. His hazel green eyes ringed with black remained unchanged. Still compelling, yet reined in by a new maturity.

"How are you, Dana?"

How dare he show his face – now, after what he did to me? Now, after the nightmares are finally behind me?

"I hope I didn't intrude...I started to telephone...but I was afraid you wouldn't... You look wonderful." He broke eye-contact, gesturing toward the window. "You have lovely country here. I see why it is important to you...why you could never leave."

Dana's eyes narrowed, her brows dimpling. "Why are you here?" Her voice was harsh once the words escaped.

Mario shifted his weight, his hands began to stretch and close as if looking for where they belonged. "I...I came to ask your forgiveness." His words were strangled at first, building in clarity but lacking volume as he looked directly at Dana. "I...I have always regretted our last... You did not invite my attentions, and I have always regretted my forcefulness with you...the stupidity of my youthful... I loved you so, but I did not contain my...lust. My letters...I begged you..."

"You raped me."

His head and shoulders dropped in shame. "Yes. Yes, regretfully, that is what I did. And I am so sorry, Dana." He looked again at her directly. "I have confessed my sin, but it continues to haunt me. My sons are becoming men, and I have tried to teach them restraint – to honor women and themselves, yet I carry such a dark burden knowing I sought gratification that...you did not choose to give. I would give anything to undo what I have done."

Dana recalled the persistent phone calls that went unanswered, the letters she threw away unopened. "Why now? How do you show up on my doorstep now?"

Mario's body continued to shift like an errant boy. "I have business in Anchorage...with Japan and others. I leave tomorrow. I couldn't come to your country and not at least try...to...I know I can't make it right. I can't undo it. I thought possibly..."

He took a deep breath, shifting his weight to center over both feet. "I guess in my deepest heart I dream that you were not, how do you say...fazed...by my shameful actions, but your face tells me that is not the case. I hurt you as deeply as I feared."

The expression on Dana's face did not change as she watched Mario struggle with his emotions. "I understand if it is asking too much. I...I'm so sorry."

Keeping his head down, he reached in his pocket. Pulling out a slim wallet, he removed a business card and set it on the side table next to the door. Looking back at Dana with a bowed head, he repeated. "I'm so sorry, Dana. If I can do anything to make it up to you...please let me. I will forever carry the shame."

Dana stood frozen in place long after Mario turned and quietly left her office. Myriad emotions roiled through her body as the memories flashed through her mind—the carefree gatherings of their study group in graduate school; seeing herself as the naive young woman away from all that was familiar and solid to her; the laughter and Friday night parties to relieve stress after exams; the infatuation she felt for the sophisticated, charismatic man that Mario appeared to be; the overwhelming fear that she would never see Hub again; the disbelief that Mario was so forceful to come into her dorm room. Then the helplessness she felt as Mario forced himself upon her.

The months following the rape were hard to think about. She could see her unkempt self holed up in her dark dorm room, hating herself for not seeing Mario for who he truly was; for letting him think she was interested in him in the slightest way; for allowing herself to be charmed by his worldliness. She longed for Hub to make it all right, but she could not admit her shame to him then—to seek forgiveness for dumping him. When she was honest with herself, she could acknowledge that the flirtation with Mario was the underlying reason she broke her engagement with Hub abruptly, even though she regretted it almost immediately and never pursued a relationship with Mario.

Dana sat down in her usual chair for group sessions. *He risked my fury at the very least—perhaps even public humiliation. Surely a scandal like that would have threatened his family name...even destroyed his reputation.*

Dana continued to think through the possibilities of his cosmopolitan life, and the courage it took for him to admit he harmed her. *He never used the word rape, but didn't deny it when I said it.* She sat for a long while trying to grasp the enormity of his visit.

The next thought blasted all thoughts of charity she had begun to entertain—Rachel! Dana began to sink further into the chair as she considered the implications for her daughter and their relationship. Mario didn't even know he had sired a child. He had no right to know, in her mind, but Rachel—their precious beautiful daughter who resembles him so much—has a right to know about him.

Oh God, we're just settling in to be a family, her roots taking hold in Juneau soil. Surely now is not the time for Mario to appear in her life. Tears of anguish leaked from her eyes, as she considered that all options would require truth. *What if she chooses him and his exciting world?*

* * *

The muscles in Hub's jaws convulsed as he listened without comment. Methodically, Dana recounted the events of the afternoon with a calmness that was surprising. Perhaps it was in counter-balance to the intensity she saw brewing behind Hub's controlled façade.

Dana knew it would be difficult for him to hear that his nemesis had surfaced after all these years, but there was no question of his need to know about it. They knew each other so well, she couldn't hide it from him. Plus, he and Rachel had a heart connection that could be threatened. Every fiber in her being wanted to soften the reality—to hedge the truth to avoid Hub's pain, but the insight she had gained these last few months about trying to control others to avoid pain was now prominent in her thinking.

She finished her account with, "I'm so sorry, Hub, that we're not done with this yet. I guess, in a way, we never will be anyway. He's part of Rachel. She's the one who has to decide about it." She squirmed in her chair before she concluded, "He does seem sincerely remorseful. He didn't have to come all this way…go to all that trouble to find me. To admit what he did. I think he risked a lot."

Hub's heavy eyebrows hooded his intense eyes that appeared to have darkened, "Did you tell him about Rachel?"

At Dana's head shake, he continued more fiercely, "Do you know where he's staying?"

"Hub, you can't...I don't want you to do anything. I...I don't know where he's staying. He just left his card and said to let him know if he could do anything, you know...to make it up to me."

"Where's the card?"

Fear exploded within Dana, her breath becoming shallow, her voice escalated. "Please, Hub, please. I don't want you hurt. Please don't go off half-cocked."

"I'm not going to get hurt, Dana — I'd like to have a word with this guy. It seems like tonight is the right time." His level gaze made it clear he would not back off.

Dana retrieved Mario's business card from her purse and handed it to Hub. Her eyes implored, but she held her tongue.

Hub gave Dana a brief hug before he left the house, saying only, "Don't worry."

Panic danced around inside Dana as she envisioned the possibilities if Hub's contempt for Mario let lose. He wasn't a violent man, but what if he lost control? What if Mario became aggressive? What if something unforeseen, something horrible happened? She wanted to stop this...to fix it. *But Hub is so strong...and grounded. He won't do anything stupid. But Mario is...is...I don't know what he is capable of doing. Actually, I do know — he is capable of evil.*

Dana stomped a path from the great room through her kitchen and back, trying to think of what to do. Her dad — he would know what to do. He could go after them — to make sure nothing happened to Hub. *But no, my father is too volatile. I can't involve him — he'd make it worse.*

Dana's worry swirled around inside like a squall building to a gale. Her intellect argued with overwhelming fear and a sense of helplessness. She cried out loud, causing Mica to whimper. Both dogs hovered until Dana dropped to her knees. Sitting on her heals, she hugged their necks.

Speaking out loud, her chin trembling. "I know I'm supposed to *let go and let God*, but I'm not sure, God, if you'll..." Dana recognized the pattern of her old thinking — she was afraid to trust even God. She had absolutely no control over the situation or the outcome, yet she was trying to find a way to manage it. To manage God...her husband...and anything that could possibly happen.

The realization caused her to see how ludicrous it was for her to *strive after the wind.* A chuckle broke through her angst as she cried to her loveable companions, "Your mama is a control freak, girls...and a slow learner."

Dana's thinking shifted, turning her attention toward God as she continued to kneel on her haunches. She poured out her heart, not telling Him how she wanted it handled, but pleaded that He would hold sway over the situation. *Please guide and protect my Hub, dear Lord.*

As she let go of the need to control the uncontrollable, the tension drained from her body, replaced by the comfort of God's love and promises. It could get ugly, but somehow, they would get through it.

Dana got her knitting and a cup of tea to settle on the couch and wait.

Chapter Thirty

IT WAS STILL PRE-SEASON in Juneau, so traffic and tourist impact were light. Hub was able to find street parking in front of Hearthside Books. Juneau didn't offer much in the way of luxury, but Hub had guessed Mario would choose the old Baranof for its reputation. The historic nine-story hotel was luxurious in its day, and was still a center for business meetings, conferences, and fine dining. One of the biggest advantages of the Baranof was that downtown Juneau was a step out the front door.

As he watched people scurrying down the sidewalks, it was obvious which ones were the Alaskans and which ones were outsiders. Even the local bureaucrats could be singled out by their suit jackets or trench coats. Hub wasn't sure how he would spot the scumbag since he had no idea of what he looked like, but he was betting that something would give him away — if his assumptions were right. It was worth a try.

Mario Santos Chavez: The man who had been in Dana's nightmares for twenty years. The man whose shadow put distance between him and his wife many times over. The man whose memory encroached in his bedroom, and caused Hub to fantasize about taking revenge in a slow and painful manner. And now that was a real possibility.

Most of the shops were closed, but the eateries created a light steady stream of foot traffic this time of night. An occasional skateboarder claimed the center of the street, or small bunches of young people meandered down the sidewalk. Hub would normally bemoan their attire and tattoos as a sign of the times, but his focus was intent on seeing a stranger...someone who looked out of place. Someone of wealth and sophistication. A Latino snake who had manipulated his way into Dana's life and cornered her. Raped her. Left her with self-doubt and fears that took away her self-confidence. It changed who she was.

Hub had a good view of Franklin and Front streets that faced the Baranof. Waiting was a little like fishing — you had to be patient — get to the spot where you think they'll be biting, and then wait.

The sun had started its decent above Douglas Island before Hub's attention was drawn to a tall broad shouldered man carrying a go-cup, walking toward Franklin. He sported a new pale green ball cap that featured the midnight sun logo. His light jacket and slacks professed elegance, not common to Juneau. He was handsome — the movie star look before scruffy beards became the rage.

Hub stepped out of his pickup, timing his step up on the curb to force Mario to look at him.

"Mario Santos Chavez?"

The look of surprise rather than confusion confirmed to Hub he was on the mark. "I beg your pardon...have we met?"

"Not directly. I'm Robert Cordell. You may know me as Hub."

Mario's face reflected bewilderment replaced quickly by understanding, then settled on weariness. He took a step back.

The two men stood silently. Mario dropped his eyelids and shoulders like a boy caught stealing. Hub never flinched, his eyes drilling into Mario's face, his stance wide, arms crossed.

When he spoke, Mario's voice was hoarse. "You must be Dana's...husband?"

Hub nodded slowly, his jaw-set and narrowed eyes menacing.

It was a moment before Mario spoke. "I guess I can't be surprised at meeting you. Not something I have relished, but certainly it's understandable." He gestured toward the Baranof, "Please, could we share a coffee, or brew? There is much to say."

Even though Mario stood four inches taller than Hub, it was Hub's bearing that was imposing. He growled, "Here's fine."

Mario shuffled, looked away as if searching for a starting point, then took another deep breath. "I...I was hoping I might find resolution to a very old...regret." Looking directly at Hub,

Mario seemed to gather new resolve. "You have a beautiful wife, Mr...uh...Hub. You are a lucky man."

Hub's glare deepened; the muscles in his jaw flexed menacingly.

"Obviously you know I met briefly with Dana this afternoon." With no change in Hub's expression, Mario stumbled on. "It...it wasn't a meeting, really...I guess I surprised her by stopping by her place of business. She had no foreknowledge I was coming."

Mario fiddled with his Rolex watch, his eyes glancing away from Hub's penetrating look. "I wanted to try one last time to settle an old debt. If she knew I was coming, I thought she would refuse to see me still. My attempts to apologize in the past were met with...she would not allow me to apologize. Back then...when we were students together. And I can see by your expression that nothing has changed."

Hub's voice was a snarl. "What you call *a debt* changed my wife. It's taken years for your shadow to leave my bedroom!"

Mario deflated like he had been punched in the chest. When his eyes returned to Hub's face, they were moist. "I am so sorry. I would give anything to take that night back, I swear to you. I pray you will forgive me. That she will."

His voice faltered. "I have two sons coming of age. I try to teach them...to be men of honor...to never have the regrets I have lived with for twenty-two years. My shame has increased knowing they will soon be...independent and full of themselves as I was. They may choose to drink too much, as I did."

Looking at Hub directly, he said, "I loved your wife desperately. I even let myself believe she returned my ardor, even though she loved you completely. I let my desire overcome my good sense, and I have regretted it every day of my life since, you must believe me. It has been a shadow over my marriage too, although in a different way, I'm sure.

"My priest has interceded for me, but...I hoped that Dana would... I had hoped for her forgiveness, but I understand. It is understandable under the circumstances. I...seek your forgiveness too."

Hub stood silent for a long moment, his eyes never leaving Mario's face. Finally, he inhaled deeply, nodding slightly while he spoke quietly. "Sounds like you've got a good handle on how big a mistake you made.

"I reckon you and God will have to settle it. I'm done with it."

Stepping off the curb, Hub looked back just before getting into his pickup. "I hope you find peace with yourself."

Chapter Thirty One

IT WAS LATE BY the time Hub returned to the valley. There was so much to sort out in his mind, he stopped by the shop first for some solitude. He clicked off the radio that had been left on when his helpers closed up, not wanting the distraction of some western song lamenting lost love. The diesel and oil odors were as familiar to him as the fit of his boots. Here, he knew clearly what was right and what was not; what was important, what could wait; how to approach a problem and look at it from all angles.

Had he handled it right with Mario? The encounter continued to swirl around in his mind. He had finally met the swine after all these years. Feeling disgusted with himself, he picked up a crescent wrench and thrust it back on the workbench. He'd been impotent about the situation for twenty-two years, and tonight he hadn't made it right. He had planned to *even the score* — at least give him some of what he had coming. For years he had dreamed of sinking his fist into this guy's jaw, loosening some of those pearly white teeth. How could he face Dana and tell her he had done nothing to defend her honor?

His jaws continued to flex as he leaned against the old oak workbench, making the solvent ripple around the carburetor soaking in a pan.

He could understand how Dana had been taken in. *That guy is smooth, that's for sure. Yet he seemed sincere.*

He was in love with his Dana. "Right." *Yet she came back to me. Eventually.*

Hub recalled his anguish when Dana broke off their engagement, returned to graduate school, and would have no contact with him for over a year. His despair was so overwhelming, he made plans to go crab fishing on the Bering

Sea, the most dangerous waters in Alaska. On some level, he recognized his underlying hope was for an accident to end his misery, but the Lord had other plans for him, thankfully. Old man Shipley asked Hub to stay and buy out his marine engine repair business. He had cancer, and was facing lengthy treatment. As it turned out, it was a blessing for them both— Hub launched a successful business, for which he was well-suited, and it provided some financial stability for Mr. Shipley. Most importantly, if he had left, he would have missed the opportunity to get Dana back.

He had thrown himself into his business, trying to block out the pain, and then he ran into her at the dock. She was launching her skiff, rigged for salmon fishing. He caught her dock line and stood transfixed, seeing the changes in her eyes that held a sorrow beyond Juneau. Neither said a word, but he knew he couldn't let her leave again. He simply stepped in her boat and pushed them away from the dock. He didn't care that the shop door was left open or that he had his heavy work boots on—he wouldn't let her out of his sight.

She never took her eyes off her destination, navigating out to Benjamin Island. The sea lions were calving, their cacophony providing the back drop to their uncertain reunion. Dana anchored, but didn't reach for her fishing pole. When she looked up at Hub, vulnerability was written all over her face. She broke down, telling him what had happened during the last year. She had gotten pregnant, gave birth to Rachel, arranged for her adoption, finished graduate school, and returned home believing she could never face Hub again. It was only years later that she told him Mario had actually raped her. He suspected coercion, or a date gone awry, but when she came to the realization she was carrying guilt for something she had no control over, she admitted it was a rape. That's when Hub's desire for revenge began to fester.

He imagined Mario would be an arrogant, sordid, womanizing slime ball. He would take pleasure in beating him to a pulp—teaching him a lesson.

Did he just fool me too...or was he sincere? Hub retraced the encounter in his memory for the tenth time, looking for inconsistencies in Mario's bearing and words. Again, he appeared to be a man laden with guilt over a really bad mistake made many years before. He admitted it haunted his marriage, and that he had confessed to his priest, but it wasn't enough. *Why else would he go to the trouble to seek out Dana half a world away? He doesn't know about Rachel.*

Hub thought about what it might be like to have sons, trying to teach them scruples while hiding a sordid past. *Kind of like a preacher talking righteousness from the pulpit while hanging with a prostitute.* He could understand Mario's anguish — if he was an ethical man anyway.

An ethical man. *Who knows? I'm called to forgive whether he is or not. But the real victim here is Dana — the forgiveness decision is hers.*

Switching off the light, Hub headed toward home, trying to sort out his thoughts about how to lead his family — a circle that now extended beyond just him and Dana.

* * *

Dana was standing in the doorway when Hub pulled in the driveway. Turning off the engine, he sat a moment with his forearm resting on the steering wheel, looking back at her. She looked tired. Vulnerable. It was well past midnight. Wearily, he got out of the pickup, covered the twenty feet of gravel drive, and quietly encircled his beautiful wife in his arms. They stood without speaking for some moments before settling at the kitchen table.

He nodded at Dana's silent offer to pour him a glass of wine. His thumbs turned the stemless glass as he studied it, looking for a place to begin.

Dana broke the silence. "Are you okay?"

"Yeah. Just...looking for a place to start."

Her eyes scrutinized him, but she waited for Hub to continue.

After taking a sip of the wine, he set it aside and folded his square hands. "I caught up with him. In front of the Hearthside book store. I figured he would stay at the Baranof.

"I can see how he got your attention, Dana. He's certainly a pretty boy."

After chewing on a few starts, Hub shared the encounter he had with Mario, trying to repeat everything Mario had said to him. The only expression Dana showed was when Hub said that Mario claimed he loved her then.

With a look of disgust, she spat, "He doesn't know the definition!"

Hub only nodded at her sentiment before he continued. "I wanted to hurt him, Dana. I left here...waited for him...with the intent to pay him back for some of the pain he has caused you. And...me. I wanted him to know how...evil he was. I have never wanted to hurt another human being like I did him—I wanted to make him suffer."

His lips jostled as he searched for what to say next. Finally he exhaled in conclusion. "I decided it wasn't up to me to hold him accountable—God is doing a pretty good job of that. He seems sincere in his remorse, and if he isn't, God will still take care of it. I...I hope I didn't let you down, Dana. I'm torn between a sense that I should defend my wife's honor—*bring back an ear*—and knowing I'm called to forgive; make peace whenever it is up to me."

Dana's weepy eyes looked at him in that way that made him as dopey as a hormonal teenager.

Her voice was just above a whisper. "You couldn't let me down, Robert Cordell. You are the most honorable man I know. I love you so much."

Reaching for her, she rounded the table before he could get out of the chair completely, and he almost lost his balance as her passion enveloped him. Dana seemed driven, intent on showing the depth of her love. Hub marveled at her abandon as their love making took them to new heights.

Later, as Dana was tucked under Hub's arm, he thought about Mario's sons being half-siblings to Rachel. He decided to keep that thought to himself for tonight.

Chapter Thirty Two

"LADIES, THIS IS THE next-to-last group—the last therapeutic session, really. Our last session will be reserved for celebration and closure."

Dana scanned the five faces around the circle, seeing non-verbal reactions to her announcement. Brandi's head shook, her eyelids closing in regret. Ruth grimaced. Sheryl shook her opened hands up as if to brace against something undesirable. Susan shook her head once in affirmation. Genie gave a playful scowl.

"I know. It's hard to think about ending, isn't it? I too find it hard to bring our group to an end. You've each become so very dear to me. But...we must."

Shifting gears, Dana reached for a stack of papers and handed them around the circle. "Unless there are urgent needs to check-in first, I'd like to incorporate this poem with our process tonight—combining check-ins and reactions to this poem. Is that all right?"

Seeing nods from everyone, she began. "This is a poem called *After Awhile*. There's some disagreement about who originally wrote it, but it's commonly attributed to Veronica A. Shoffstall. It's been very telling to me in my life's journey, and I want to share it with you now."

Dana read aloud as the women followed along with their handouts.

> *After a while you learn the subtle difference*
> *Between holding a hand and chaining a soul*
> *And you learn that love doesn't mean leaning*
> *And company doesn't always mean security.*
> *And you begin to learn that kisses aren't contracts*

And presents aren't promises
And you begin to accept your defeats
With your head up and your eyes ahead
With the grace of a woman, not the grief of a child
And you learn to build all your roads on today
Because tomorrow's ground is too uncertain for plans
And futures have a way of falling down in mid-flight.
After awhile you learn that even sunshine burns if you get too much
So you plant your own garden and decorate your own soul
Instead of waiting for someone to bring you flowers.
And you learn that you really can endure
That you really are strong
You really do have worth
And you learn and learn
With every goodbye, you learn."

As she looked around the quiet room, Dana could see that the poem was resonating with the group. She sat back and waited, giving them time to think about it.

Uncharacteristically, Genie started by waving her copy of the poem toward the center of the group. "She's got it right. If you don't get it, you go under. You gotta plant your own garden and not let some scumbag chain your soul."

Dana simply nodded in acknowledgment, continuing to sit with her hands relaxed in her lap.

Brandi was tentative. "There's so much, it's…I'm going to have to read it a few more times to really grasp the depth of it, but right now that *presents aren't promises* is standing out to me. Maybe it's because of how Goodell has always made promises or been on his best behavior when I planned to leave him, but I see through that now and he's…floundering. He doesn't know how to act around me because I am strong. I do have worth.

"Shall I go ahead now and check-in, or wait till everyone has a chance to talk about the poem?" With a nod from Dana, Brandi continued. "Well, I wanted to update you all about what's happening. My mom is here, and it's been…interesting. Helpful—she loves my children and is a lot of help with them. I come home from work to a clean house, homework done, and a balanced meal."

Brandi hesitated, searching for how to express her next thought. "In a way, I was dreading her visit, because I thought she would...disapprove of my decision to leave Goodell. I know it was hard for her, but she didn't pry. I asked her last night why she stayed with Daddy, knowing he was unfaithful. Her response is still a puzzle to me — she said, *because he needed me. And I knew that one day, he would realize it.*"

Shaking her head, Brandi continued. "I always thought it was the other way around — that she was afraid to be on her own, but she said in no uncertain terms she could have been very comfortable on her own. She made the choice to stay."

Ruth asked, "Are you feeling pressure to make the same choice, Brandi?"

"In a way, but not really. She said I had to make my own choice, that we're different, and times are different. But I think about how her choice...her decision to stay...allowed my sister and me to grow up with an intact family. I love my dad, even though he used to be a jerk to my mom. And...I would love for my children to have that...security."

"Anything else?"

"No. Well, maybe. I just think about the difference. I have some tools that my mother didn't have, like this group. And picking up on some of the twelve-step philosophy from Genie. So that's what I'm doing now — just taking it a day at a time."

Seeing that Brandi was finished, Dana looked around, her expression inviting the next person. Ruth motioned with her head to indicate her readiness.

"What strikes me about this poem is the poetic reference to boundaries — *the subtle difference between holding a hand and chaining a soul.* And that *even sunshine burns if you get too much.* There's such a balance between holding and letting go, between controlling and guiding, between getting what you need and getting too much. It is subtle. Growing up, there was no exploration of that concept — you just obeyed. Maybe that's why I get offended at times, because it's hard for me to see the subtleties...or humor.

"But the good thing is — I'm learning to accept those last lines about me: I am strong. I do have worth. I'm learning...and learning."

Dana invited Susan to go next, sensing she was ready.

"A lot of it doesn't apply to me. I don't have those relationships, but I know I am strong. I'm good at enduring and not putting too much emphasis in a future that might collapse. It just works better for me that way."

"Thank you. Sheryl?"

Sheryl's chuckle percolated, settling in her throat. "Subtlety is lost on me...and when I think of chaining a soul, I think about my students in these last weeks of the school year. And prison — that's where they'll put me if I try to subtly chain their little souls to their chairs!" Her laughter burst forth like a tossed water balloon, eliciting head shakes and chuckles from the other women.

"*Oy vey*, Dana, your good efforts have been for naught." Sheryl wiped her eyes as she became more serious. "Not really. This has been good for me — I've learned a lot and it's made a huge difference in my life.

"I have to admit, though, poetry is lost on me. I'm so left-brained, it's hard for me to relate to it. Maybe that part about security — *company doesn't always mean security*. If I relate that to *things*, it resonates — *things* don't equate to security. I know that in my head, but it doesn't follow through to my actions — I hold on to *stuff*. I still have a problem with surrounding myself with *things* to feel more secure, even though it's nonsense. It'll take another nine-month session to get me past that one, though!" Sheryl's voice mimicked Forrest Gump, "And that's all I have to say about that!"

Dana's voice signaled a shift in topic. "Interesting. We all have such different takes on the few paragraphs, don't we?

"Okay. Let's use some art supplies and take a few moments to contemplate — what does healing look like for you? Or recovery...whatever you want to call this journey we've been on. Take ten minutes or so to come up with a visual that says something about your healing...recovery...personal growth."

As the women mulled around the side table selecting card stock and art supplies, Dana considered each person in her mind, thinking about what tools she might still be able to incorporate in this last hour. They would have a celebration for closure in two weeks, but tonight was really the therapeutic ending. Genie was invested in the NA program, and it would be an easier transition for her. And she would likely continue with individual counseling for awhile yet. Brandi has her mom, who sounds like a pretty good resource for her. Sheryl is content with her progress. Susan. *Susan seems content with her progress. I think I was projecting my goals onto her, instead of supporting hers.* Ruth. *Have I failed her? No…her presence is less domineering. At times, she's downright humble in this group.*

Dana's thoughts were interrupted by the women as they ambled back to their seats. They all seemed subdued — even Sheryl.

"Who would like to start?"

Sheryl raised her hand, reminding Dana of her classroom environment. "I'll go." She showed her drawing of a large steering wheel with a steering knob. "This reminds me of the control I have taken over my life. Up until this winter, I let others control my time and energy. My stress level was sky-high because I wasn't in charge of my own life. Now I've got a pretty good handle on how to drive my own vehicle." She stopped to laugh at herself. "And in case I feel weak, I can always grab this steering knob like my dad used to have on his old pickup. That'll turn me around in a minute!" She made eye-contact with each woman as she beamed.

Brandi held up a drawing of two children shaped like gingerbread figures. Two hands entwined in front of them, one obviously male, one female. "I don't know what this will look like in the future, but I want my children to have both their parents involved and active in their lives. I hope Goodell and I can come together to guide and protect our children, even if we don't get back together again. That would be the best for them — to have us both. I think…I guess healing for me looks like strength. I purposely made the two hands the same size, because regardless of how Goodell and I work it out, I am a strong woman, and I can plant my own garden.

"I will get through this. I plan to proceed with selling the house — we'd have to anyway. Even if we got back together again, we wouldn't be able to afford it for awhile. But I've decided to not move south yet. The children need their father, so we'll move to an apartment for now. And I think that looks like success, under the circumstances. Healing."

"Very nice. Susan?"

Susan turned her card stock over to show a drawing of a wide building with large double doors and a stick figure standing before it. A small airplane was in the sky overhead. "This is me going to summer semester at Stanford. That's the plane I flew in to San Francisco – without incident, and I'm ready for classes." She laid her drawing in her lap, "And that's it."

"Wonderful. Your students are getting the best!" Looking around the circle, Dana's eyes met Ruth's. Her face held a hint of a smile.

"My family united." Her drawing was reminiscent of Rie Munoz Alaskan paintings with an aerial view of five people holding hands. "Healing for me is to have my girls back, not just in my life, but close like we used to be...holding on to each other. I know it'll take time, but God isn't through with me yet, and I know he has good things in store.

"That poem keeps going through my mind – the subtle difference between holding a hand and chaining a soul." She took a deep breath. "I'm going to hang that on my refrigerator."

Grinning, Dana transitioned to the last person to speak – Genie.

Genie held up her card that showed one word printed in bold, black, block letters. "Beth. My name is Beth." Her voice was resolute, but Dana detected the slightest tremble in her chin. She took a moment before she continued.

"Healing is claiming my own name...the one I was given in love. The old name is one *the beast* gave me before I can remember, but I know it was for his perverted ways. It's not descriptive of me. He manipulated me in that identity, just like he did my mother. She was mentally ill, and I was just a little girl."

She sat up taller in her chair. "Tonight, I will destroy every-single-object or reminder of that name. He no longer defines me. He is irrelevant. I will no longer answer to the name he labeled me with so many years ago. I am Beth."

* * *

Dana drove home after group, her heart overflowing with gratefulness. She couldn't have hoped for greater insight and progress than she had witnessed tonight with every one of her group clients. *Yes! That's why I love group work!*

Pulling into the driveway, she hopped out of her Subaru and up on the deck. She couldn't wait to share her excitement with Hub—her best friend and confidant. He had dinner on the table when she walked in.

Dana chattered through dinner, praising the resiliency of her clients, especially the admiration she held for one young woman who had claimed a new identity. "Hub, she had a horrible, horrible life, and spent nearly twenty years addicted to drugs. She's thirty-two years old, and has begun walking a whole new path. She's amazing. I don't know if I could have come through what she has and kept my sanity."

"You've come through a lot, Dana. You're pretty amazing, in my estimation."

"Oh, you charmer, you. You know how to get a gal's attention."

The couple continued to flirt and play as they cleaned up the kitchen together and Dan stoked the fire in the woodstove.

Having spent her considerable energy, Dana spoke quietly. "They've taught me so much about resiliency, Hub. And not getting ahead of myself...to take things one step at a time. I've decided to let Mario know I forgive him. I don't want to make a big deal of it...just send him a text. Be done with it." She looked over at her husband. "You inspired me to do that. One of these days...soon maybe, I want to forgive my dad. This has gone on too long. If he can't understand me, so be it. I'll just have to let it be."

"Are you ready to talk to him yet? See him?"

Dana knew Hub longed for resolution between the two people he loved the most...and now Rachel. Harmony—that's what he treasured. She wished she could give that to him. "Not yet, but soon. Maybe next week. I know he and Rachel are planning to hike tomorrow if the weather holds. She seems pretty excited about it. I still can't imagine my father hiking a trail when there are no fish at the end of it!"

Hub brought a mug of hot chocolate he had just stirred, and sat close to Dana. "Pretty amazing what a difference our girl has made in all our lives. One of these days, you're going to have to tell her she's got a couple siblings, and about Mario, don't you think?"

Dana groaned. "Yeah. But it can wait. Let's take it a step at a time."

Chapter Thirty Three

IT WAS THE PERFECT day for a long hike — still cool with clear skies. Dan wouldn't have cared if it was pouring rain because he was getting to spend time with his beautiful granddaughter.

Lucky for him, her boyfriend had to cancel the planned hike — his company had redirected him to the Caribbean on business, so Rachel had invited her ole granddad to tag along. *That's better than the Caribbean any ole day!*

He'd never hiked for the purpose of just taking a walk. His hikes had been to get to the lake so he could fish, or get to the cabin for an overnighter, or walk out to find help when he was broken down. This was a new knot in his rope.

Dan paused from stuffing extra socks and a shirt into his daypack to contemplate the changes in him since Rachel had come into his life — his move back to Juneau, getting with a trainer to drop those two inches around his waist, being more deliberate about how he spent his days. She'd given him purpose again, something he hadn't had for a long time. He felt good about how much his health had improved. *Maybe I'll be around long enough to see my great grandchildren!*

They were going to hike the Herbert Glacier trail, an easy but long trek. The glacier was a familiar site to Dan from a distance — it could be seen from the middle of Lynn Canal, but it would be good to check it out close-up.

He finished packing a few personal items, and then went to the kitchen to load water and the sack lunch he had prepared. As if on cue, there was a knock at his door. *There's my girl.* They hugged each other, loaded their gear in her Jeep, and headed out the road. It was a twenty minute drive to the trailhead, giving them lots of time to talk about hiking gear and potential conditions of the trail. Dan was amazed at how this girl stirred his enthusiasm about the simplest things—she reminded him so much of Dana at that age. A slight grimace crossed his face at the thought of his daughter and their estrangement for nearly a year.

One other car was in the parking lot when they arrived, a mountain biker if his bike rack was any indicator. Dan thought it was a little muddy yet for riding a bike, but who knows what young people and their high tech equipment did now days.

They made quick work of retrieving their packs from the back of Rachel's Jeep and making adjustments to the straps. Rachel showed surprise to see him strap his revolver on his hip.

"Oh. You came prepared. You think we might need that, huh?"

"Better be safe than sorry."

"I've got bear spray...right here."

"That's good, but this is a good back up...just in case. And we'll make lotsa noise. Bears appreciate it when they have time to hightail it off the trail, and I'm partial to seeing them from a distance."

Rachel laughed as they walked to the trailhead, a sound that filled Dan's heart. They settled in to a steady pace on the wide gravel flood plain, her long stride matching his. "It smells...rich. Even the air is more intense here, G-Dan. The trees really do create more oxygen, did you know that?"

"I reckon so, although a morning on the water has that same effect on me. There's probably some science that explains it."

"And that's next. When are you going to teach me about navigating those waters, G-Dan?"

"Just name the day, sweetheart. My little boat is gassed up and ready to take you any time you can get away. The kings should be running any day now."

They made small talk as they walked for a few hours, taking periodic breaks along the river that led to the glacier, and enjoying the views when the forest opened up. Rachel had her camera clicking, too often capturing Dan's ole scraggly face, to his way of thinking.

They found some great rocks near the face of the glacier to sit for lunch. Dan removed his gun and holster, stretching out in a perfect hollow in the rock. He was not only relaxed, he was content. It felt good to leave everything except this moment behind.

"This is nice. I'm more of a mariner than a hiker, but seeing this with you, Rachel, has been stellar."

Dan wasn't sure how the topic drifted to the *what ifs* — *what if* she hadn't been given up at birth? *What if* she grew up in Southeast Alaska as Dan's treasured granddaughter? *What if* there weren't twenty years lost to him — years he had no idea of her existence, years he could have loved and guided her? But with Rachel's innocent questions, the agony he tried to keep buried catapulted him right back in the middle of the angst.

Am I going to forgive Dana? Is she like her mother? Just thinking about the questions was enough to stir the wrenching in his gut. He knew he had to talk to Dana about it — he just wasn't ready. Yet here was his precious granddaughter, the spitting image of Dana. And Mae.

Rachel was speaking, but Dan had been so preoccupied with his internal yelling, he didn't catch it all. *She's apologizing for asking me questions?* "Oh honey, you don't need to apologize. I hope I didn't bite your head off. It's just…"

Dan sat up straighter, hooking his boot on a ridge in the rock so he could lean his elbow on one knee. "You've a right to know. You carry their genes. You're just as pretty — prettier. And I see a lot of similarities between you and Dana…and her mother." Dan sighed, aware of the weariness in his chest.

"I'm glad you're getting to know Dana — she's a good woman, and I'll get around to forgive her one of these days. It's just…she kept you from me. For twenty-one years! That's a lotta lies, and it still rankles me."

Brushing the gravel off his jeans and strapping the Colt .45 back on his hip, Dan pushed back the squabble about Dana. *No use dredging up old stories that'll hurt people.*

"I suppose we ought to head back down the trail, don't you think? It'll be a few hours to your rig."

As Dan followed Rachel back down the trail, he couldn't help but think it could be Dana ahead of him, they looked so much alike. A lot of their mannerisms were the same too — strong slim hands that gave poetic emphasis to whatever they were saying; the tilt of their heads when they looked ya in the eye; the way they moved like they owned the sidewalk.

Rachel's got a lot more self-confidence than Dana did at that age — more bold. She expects privilege…in an innocent way. Might be youth; maybe it comes from growing up with money.

Dan noticed the ham sandwich sitting heavy in his stomach. *Dana had to raise herself much of the time. Not many extras in those early years.* He frowned, brushing off the angst that threatened to encroach on this outing. He missed his daughter and wished they could get this disagreement behind them — *it's all in the past!*

Returning his thoughts to the present, Dan scanned the area. *Perfect habitat for bears.* He stopped to adjust the leather string on his holster, then started to sing loud to give critters fair warning. Shortening the gap between him and Rachel, she laughed over her shoulder, teasing him about his raucous ditty. He thought his heart would burst. *She gets me. This beautiful, sophisticated, young woman, for some reason, cares about me. Lord, I am blessed!*

Rachel stopped suddenly mid-stride. She started to speak, but Dan couldn't make out what she said. When the trail opened up to Dan's view, he immediately sized up the situation: Two bear cubs on the trail beyond and mama was nowhere in sight. Just as that thought formed, he heard a rustling in the brush to his left. *Not good.*

Rachel was still several yards ahead of him, the cubs beyond her, and mama lifted up to look over the brush at them. Dan's thoughts raced as he sized up the situation. *Not much of a breeze, so she might not smell us.* Bears have poor eyesight, but she was pretty close — not fifty feet from him, a little closer to Rachel.

He inched his hand up to pull the .45 from its holster. "Easy now, mama, we don't want to do you no harm." His voice was low and steady as he inched closer to Rachel. Dan stretched out his shoulders to look as big and broad as he could, while speaking to Rachel in the same tone of voice he spoke to the bear, not taking his eyes off the bear. "Don't panic — move slow. We're going to step off the trail to the right. That's right mama, we're gonna leave you right here. Now stay calm. We're not gonna hurt ya."

The cubs had paused to watch them, but were now getting frisky again. Dan feared their curiosity would draw them closer to Rachel, which would surely cause the sow to attack.

Rachel stood rigid, staring at the cubs. By now, Dan had his gun in his right hand and was coming up behind her on his right. It was poor positioning...he wouldn't have the correct angle to move Rachel behind him with his left arm crossed over his front and still keep his eyes on the sow.

The sow growled, hurling saliva as she tossed her head.

Rachel's high pitched voice was directed to the cubs, "Git. Git. Go away."

Dan could see movement out of the corner of his eye. He yelled at Rachel, "Get behind me – get out of the way!"

Firing one shot in the air, Dan hoped the bear would be scared off, but she dropped down, still moving in the bushes between them. He sensed the cubs had been frightened by the noise because he couldn't see them now. Rachel was somewhere behind him. He fired another shot in the air, yelling and waving his left arm.

It could only have been seconds since they spotted the bear, yet it seemed like many minutes had passed. The bear was moving closer. Dan pointed his revolver directly at where the sow had dropped down, holding his arm steady with his left hand. He hoped she would veer off before he had to shoot, but he was prepared. It was against his nature to kill unnecessarily, especially when it would mean two cubs starving, but he knew a protective mama bear had the ability to do serious harm, to even kill an adult.

He zeroed in on the bear, cocking his gun as she continued to crash through the bushes. With only a few thick bushes between them, he thought she may have broken stride. Citing the revolver on her center, his finger curved around the trigger, his jaws set. He leaned forward, bracing for the kill, measuring the split second before he had no choice but to shoot.

Suddenly, she side-stepped, slowing to growl a few more threats, her head swinging away from them. Then as quickly as she had appeared, she was gone. Dan could see her turn to her left, which he figured would have been toward her cubs.

He stood up straighter, still pointing his gun in the direction the bear had turned, and continued to scan the brush for any sign of her return. "Where are you, Rachel...are you all right?"

"Yes." She was breathless and shaken. Coming up on Dan's left, she slipped under his shoulder. "Will she come back?"

"Probably not, but we'll give her more time to get those cubs a distance from us." He glanced at Rachel and held her tighter, yet maintained his vigilance for danger.

He couldn't see the bear any longer or hear any rustling in the brush, but the trail ahead was curved, so his view was limited. Hopefully she veered away from the trail. Continuing to watch for signs of the sow's return, his attention turned to Rachel. She was trembling, still holding her bear spray ready, her finger on the trigger.

Her voice was loud and shaky. "G-Dan...that was so scary! It came so close—it could have killed you!" Breaking down, she sobbed. "And you protected me! I...I panicked. She was so big...was that a brown bear?"

"No. No, she was just a black bear—but the biggest one I've ever seen. They'll usually avoid people, but they can be fierce when cubs are involved. Actually, that was unusual for her cubs to be so far from her. I would have thought she heard us coming."

Still holding her close, Dan said, "Let's head on down the trail and make lots of noise. Stick real close to me, honey. I want to keep my right side free though, just in case she decides she wants another look at us."

Dan spoke loudly as they walked, alternately speaking to Rachel and directing his comments to the bear if she was still in the area, assuring that she was safe and they just wanted to get out of her territory.

The two walked fast, their boot steps and movements creating a disturbance above their voices. Otherwise, the forest was silent. After thirty minutes, they came to an open space by the river. He saw fresh tracks in the mud from a mountain bike, and figured it was likely a safe place to take a break. Slipping his revolver back in the holster, he realized how tired he was.

Exhaling through a *whew*, he added, "I don't want to do that again anytime soon!" He took Rachel by the shoulders and bent down to study her face. "Are you okay, honey? That was quite an adventure."

Rachel nodded, but she looked as tired as he felt. Wrapping her arms around him, she clung to him for some minutes. Speaking into his chest, she mumbled, "I'm glad I was with you, G-Dan. I love to hike, and I wouldn't want this to stop me from other trails, but that was really scary. It helped to keep walking." She looked up at him, standing back to see his face. "I can't believe how it all happened so fast, yet it seemed to go on forever. Those babies looked like they were going to come right to me to play. I...I was afraid they would come to me and then their mother would get me. Then seeing her come toward you..." She put her hands to her face. "I can't get that image out of my mind! She was so close to you, G-Dan!"

Dan reached for water for them both as they continued to talk about the incident. Even though he believed they were probably safe now, he was vigilant with their surroundings.

After they talked about how rare it was to have such an encounter with a bear, how fearful it was, and how Rachel regretted not having a camera going, they headed out for the last stretch of the trail.

With their gear stowed in the back, Rachel asked, "G-Dan, would you mind driving back? I'm still pretty shaky."

"Sure honey." He sat with his forearms on the steering wheel a moment. "Me too. That was enough to send me to confession!"

Rachel laughed, "You're not Catholic!"

He chuckled as he started the engine, letting the thought hang.

* * *

Dan slept fitfully that night. Images of the bear lunging toward him intruded in his dreams. He had nightmares of his precious Rachel being in danger and he couldn't reach her. Then Rachel would become Dana and he couldn't save her.

Lying there, trying to find sleep, his mind reached back to times when he and Dana were in danger. He'd told the story of them being stranded off Baranof Island with a malfunctioning engine a hundred times; how they lived on beans for two days while he worked over the engine in rough seas. It was a captivating story, yet as he looked at it now, he saw Dana's...forlornness? She was such a good sport, he didn't see it before, but there was a look in her eyes. *She was only twelve – how could she not be lonely? Afraid. But there was something more in those eyes.*

His mind raced through the years, jumping from the present discord about her deception to her growing up on the boat. The gap of whole years in his memory gnawed at him. He could remember scaling back his fishing territory and settling in Juneau, but the details of Dana escaped him. *How did she get along? What else was important to her...before Hub, and besides me?*

Finally giving up the struggle to sleep, he started coffee about three in the morning. Leaving the light off, he sat at the kitchen table and stared into the darkness out the window. Snatches of memories surfaced of the early years – a few incidents of Dana getting her sea legs as a toddler; Mae fussing about their need to move to shore. He felt his gut twist as he touched on the memories of his wife. He pushed them away, only to be replaced by Dana coming to his front door a few months back, demanding to know the story of her mother. And her attempts to talk about Rachel.

He tried to sort out the sequence of his actions – to reinforce why his anger was justified. He brought her up to know right from wrong; that a lie was worse than a thief; that they were hardy people, and could conquer just about anything if they stuck together. *Why didn't she keep Rachel?* They were family, and they could take on the world together. How could she deceive him, especially about something as important as his granddaughter?

He needed a drink. Looking around the kitchen, he wondered if he might have a bottle stashed somewhere. He checked the time to see how long before the liquor store would open.

He thrust up from the chair with such force it toppled. His long stride took him to his small living room in three steps where he stood staring at the narrow closet door for a long moment, his mind racing through the years. Opening the door, he couldn't see the boxes stacked neatly on the top shelf, but even in the dark, he could locate the old boot box. He used to put Dana's papers and keepsakes in it.

Pulling it down from the shelf, he returned to the kitchen, turned on the light and poured another cup of coffee. He couldn't remember the last time he'd opened the box. *No need to since she grew up,* he told himself, yet he hesitated to lift the cover. It wasn't just Dana's mementoes — Mae had been shut up in that box too.

Dan's face scrunched as he rubbed his whiskered cheek. Setting the top aside, he began to reflect on the drawings, stories, and child creations professing her love for her daddy. Dan's heart squeezed in his chest as he sorted through them.

There were few pictures. Dana had created picture albums as a teenager and organized what he had, but a few remained here — one of her as an awkward pre-teen surrounded by boxes in their first apartment — a pose she wouldn't have treasured. There were a few sheets of school photos left uncut. Multiple prints of prized catches on the boat had been left, along with poor scenery shots with a black dot out in the ocean — likely an orca sighting.

Dan shuffled through the various pictures, pausing over a colored photo of him on deck, readying the fishing lines. His hair had grown over his ears and he hadn't shaved in a few days. He was unkempt, even for a fisherman. The memories hit him like a wave over the bow — the years when Dana was little! He had tried to drown his sorrows in the bottle after Mae left. Guilt twisted his gut even more. That instant captured on film took him back almost forty years. He felt off-balance, much like the image of his younger self — unsteady as he readied the boat for the day, oblivious to the needs of his little girl.

Picking up another picture, he stared at the image of Dana as a pre-schooler, and tried to recall how he attended to her needs. Books — there were a lot of books. But he could only recall snatches of her younger years — Santa showing up at the harbor house, friends who would take her for a week or two when their own kids were out of school.

She was such an easy kid — whatever he was doing, she'd join in like a trouper — quick to pick up on things, determined to learn everything he taught her. *Easier for me to drift...*

Dan shoved the box aside, telling himself he made up for it after he got sober. He put a lot of energy into her schooling, he was more structured. He incorporated their life on the water with book learning — trying to make it rich for her. *But there was so much I didn't give her.*

The internal debate raged on, but Dan's gut told him his rationale didn't hold water. His argument shifted to Dana's blame, imagining what it would have been like if she had kept Rachel. He envisioned the threesome navigating life on the water, how he would have shown Rachel the beauty of Southeast Alaska, and created adventures for his granddaughter. He would have been smarter about her education, and exposed her to larger ideals and opportunities. Maybe Dana and Hub would have raised her, but he would have been a big part of shaping her destiny.

He picked up the picture of him on the boat again. That's when it hit him — the truth of his history. Life on a shoddy fishing boat would not be glamorous to Rachel. He could never have given her the travel experiences and ease of the life she had with her adopted family. They couldn't have love her more than he did right now, but she wouldn't have preferred his paltry life. And maybe Dana didn't either — she just didn't have any choice. She went along with him because that's what he wanted.

And Mae didn't.

The anguish overwhelmed Dan as the truth washed over his selfish grudge. He clenched his jaw and gripped his coffee mug, but the wrenching in his gut would not let up. It swelled inside and leaked out his eyes as he stifled his cry, "Oh God, I've made a mess of it. How can I fix it?"

Dan wept as he acknowledged how precious his daughter was to him. *She made a mistake, and I condemned her for it. All the mistakes I've made, and she still loves me. How could I be so blind?*

Dan's attention shifted to the God he knew, but had ignored for so long. He poured out his heart, promising to be a better man and make it up to Dana if only she would forgive him. *I've been such a self-centered buffoon!*

It wasn't yet six o'clock, but Dan knew what he had to do, and it would not wait another moment.

Chapter Thirty Four

SITTING IN FRONT OF Dana's dark house, Dan had second thoughts about his impulsiveness to drive out here at this time of morning. The sun was just appearing. He wasn't sure how early Hub got up, but Dana wasn't an early riser. He considered returning to his apartment, but knew he would never have the nerve to do what he needed to do if he left.

It wasn't long before a light came on and the dogs came out barking. Upon seeing who it was, they side-tracked to take care of business. Hub stood on the porch bare footed, motioning him to come in.

Dan set his jaw, and stepped out of his pickup like a man in deep water letting go of his life preserver. By the time he and the dogs entered the kitchen, Hub had the coffee started.

He greeted Dan warmly as if it was common to see his father-in-law at such an early hour. "You okay, Dad?"

Nodding his head, Dan responded, "Fine. I need to get some stuff off my chest...with Dana. Sorry to have got you up so early."

Hub held up his hand to stop further apologies. "The dogs were letting me know it was time to go out—I didn't even hear your rig. Sit."

Over coffee, the two men caught up on business and fishing reports, planning when they would get the boats out and see who could catch the first king. The comfort level between them was testimony to the many years of close relationship, starting when Hub hung out with Dan while waiting to take Dana on a date. Their ties were strong.

"Can I fix ya some breakfast, Dad? I've got some links and hash browns; eggs."

Dan rubbed his belly and shook his head. "Sounds good, but I'm a little queasy. Had a pretty harrowing day yesterday. Made me think of things differently, and...uh...I need to settle it with Dana."

"Sure. I'll leave you two alone 'soon as she gets up."

"'Preciate that, son."

It wasn't long before the sound of Dana's slippers clopping down the hall stopped their conversation. She was still tying her bathrobe belt as she entered the kitchen. "Dad, are you all right?"

Dan had to fight back his angst a moment before he could speak.

Hub set Dana's tea mug on the table. "I think I'll go shave and let you two talk."

Sitting down across from him, Dana's eyes were huge, making her look vulnerable to Dan. He reached his hands across the table, covering half the distance. Ducking his head before starting, his voice was raspy. "I'm fine. I just needed to tell you how sorry I am...for everything."

Dan struggled to control his emotions, praying for help in finding the words to express his heart.

Tears came to Dana's eyes immediately, but she didn't move.

With stops and starts, Dan asked for Dana's forgiveness for not being there for her in the early years, for expecting her to grow up on her own and be satisfied with the life style he chose. He admitted it had to have been hard for her to have a *lug head* at the helm of her life, not seeing to her needs even when she was a blossoming young woman.

She tried to interrupt him at times, denying the need for apologies, but Dan wouldn't let her. He insisted on saying his piece.

"You...made a mistake years ago, and instead of understanding, I made it harder. I wouldn't even have Rachel if it weren't for you—she's the greatest joy in my life...at this age, and instead of making it good for you both, I undercut you."

Dan was trembling, just barely holding it together.

"Can I say something now?" Her voice was soft, but not haughty.

He nodded, preparing himself for whatever wrath she might give him.

"I didn't *make a mistake*, Dad. I was raped." Her tears fell freely as she watched her father crumble emotionally. Her chin trembled as she continued, her eyes not wavering from his face. "I didn't want to burden you – to ask you to give up more than you already had to raise me."

She held up her hand to stop his interruption. "You did, Dad, you sacrificed a lot for me, and I am grateful. I wouldn't have wanted it any other way. But I was afraid. I was afraid I would ruin her. I felt so incompetent...as a woman. As a mother. And I had let Hub go, never thinking we might ever get back together. I was afraid to face him again. Afraid to *not* come back home. Afraid to tell you the truth. So I did it – I gave her over to be raised by...strangers. A couple who had no children. I thought she would have a better life with them. And I have regretted it every...day...of...my...life."

Father and daughter rose at the same time, navigating around the table to encircle in each others' arms. They both sobbed, clinging to each for the grief that Dan now understood and shared. His heart burned thinking about his little girl going through such sorrow by herself. Not only did he not protect her, he made it harder on her. How could he not know she carried such pain? *I should have seen the signs. I don't even know what she went through – whether they caught the buzzard that hurt her.*

When he thought he couldn't handle any more emotional strain, he held Dana back from his chest, looking at her face. She looked like he felt – her mascara smeared, nose and eyes red. He couldn't speak, but managed to mouth, *I am so sorry.*

She whispered, "I'm so glad you came...that we talked. There's so much more to be said – so many more questions."

After embracing again for a few moments, she asked, "Can you stay? Can we talk today?" With his nod, she suggested they get Hub and have breakfast first so he could escape the bedroom.

Dan walked out on the deck while Dana rescued Hub. Looking over the canal, he saw the perfect microcosm of Southeast Alaska – vast blue waters, tree covered islands, and endless skies with the majestic Chilkat Mountain Range as the backdrop. It was more magnificent today...hard to take in the vastness, even though he'd lived in it most of his life. He was aware of a trembling in his chest. He dropped his head in humility and gratefulness for this moment of his life. *Thank you, Lord, for my daughter and her forgiveness. For another chance to...to be a better man.*

When Dan walked back inside, Hub and Dana were fixing breakfast. Dan reached for the plates on the side cart to set the table. Hub gave him a warm grin. "Thanks, Dad."

Dan could only respond with a nod, his emotions were so close to spilling over. He wasn't ashamed of the tears pooling in his eyes, although he didn't want to hash it over with his son-in-law. He just felt so light. He hadn't realized what a burden he had carried for the last year.

Conversation was subdued while they ate breakfast, but love blanketed the table. Dan told about the bear encounter of the previous day, and what a trouper Rachel had been. His kids were astonished, but could now better understand why the urgency to clear the air.

Dan wasn't sure how to dwell in this kind of openness, but he was determined to see the whole thing through. His stomach rebelled as he thought about the next truth to reveal—Mae.

Hub interrupted his thoughts, "I think I'll work in the shop this morning and give you two some time together."

Dan and Dana's eyes met, affirming that it was Dan's call. "You don't have to leave, son. This involves you too."

Looking at Dana for confirmation, Hub nodded and finished setting the dirty dishes aside.

It was time to speak of the most painful events in his life. He'd refused to even think about it for so long, he wasn't sure where to start. Unseeing, he watched his big hands tip his empty coffee mug north, south, east, west. His voice was hoarse when he finally started.

"Mae was a beautiful woman." He nodded toward Dana, "I see her a lot in you and Rachel. She was sweet; quiet. We were just kids like you two when we fell in love; married just out of high school. She came to visit her aunt in Petersburg for the summer, and never went back.

"I got the first boat when I was nineteen; she was twenty. We were happy as clams...I thought. Then Dana came." He looked up with pride at his daughter, who returned his look of affection. "I thought it couldn't get any better than this – beautiful wife and daughter, incredible life on the water.

"We worked hard. It took long hours to keep us afloat. It wasn't perfect, but I thought things were good. As I looked back...later...I could see I missed a lot. Mae had gotten more quiet. Sad. I wasn't...a thoughtful husband. Took a lot for granted.

"We were docked at Ketchikan for the winter. I had gone for supplies in town. Had a few beers. Probably more than a few. When I got back to the boat, she – and you – were gone."

Dan paused to collect himself. The images of that day were so clear in his mind, it was like he was taken back there – the cold and rain, the sound of his boots as he walked down the planked dock, his anticipation of their cozy nest and Mae's chowder for supper, followed by disbelief at the cold empty cabin.

Shaking his head to clear it, Dan went on. "She was gone. Left a note that said: *I'm sorry. Take good care of my darling girl. She is at Jenny's. I'm so sorry, Dan, but I can't take it anymore.*" The note was branded into his brain – he would never forget her words, or the devastation to his soul.

"I learned much later that some...smooth talkin' cowboy had been after her for some weeks. She left with him. To Montana." Dan's Adam's apple pistoned as he tried to regain control of the anger that welled up inside. He knew he was capable of murder if he ever came across that guy.

"He dumped her shortly afterward, and she was working as a care taker last I heard. Her aunt moved south and I lost track of her. That was...that was all within six...eight months. Her aunt wouldn't tell me anything, so I didn't even know where to start a search for her.

"Far as I know, she's still there and we're still married."

Dana's hand on his arm and her soulful brown eyes were almost too much to take.

"I'm sorry, Daddy." Then she broke down and sobbed.

Dan held back, allowing Hub to comfort her since he was barely holding it together. He excused himself to step back out on the deck for a few moments. He drank in the brisk air like a skin diver surfacing after too long underwater. Seeing the pain in his daughter's face was overwhelming. *That's why I never wanted to tell her. How do you dress up something like that?*

When he came back in, his red-eyed, snot-nosed little girl slipped into his arms like always. He couldn't speak, but the reconciliation with her began to patch the holes in his heart. He whispered, "It's gonna be all right, honey."

Still holding on to her dad, Dana finally asked, "Couldn't you learn anything from her friends or other family?"

"I...begged them to help me — Jenny who had you that first day; her aunt. It was like they thought I was a monster, or something." He gulped, then whispered, "Maybe I was. I was pretty rough around the edges, and she was so...tender."

Recovering his voice, he continued, "I was out of my mind for awhile...with hatred for the man who took advantage of her. Rage at those who knew about it and didn't tell me. I got lost in the bottle for some years...'til I saw what that was doing to you."

He held her tighter, his shame slipping away. "I'm so sorry."

Chapter Thirty Five

THE COALS HAD BURNED down, perfect for toasting marshmallows, while the incoming tide had reached within twenty feet of the family surrounding the fire pit on the beach. It was cool enough to require light jackets, yet the promise that winter was nearly spent held them close. The sound of the waves accompanied the pause in conversation.

Dan and Rachel had retold the story of their bear encounter of a few days before, rehashing the experience and exploring it from every angle. Hub and Dana relived the terrifying moments with them, trying to comprehend the reality of how their loved ones were in such great danger.

"I honestly thought this might be it—twenty-one years is all I get. It happened so fast, yet I had all this time to think, like *What if my bear spray misfires? What'll I do if it gets G-Dan—do I run for help or stay and try to save him? What can I use for a tourniquet? Should I climb a tree and wait for her to leave? What if she takes me down too and we die together...or will someone come along?*

She took a ragged breath before continuing. "I wondered if God would let me in heaven, and I promised I'd do better if he gets us out of this. And...I guess he did.

"I even called my mom last night and thanked her for the life she gave me growin' up. She cried a bucket. Well, half a bucket—I filled up the rest."

Hub grimaced. "Sounds like you had an angel watching over you all right—it could have turned out very differently. I hate to think about that."

Dana shuddered, folding into her jacket. "I...I can't bear to think about that. Instead of getting my family back, I could have lost you both."

Dan stirred the fire with a stick. Without looking up, he spoke in a quiet voice. "Funny how that works – what ground we can cover in our minds in a split second. I wouldn't want a repeat of that day, but it did make me realize some things. Today is important – I shouldn't a been putting off...taking care of business."

Looking at Rachel and then Dana, trying to keep his composure, Dan continued. "Dana did right by you, Rachel. You've had a good life. I regret making it harder for her this last year...and many times before. I've been pretty...pigheaded thinkin' I was the only one ever betrayed. And I probably caused that."

Dana slipped under Dan's shoulder, tears in her eyes.

The fire was burning down in spite of the occasional stick that made sparks shoot skyward. Rachel laughed as she maneuvered a browned marshmallow in her mouth with a long stick, garnering smiles from the others.

Taking a deep breath, Dana swallowed a few times before she could speak. "Speaking of *taking care of business*, there is something I need to share with you, Rachel. Mario, the man who...is the other part of your genetic makeup, came to my office a few weeks ago." She hesitated when Rachel looked at her, open mouthed, rounded eyes saying so much, and yet her face said so little.

Dana continued, choosing her words as if stepping over unstable rocks on the beach. "He said he was in route to Anchorage for a meeting...and he stopped over because he wanted to apologize for what he did to me. That it's bothered him all these years – that he forced himself on me."

Rachel stared at Dana without revealing how she was taking this news.

"He said he has two sons who are becoming young men, and in trying to teach them right from wrong, he felt like a hypocrite – something like that anyway.

"His showing up stunned me – I couldn't respond...I had to process the...shock of it all." Glancing over at Hub, she said, "I think he was sincere...and I have forgiven him.

"Rachel, I didn't tell him about you. I think that's not my...right, not without your permission." Her shaking coat betrayed her trembling inside. "And so you have it: One more crazy piece of your history. Oh...he left his card with his contact information on it."

Rachel's intense eyes tracked the thoughts zipping through her mind, although she continued to look at Dana. Finally, she nodded once. "Thank you, Dana. You're right...it is my choice now. That's good to know. I'm glad he apologized to you."

Returning her attention to the fire, her hand touched her heart. "Wow...I have brothers." The lopsided grin held Rachel's mouth, her eyelids flashing. "That's a lot to take in. How old are they?"

Dana shrugged. "He didn't say."

Seagulls clamored in the distance, finding refuge as the night settled over the water. The dwindling fire held the attention of the beach dwellers, as if to give Rachel privacy to contemplate the enormity of Dana's revelation.

After several moments, Rachel slowly looked around the fire circle at Dana, Hub, Dan, and back to Dana, her beautiful face full of love. "I think I've got all the family I can handle right now. And I'm so glad you found me."

Some of the Books on Dana's Bookshelf

- *Adult Children of Alcoholics*, Janet G. Woititz
- *Alcoholics Anonymous, The Big Book,* Anonymous
- *Battlefield of the Mind: Winning the Battle in Your Mind*, Joyce Meyer
- *Boundaries: When to Say Yes, How to Say No, How to Take Control of Your Life*, Henry Cloud and John Townsend
- *CoDependent No More: How to Stop Controlling Others and Start Caring for Yourself,* Melody Beattie
- *Courage to Change: One Day at a Time in Al-Anon II*, Al-Anon Family Group Head, Inc.
- *Every Man's Battle*, Steve Arterburn
- *It Will Never Happen to Me: Growing Up with Addictions as Youngsters, Adolescents, Adults*, Claudia Black
- *Love Must Be Tough*, Dr. James Dobson
- *Perfect Daughters: Adult Daughters of Alcoholics,* Robert J. Ackerman, Ph.D
- Holy Bible
- *Redeeming Love,* Francine Rivers
- *The Dance of Anger*, Harriet Lerner
- *The Dance of Intimacy,* Harriet Lerner
- *The Enabler: When Helping Hurts the One You Love*, Angelyn Miller
- *The Glass Castle,* Jeannette Walls
- *There's a Hole in my Sidewalk: The Romance of Self-Discovery*, Portia Nelson
- *Women Who Love Too Much*, Robin Norwood

Book Club Questions

1. Dana Jordan, an expert in human relations, was powerless to create the *mother-daughter* relationship she desired with Rachel. What realities made that so hard? In your experience, what is helpful and NOT helpful in mending relationships with a *reluctant other*?

2. Why do you think Rachel was so resistant to bonding with Dana, her birth mother? What did she have to lose if she continued to reject Dana? What did she have to gain?

3. Dana and her father were always close-knit. How could that bond have been so damaged by the secret of Rachel's birth? Is it reasonable to keep the truth of a surrendered child from their grandparents, or other family members? What are the *pros* and *cons* of disclosing such a reality?

4. Hub Cordell and Dan Jordan were both drawn to Rachel, long before they knew she was Dana's daughter. Why do you think they formed early friendships so readily?

5. Becoming a grandfather changed Dan Jordan dramatically. How was he different because of Rachel? What changed in his thinking and his behavior with Dana?

6. Women in the therapy group made different alliances, but Genie made it hard for the others to like her. Why do you think she was so belligerent to the others? Have you had people in your life who put up barriers like Genie did? What enabled you to see past the façade and empathize with the hurting person?

7. Brandi found herself in the same position as her mother had been—married to a cheating husband. Her mother stayed in the marriage, while Brandi separated. Although Brandi wanted to keep her family together and to honor her vows, she felt she had no options. As a friend, how would you encourage Brandi?

8. What do you think about the need for the therapist to get therapy?

9. The sudden appearance of Mario seeking forgiveness from Dana threw Hub for a loop. How was his reaction typical or atypical of an honorable, Godly husband? What do you admire about how he handled the situation? How could it have turned out differently?

10. Dana chose to keep the truth of Rachel's existence from Mario, her biological father. What are the implications of such an enormous decision?

11. Do you think Dana has finally found contentment with having a *normal* family? How might it work out? What is a *normal* family in your mind?

If you missed the first and last books in the *Tethered Trilogy*, you can find them on Amazon:

Tethered to Shadows: *The Healing Journey of Six*
Tethered to Shame: *The Search for Grace*
Untethered Heart: *Redeemed by Love*

My prayer is that this series has blessed you in some way.

I love hearing from my readers. Please visit my blog,

UntetheredVoice.com and or
Facebook Page, Judy Hudson, Author

As always, authors greatly appreciate your posted reviews on Amazon.

Made in the USA
Columbia, SC
06 November 2024

45492595R00138